KNIGHT

THE WORDSMITHS BOOK ONE

CHRISTOPHER HARLAN

Knight
Book 1 in the Wordsmith Chronicles
By Christopher Harlan

Cover design and Formatting by Jessica Hildreth
Beta-Reading by Lauren Lascola-Lesczynski & Stephanie Albon
Proofreading by Jessica Kempker

DEDICATIONS

To the indie writing and reading community—you never cease to amaze. These words are for you.

To my wife and children, without whom none of this would be possible.
#potato

To the guys of the R&E Fraternity who I got to meet at the signing—BT Urruela, Golden Czermak, Seth King, Mickey Miller, Rob Somers, Derek Adam, Chris Genovese, and Jackson Kane—the conversations we had lasted way past that weekend.

And a very special thank you to Scott 'fucking' Hildreth—
thanks for helping me find True North

FOREWORD

MY DINNER DATE WITH SETH
GETTYSBURG R&E FRATERNITY
SIGNING, MARCH 2018

Okay, that title is clickbait 101. Fake news. Or, if not fake, intentionally misleading. I did have dinner with Seth King, but so did about three hundred people simultaneously. Some of you reading this were undoubtedly there, but for those who weren't, allow me to contextualize a bit.

I always like to include my thoughts at the beginning of a new series, or at the beginning of a particularly impactful work, as was the case with *Away From Here*. For my *New York City's Finest* series I wrote my inspiration at the start of *Calem*. For this, I feel like explanation more than inspiration. As many of you reading this know (or, as those who are new to me will shortly find out) I wrote almost nine books in my first year and a half. I wrote a two book series (The *Impressions Series*), started the *New York City's Finest*, and finally completed *Away From Here*—my first Young Adult novel. By the time I was getting ready to leave for my first signing in Gettysburg, Pennsylvania, I was at a complete loss as to where to go next.

Perhaps some authors have a cache of hundreds of plot ideas swimming around their heads at all times, but I'm certainly not one of them. I had just finished writing *Riley*, the 5th and final book in the NYC Finest, and I was done with *Away From Here*. It was at that moment (and, honestly, way before) that I had to ask myself that most loaded of questions: what am I going to do next?

The answer came at the R&E Fraternity signing in Gettysburg. Saturday night there was a dinner hosted for all the participating authors. By happenstance I was seated next to Seth Nicholas King, author of *Daddy Issues* and many other great books. We discussed all manner of things, from sociological insights, our favorite books, to all things romance related. He thought of the basic idea for the story—that of a wounded male writer who's saved by a woman he meets at a signing just like the one we were sitting at. From there, I came home and thought up the basic framework for this story. Like all stories, it took a million twists and turns that I hadn't anticipated along the way. But, after all, that's the fun of writing.

Enjoy! More to come!

Christopher—2018

A WORDSMITH.

A *Wordsmith.*

That's what she called me. Why? Because I could make her feel things with my books that no one else ever could. My name is Michael, but everyone knows me as *Knight*.

I write the books that you don't want your family to know you're reading. The ones whose spines you hold down so that passersby can't see the cover, the ones you enjoy in the privacy of your bedroom, where no one can see the beads of sweat my words inspire forming on your forehead.

My last book brought two women into my life—the one who broke my heart into a thousand pieces, and the one who may have the power to mend it.

Everleigh.

My lingering blank pages needed inspiration, and that's exactly what she was.

I know two things for certain—that my heart beats only for her, and that my best book is still inside me, if only she can help me pull the words from my wounded heart. I can be the writer that makes her heart pound in her chest. And soon, everyone will read my masterpiece.

I'm a Wordsmith.

Let me tell you my story.

Michael Knight

- Author of *Into Your Eyes*, the *Lost Lovers* series, and an upcoming work, title TBA
- Co-author of the upcoming *Wordsmith Chronicles Anthology*

Colton Chase

- Author of the MMA themed *Battle Tested* series featuring alpha bad boy Aidan Paul. Book 1 is titled *Fist*. He's currently working on book 2, *The Gentle Art*
- Co-author of the upcoming *Wordsmith Chronicles Anthology*

Grayson Blackman

- Author of the Rom-Com series *Benefits for Friends*, and the Dark Romance *Stolen* series
- Co-author of the upcoming *Wordsmith Chronicles Anthology*

The Brotherhood

- KL Steiner
- Roland Rays
- Johnathan Logan

Authors

True North

- Author of *The Furious Pricks* series, *The Rotten Scoundrel* series, along with 50 other novels, most of them bestsellers

Greg Olden ('G. Olden')

- Author of the *Flexed* series/renowned photographer/fitness model

THERE YOU ARE.

Sitting at that table, shaming all of those other women who only think that they're beautiful, the ones who probably worked on themselves for hours just to achieve the type of beauty that comes so effortlessly to you. This whole dining hall is a sea of women, but not a single one can hold a candle to you in any way.

When we met you didn't crowd me, or treat me like a rock star, or try to stroke my ego. You were just you—smart, sexy, and touched deeply by a book I'd convinced myself didn't impact anyone except me. And more than anything, I could tell that you didn't know how gorgeous you really are.

Just like now.

You sit back in your chair, never too concerned with anything going on around you, and never trying too hard to be anything but yourself. Others might see that as arrogance, but I know that it's the epitome of confidence. And you have every reason to be confident in yourself. Right now your hair is down, and I'm mesmerized by those brown curls draped gently over one shoulder, falling at your breasts, and driving me absolutely insane. Even from this distance at the author's table I can make out the emerald green in your eyes—the light reflecting off of them perfectly. When they look my direction you hold me in place, and all of the sounds around me become white noise, as if I'm in a dream that I never want to wake from.

I didn't know what I was doing here at first, in a place where everyone looks at me like I'm on display. Grayson and Colton asked me to be here. Better to be a good friend than a bad one, right? But I'd convinced myself that being here was a favor that I was doing them, even if they thought it was the other way around. How could I have known that coming here would bring you into my life? I guess the universe has its mysteries to keep.

I'm the most reserved of us, even though I write steamy novels for a living. I'm a contradiction like that—a quiet, reserved, author who's a romantic at heart, yet I write the kind of books that can make a tingle appear between your legs and get your heart racing in your chest. That's me. I write the books you don't want your family to know that you're reading, the ones you'd hold down so that passers by couldn't see the cover. I write the books that you enjoy in the privacy of your own room, where no one can see the beads of sweat my words make appear on your forehead.

The other guys are the loud and boisterous ones—the ones who'll keep the crowd of our fans and readers happy and laughing all weekend. I mostly smile. I mostly sit. I mostly use my energy to look at you and think the kind of thoughts that get me in trouble. There must be three hundred readers here, each dressed to the nines, each here for us, each busy taking selfies and drinking enough wine to give the entire hotel a hangover. The music is loud enough to drown out almost anything else, but it's powerless to stop the thoughts running though my head.

I'm used to having my thoughts dominate my life. I'm a writer, after all, and that comes with the territory. Only tonight I'm not worried about plot, or characters, or cover models, or blurbs that'll catch a reader's attention. No. Instead I'm wondering what your lips would feel like when they're against mine, how much pressure I'd feel with your legs wrapped around my waist, squeezing me as I kiss you harder than you've ever been kissed before. I think about my body suspended over yours, promising to descend and bring you to unthinkable levels of ecstasy. Then I imagine the noises you'll make as I slide inside of you, how your back would arch and your mouth would open to take in more air, because you're going to need it.

I see you stand up and start to walk out. You catch my glance, and we both understand each other without a single word needing to be spoken.

I'm on my way, Everleigh, just like we arranged.

I'm about to find out the answers to all of my questions, alone with you in the darkness of your room.

Before I started my full time gig as a romance novelist, I had a lot of odd jobs, and I almost ended up as a full time pastry chef, but the itch to write was too strong. I've been a writer all of my life in one form or another. When I was a little kid I used to annoy my parents by making up bad sci-fi and fantasy stories that were total Tolkien rip offs and force them to listen to me read them over dinner. In high school I wrote articles for my school's newspaper, and when I finished college I had a bachelor's degree in literature to call my own. Eventually I grew the balls to take the plunge into self-publishing my own books.

I like doing things my way. I'm an independent person, and I don't like seeking acceptance from anyone. Just not in my personality. When I was a kid the only way to get a book published was through a company—one of the heavy hitters that everyone knows about. Query letters, agents, meetings, lots of rejection. Yeah, that shit isn't for me. Back in the day I wouldn't have had a choice in the matter, I would have had to eat the same type of shit all struggling artists have to eat in order to have guys in suits hand you a check and get your book in window displays. But the world's changed, and the huge publishing companies aren't the only game in town.

Getting into this business was a group effort. Me and my two best friends, Colton and Grayson, got into this together. We met in college and hit it off right away. The original idea to get into publishing was mine, and when I first brought it up I got the skeptical eyes. I remember their faces as we sat over one too many drinks at a bar near NYU. Colt almost spit his beer right in my face because he was laughing so hard. "Romance? Like *Fifty Shades* kind of shit? You want me to take my very expensive college degree and write about women getting tied up and whipped?"

"There's more to it," I told him. "I've been doing some research. It's not all '*Fifty Shades* shit.'"

"Research?" Gray asked, giving me the raised eyebrow. "So what I'm hearing is that you've been staring at half naked dudes on book covers every night and whacking off? Is there something you want to tell us? Did you need a few drinks to help you come out of that closet?"

"No, dick," I said. "I mean I've been looking into the industry—into books that aren't *Fifty Shades* to see what else is out there in the romance world. It's not all bondage and whips. There are actually a lot of different sub genres."

"My sisters read that shit. All the time."

"Mine too," I told him. "Not just my sisters, but my mom and about every other woman I know."

That's when Gray jumped in with a healthy does of skepticism. "But don't you think everyone is going to be doing exactly what we're doing? Trying to jump on the *Fifty Shades* train and ride it to the bank?"

"No pun," Colton joked, amusing mostly himself.

"I can't believe you're a writer. Do you put those shitty puns in your work?" Colt didn't answer, just gave me the middle finger.

"Maybe," I said, ignoring Colt and responding to Gray. "Okay, it's more than a maybe. It's probable, but I honestly don't think that matters as much as you think. I joined a few readers groups on Facebook and found some stuff out."

"As part of your research?" Colton joked.

"That's right. And what I noticed is that the women who read romance read a lot of romance. I mean A LOT."

"Like how many books are we talking about?" Gray asked.

"Some were reading ten a month, some were even as high as twenty to thirty a month."

"Jesus, I don't think I've read that many books this year."

"That's 'cause you're a fucking caveman, Colt. But think about it, in a market like that we're not competing with other authors in the same way as if we were in another business. If there were 10 people who all opened up a pizza place in the same neighborhood, then probably only 1 or 2 of them would stay open. People would have a forced choice because it's the same product. But if someone's reading 300 books a year over several years, then they're not choosing between authors, they're reading all of them."

"See," Grayson said, smiling. "That minor in economics is paying off dividends. No pun."

"I think it's a worthwhile experiment. What do we have to lose? If it works, then we can all have great careers. And if it doesn't, hell, we can always get regular jobs."

That was how it all started. A longer conversation got Colton on board, and before we knew it we were all on the road to becoming indie romance authors. That seems like forever ago, when we were still in the honeymoon phase of our careers. Everything was potential. The reality has been a little different, at least for me. The God's honest truth is that Colt and Gray are far from bestselling authors, but they're definitely more successful than me.

Colton is on the steamier side. He started writing MC, or Motorcycle Club, books but his new series is about an MMA fighter since he used to train himself. Grayson leans towards the dark romance, and he has more books out than either of us. That kid's always writing and always working on building himself up. Me? I have my own niche. I like to blend mind-blowing sex with characters that are real—guys who are everything men should be: strong but sensitive, tough as hell but kind, gentleman when they need to be, and dominant bastards in the bedroom. I like complexity.

I like to write about real guys who can fuck like women only dream of.

Now if only I can get more people to read them.

Jenny was my first for a few things, but how we met was when she gave me my first five star review on Amazon for my fourth novel. That may not sound like such a big deal, especially now, but trust me, at the time it was a very big deal, the kind of encouragement that the new author I was so desperately needed for some kind of proof of concept. I had already published a few typical romance books before that. Your standard issue sexy, bad boy stories. The hot guys who have their middle fingers up to the world at all times, but who end up hooking up with some hot woman by the mid chapters —not that original, I know, but they were fun to write and got me the small but loyal following that I enjoy now.

I'd never write books like that anymore. I still have the usual checklist of things you need in a romance book: hot guy, hot girl, and, of course, lots of sex, only now I like to tell deeper stories—and no, that's not a pun.

Jenny was a blogger, which is actually how we met, if talking to someone online without seeing them in person counts as meeting, which I guess it does in our society today. It wasn't a Catfish kind of situation, which I was worried about when I first asked to see her in person. Before she walked into the bar that night and I got to lay my eyes on her in the flesh, I'd convinced myself that there was a 50/50 chance that *she* might actually be a *he*, smiling and holding a copy of my book with his five o'clock shadow showing from across the room.

My best friends and fellow authors, Grayson and Colton, told me that I was batshit crazy for agreeing to meet some reader at a bar, but I ignored their pleas for my sanity. What if she's nuts? What if she's a stalker? Yeah, Yeah, I told them,

I'll be fine. Jenny lived in New York also, so it seemed easy enough of a hypothesis to test, even though it wasn't my style to meet up with a female fan or reader. There was just something about the way she described my work that made it a necessity to meet and talk to her. It was a just supposed to be a meeting at a bar, something friendly, something without any further intentions on my part.

As they say, one thing led to another. First, Jenny was all woman. No buff dude with a beard looking to hook up. She was beautiful, and loved my work almost as much as I did. Drinks led to me asking her out. One date led to another. And before I knew it we were in a full fledged relationship. Dating became an engagement, and the rest is history. For a while there we were really happy.

At least that's what I thought at the time.

By the time I DM'd Jenny I'd written four romance novels. Each of my other three had done just okay. I was hardly E.L. James. Hollywood wasn't exactly calling to try and cast the lead in the movie adaptation of any of my books. My sales were nothing special, nothing groundbreaking, and sure as hell nothing anyone would describe as lucrative. I don't know why I'm using euphemisms to describe the situation—my sales sucked. By the time I met Jenny I'd done a pretty good job of burning through all of my savings trying to make it as a full time author. At that point the glitz and glamour fantasies about writing the hit novel that made me millions had long since passed, and I was facing the harsh reality of the indie book world. Going to events, buying my own books to give away, and spending untold fortunes on swag drained the little bit of profit I made off of each book, and the bills were piling up way faster than the royalties were coming in. And then, at a certain point, they weren't coming in at all.

I almost gave it up on the entire idea of being a professional author, but it was my fourth book, *Into Your Eyes*, that helped me turn the corner. Not only did it bring Jenny into my life, but it was easily the most successful of the four—and when I say successful I don't mean that I was balling, but it did help me build my confidence and make a little profit. I gained more newsletter subscribers, more friends and followers on social media, and my Facebook reader group was getting more and more joins from readers by the day. Things were going well.

But back to how I met Jenny.

I'm an indie author, which means that I release my own books, and that I'm not contracted with any major publishing company. Authors like me, especially ones trying to get their careers off the ground, don't just need readers, we also need the writing *community*. The bloggers, the advanced readers, the PA's. All of them are an absolute requirement to help get our work out to a larger audience. You can only have so many friends and followers on social media. That's not enough to make it big. You need help to get your books seen—word of mouth—people who couldn't get enough of your book and would tell all of their friends about how hot and steamy it was.

That's where the bloggers come in, especially.

I'd sent out advanced copies to about 100 of them, hoping that the women who ran the blogs didn't think I was a terrible writer, and that they would give me a decent review to however many followers they had on their sites. I didn't care how many. No blog was too small for me. 10 followers or 10,000, anything that helped get my work out to readers was fine by me.

Jenny was one of those bloggers, and she loved *Into Your Eyes* more than any of the other ninety-nine women did, even though the majority of them gave me good reviews. But Jenny was extra excited about it. She spoke about it like I was the second coming of Shakespeare, like my words touched her in ways that no other author's possibly could. Not only did she give it three stars on her blog—the best rating she gave to anything—but she was the first to post her review of the book once it was live on Amazon, Barnes & Noble, and all the other digital platforms that were available. Five Stars. And, more than that, it was how she wrote it.

A Wordsmith.

That's what she called me.

". . .Knight, who many of you know from his previous books, is truly a master wordsmith, someone who can make you feel things that you've only ever fantasized about. . ."

That review was everything. My confidence boost. The cause of my smiling face when I woke up on release day to read it. The reason I reached out to her and asked her to get a drink at the bar.

Those were the good times.

Until Jenny called me a wordsmith I'd never thought of myself in those terms. I was a writer, an author, a storyteller. But never a wordsmith. It's not something I ever would have called myself, of course, but I was happy that she bestowed that title on me. *What's the difference*, I asked her on our first real date after our introduction at the bar. "The feelings," she said, sitting next to me at the bar. "There are thousands of authors, and ten times as many readers. Those are too common. You're a wordsmith, and wordsmiths know how to manipulate language in ways authors can only dream of. They know how to make people feel things."

Manipulate.

In hindsight, it's interesting that she chose that word specifically. They say that hindsight is 20/20, right, so I guess that I can look back and see all the little things that I should have picked up on as red flags leading up to the end of our brief marriage, but life isn't like a movie that you can rewatch and catch things you missed the first time around. Life is a single screening of events, and apparently I missed all kinds of shit I should have been paying very close attention to.

Gabriela's her name. A friend, right? Just a friend. Another blogger who she'd met through social media. A fellow New Yorker, what a coincidence? Just like Jenny and I, right? Indie romance is a woman's world, so I didn't think anything of it when Jenny made some close friends in that tight-knit online community. So what that Gabriela lived only ten minutes from us? *Isn't that cool*, Jenny would ask me? We have friends in the community who can be our actual friends. So what that she didn't seem to like me, or that her and Jenny were spending more time together than Jenny and I were. Nothing to worry about. No need for paranoia.

It was last Monday—a week ago today—when I came home to find them in bed together.

It's still so fresh in my memory that it feels sore, like a wound that still bleeds through the band-aid. I had been out that afternoon trying to pitch the owners of some local bookstores to carry a few paperback copies of each of my books, and I'd gotten home earlier than expected. I remember being so thrilled to tell Jenny all about how the biggest bookstore in town had passed on the other three, but had agreed to sell *Into Your Eyes* right in their front display. My heart was racing as I drove home, and I'd rehearsed just how I was going to tell her. I even stopped at a wine store and bought the most expensive bottle of Champagne that they had, even though we couldn't really afford it.

I saw the car parked in front of our house when I pulled into the driveway, but I didn't think anything of it. When I went in I didn't call out to Jenny like I usually did because I heard something from upstairs. It seems idiotic now, but my first thought was that someone had broken in because I heard what sounded like muffled cries coming from upstairs. As I rushed up to see what the hell was going on I was thinking the worst. Once I got up to the top I saw that the bedroom door was closed, but slightly ajar. The sounds got more and more intense the closer I got, and once I pushed the door open I realized that things were wrong in a completely different way than I had anticipated.

That visual will never leave me.

It's supposed to be a fantasy for every guy, right? Two women together, naked in your bed, rolling around. Bullshit. That sounds great in a porno, but it's only a fantasy if it isn't your wife cheating on you during what you thought was one of the happiest days of your life. When that happens, it isn't a fantasy, it's a complete nightmare.

We broke up the next day. Well, technically it was the next day. We had been screaming at each other through the early morning hours. It was about 3:00 am when I threw her cheating ass out of my house. Maybe that seems cold, but there was no way she was going to live in the home I worked tirelessly to pay for while she was screwing her new girlfriend in the upstairs bedroom. *If you need a place to stay*, I yelled, the tears still swelling my eyes, *go stay with Gabriella. She's local.*

Now I'm sitting on my couch, staring at the TV, with a half empty bottle of Grey Goose sitting only a few inches away. Funny, it was full not that long ago. I shouldn't be sitting here, falling to pieces inside and feeling sorry for myself. I should be writing. I should be working on things.

But I can't. . .I just can't right now.

Jesus, what has my life become?

2

KNIGHT

Six Months Ago

The phone rings and wakes me out of yet another shitty nap. I've been taking a lot of them lately. I wipe my eyes and look around a room that used to bring me comfort, but now only serves as a reminder of what a mess my life's become. Empty beer and liquor bottles, too many to count, line my countertops, a reminder of the lengths I'll go to self-destruct. My laundry is all over the damn floor, and my face hasn't see a razor for a while now.

Lucky me, I got to keep the house in the divorce proceedings, but that's not saying much since it was mine to begin with. I've been sleeping on the couch a lot lately because the bedroom brings back too many bad memories. I can't walk in the room without seeing what I saw that day with Jenny and Gabriela, and that's about the last visual I need these days. I guess it's some kind of bizarre silver lining that Jenny moved out and didn't contest much in the divorce. I'm fucked up enough as is, the last thing I needed was a long, drawn out fight over every knickknack in the place. At the very least I take her lack of a fight as a concession that the end of our marriage is pretty much a one sided thing. I'll relish the small victories. Sometimes it's all I've got.

I've been going out a lot, drinking a little too much—okay, more than a little—and usually when I get home I either try to write in the study—my version of a man cave—or I pass out drunk on my couch. Usually it's more of the latter than the former. I've gotten so used to waking up hung over that it doesn't even bother me anymore. It bothers me that it doesn't bother me. "Hello," I say, answering my cell without even looking at who it is. Not that I need to. I don't get many actual calls these days except for my agent, my attorney, or. . . "Oh, hey Colt, what's up? Shit, that's right. Okay, can you guys give me like a half hour. Thanks."

Colt and Gray are writers also, only they're the more successful versions of me. The three of us met when we were all college students taking the same creative writing classes at NYU, and now we all have degrees in either writing or literature. I don't think this is the kind of writing that our professors thought their students would be doing one day, but, oh well. Right after we graduated *Fifty Shades of Grey* blew up and took the world by storm, bringing romance and erotica into the mainstream like no other time in history. Simultaneously, self-publishing was becoming more and more of a valid way to get content out to people, so the three of us made a decision one night over drinks. We decided that we were each going to take two years, write the best romance novels the world had ever known, and try to ride the wave of success.

Things didn't quite go that way, but we're still doing the thing, trying our best to be successful. They stop by about once a week now, since I've been depressed. They call me up and find some pretense to come over, knowing that I'm probably hung over and sitting on my couch doing jack shit.

That's when they come by and offer to take me to dinner, or cheer me up by talking about how huge my next book is going to be even though I've barely written a word. These days I only have author friends. My other friends. . .actually, our other friends, were the one thing Jenny took in the divorce. Fuck 'em. They all deserve each other. I have my guys.

I run up to the bathroom to get my shit together. Five o'clock shadow doesn't begin to describe what's happening on my face right now. Stubble can be sexy, and a well groomed beard can work if you have the right look, but when you're in between those stages you just look like a straight dirtbag. That's me right now—I'm in the dirtbag stage of facial hair growth, which means that it's time to introduce my face to a razor and start from scratch.

When I'm done taking a shower and clear the steam off of the mirror I take a good, long look at myself. What the hell happened to me? I used to be full of piss and vinegar, ready to take on the world, but now I just look and feel tired all the time. I have to get over this shit. Lord knows my ex wife did. She's onto a whole new life with her girlfriend in a new place, and I'm here feeling sorry for myself. This has to stop. I have to get back to the old Knight.

As I'm finishing getting dressed I hear them downstairs. They both have keys and just let themselves in like the savages they are. "I'll be right down!" I shout, the towel around my waist barely holding on my hips. "I need to dry off."

"Don't bother," Colton yells up. "I like you wet."

"Yeah I know you do," I yell back down. "Help yourself to whatever's in the fridge."

"What do you think we're doing?" Grayson yells back. "Dry off and get down here, we have shit to talk about."

When I get downstairs I see them both sprawled out on the same couch I had just been sleeping on not an hour earlier. Colton's been working out a lot recently, and like all people who add some mass to their bodies, he's been wearing these tight-ass tee shirts. "You put all your shit in the dryer for too long again?" I joke. "Cause it looks like you raided your little brother's closet before you got here. Seriously, you buying XS shirts now?"

All I see is his middle finger. He doesn't even look at me while he gives it, he just keeps staring ahead at my flatscreen, an episode of Narcos season 1 on Netflix on in the background. "Asshole," he says. "You wish you could pull these shirts off."

"See that's where we differ," I answer back. "My shirts are tight because I fill them out. Yours are tight because you shop at Baby Gap."

"Burn!" Grayson jokes. "I like that line. I might steal that one."

"Thanks. I am a writer after all."

Grayson and Colton are both smiling. Colt's middle finger finally comes down and he gets up to give me one of his overly aggressive bro hugs. He loves hugging me these days. "Thanks, man. I don't know what I'd do without you pounding me on the back at least once a month. It's my own type of therapy."

"You love it."

"I do," I say, separating from him. "But for sure, relax."

"I'll do no such thing. Not until you snap out of this shit."

"I was just thinking about that while I was upstairs, actually," I tell them.

"You're a master of transition," Grayson says, and we look at each other. My eyebrows shoot up and I give him my skeptical eyes because I know these two have some plan to cheer me up. They always do. Two weeks ago it was the strip club, but I've never been a strip club guy. I think Grayson just wanted to go, and somehow he convinced himself that the trip was for me. Colton wanted to go cart racing the week before that which, for me, was definitely more fun than the strip club, but not really a cure for the kind of depression that comes from your marriage ending because your wife is a closeted lesbian. They try, and that's why we're brothers, because we help each other out when one of us is down. So I brace myself for whatever crazy shenanigans they're about to present me with.

"Okay, so what are we doing today? Sky-diving? Matching tattoos?"

"I didn't even think of that stuff," Colton says, looking over at Grayson. "Let's do that instead. I could definitely jump out of a plane right now or get some ink drilled into my skin."

"You'll be doing that shit alone if you do," Gray says to Colt. "And you know why we're here, so stop being ridiculous."

"Alright, fine." Colton throws his hands in the air while I look at both of them, confused as hell. "We'll talk about your thing instead."

"What's going on?" I ask them.

"We have an idea that we wanted to run by you. I know we've been going on some adventures recently, but this is business related."

"Business?" I ask Grayson. "What do you mean? Book business?"

"Yeah. Colt and I have an idea that we've been discussing among ourselves that we wanted to run by you. Pick your brain a little. You up for it?"

"Absolutely. Let me sit down."

The book world.

It's a little bit of a sore subject for me at the moment, and it has been for a few months now. I've never been one of those artists who thrives on drama. I'm the opposite. When I'm stressed out or preoccupied I can't write anything. Or, worse yet, I write stories that are total crap and delete the entire file the next day. I need peace of mind to write stories. And even though the literary snobs out there look down on what I write as some kind of glorified porn, I'm a storyteller, and that takes way more time and effort than anyone realizes.

I've been in a creative slump since Jenny left. I had a decent launch for *Into Your Eyes*, but sales have been total crap since release week because I haven't written anything new. Writing consistently is one of the keys to being successful in the self-publishing world. Websites like Amazon reward you for publishing more often because you get picked up in their algorithm if you're on there more. It makes sense—the more books people publish, the higher the percentage of royalties that Amazon gets, even if the book isn't a bestseller. There are so many people self publishing that Amazon makes money on the volume of books alone. But when you don't publish for a long time sales can slump because your book gets lost in the shuffle.

That's where I am right now. Of course the end of my marriage is the main reason that I'm depressed, but I was really hoping that *Into Your Eyes* would do much better than it did. When sales aren't what you want them to be—and so far they haven't been—I start to question everything about my career. Am I as good as I think? Are my books terrible? Why aren't sales better? A lot of questions that just lead to self doubt. Thank God I have these two, because every time I get down on myself they're here to cheer me up.

"So, here's the idea," Grayson begins. "Come, sit first." I

plop my butt down on the couch next to Colton and listen as Grayson continues. "We were thinking of pooling our talents. The three of us, I mean."

"How's that?" I ask.

Colton jumps in. "Kind of like a writing group. Something that we can promote and capture all of our different fans in one place. We're all romance authors, and we all do okay, but we write very different types of books from one another."

"Yeah," Grayson jumps in smiling. "I write good ones."

"That's not what your last few reviews said," Colton jokes.

"What do you mean a writing group? Like we'd write stories together or something?"

"Well, maybe," Grayson continues. "But it's more about pooling all of our talent into a social media group, so that we can expose fans to all of our different genres of books and they get to see and hear from all of us in one place. We can have a multiplier effect on each other's careers, potentially."

I think about it for a second, and only a second. Some ideas require a lot of contemplation—weighing the pros and cons—and others, like this one, just make sense the second you hear them spoken. "I like it," I tell them. "I like it a lot."

"Nice," Gray says. "We thought we were going to have to twist your arm a little more."

"You thought wrong," I tell him. "This is a great idea."

"We need a name. We can call ourselves. . .well, we're kind of stuck on that part, but we can figure those details out later. We were just thinking that it might be a cool way to tie our writing together. We could do social media posts, and maybe even co-write some books or something."

"And," Colton jumps in, picking up where Grayson left off. "We thought that we could start this off by creating a

Facebook group this weekend, then hosting an event for readers once we get a following, which shouldn't take long. What do you think?"

"What kind of event?" I ask.

"We were thinking a signing and meet and greet kind of thing. Maybe a weekend event that's just for the three of us, where readers can take pictures, get their books signed, and maybe we can organize a dinner afterwards. Something cool that all of our readers and fans can get involved in."

I listen closely and even before Colton finishes with that last part about the event, I'm already excited, even if it isn't showing on my face. I'm honestly not sure what face I'm making, but I know that for the first time in a few months the idea of my writing career is inspiring something in me other than stress. "I love the idea, man. You guys are brilliant."

"Oh," Grayson says, looking over at Colton. "We both thought you were gonna take much more convincing than that. We had all these speeches prepared to get you on board."

"No need, dude. I'm on board, it's a killer idea. You can save the speeches, I'm in."

"Well, holy shit," Colton says, smiling at me. "I'm psyched about this. It's gonna be awesome."

"I think it'll be more than awesome," I say. "It's going to help all of our careers."

"Speak for yourself," Colton jumps in, joking around. "My career is doing just fine."

"Save that bullshit," Grayson says. "I read your last book, it was shit. What the hell were you thinking killing off three of the main characters in a shoot out? You think women want to read that shit? What are you, the George R. R. Martin of romance? You basically wrote the Red Wedding into a romance novel."

Gray's not kidding. I haven't written a lot but I have been

reading plenty of books. I personally really enjoyed Colt's last one, but he made the classic mistake of writing for guys and not for women. It started off like a romance novel and then it became a Tarantino film where people were getting shot left and right. It was a good book, but it strayed a little far from what readers usually want in these books.

"I know, I know. I got bored and I started just entertaining myself. I'm almost done with my new one. It's not like that at all. It's about an mixed martial arts fighter trying to make it on the amateur circuit. Then he meets this amazingly hot woman and. . .well, I'll save the whole blurb for the book. But I have a good feeling about this one."

"That sounds cool." I tell him. "Hey, is that why you've been training again?"

"Yup. I'm going full Daniel Day Lewis on this one. I want to get into the head of my character."

"Just don't get too far into it and get injured," Gray says. "We need you for the group."

"Speaking of which, there's only one issue," I say.

"What's that?" Gray asks.

"The name? I know you said we can figure it out later, but did you guys have any ideas?"

Colton and Grayson look at each other like they've already had this conversation a few times over and come up with nothing. "We don't have any ideas," Colton says. "We did, but they all sucked."

"Like what?" I ask.

"The Writers. . .the Bad Boys of Romance. . .yeah, they're all shit, unfortunately."

"The Wordsmiths," I say, jumping right in, as if I was meant to give us all a name. "Let's call ourselves the Wordsmiths."

My words linger in the air and the guys look at each

other, and then me. Grayson raises an eyebrow and I detect a faint grin on his face. Colton does the same. "Where'd you get that one from?" he asks. "I think I like it."

"It's a long story," I say, not wanting to discuss Jenny right now. "But it's fitting, isn't it? I think it describes what we do pretty well. And it's original. If you guys are down I think we should make that our brand."

"Amen to that, brother." Colton pats me on the back. "I love it. Gray?"

"Me, too," he agrees. "See, that's why three heads are better than two."

"I think you have that expression wrong," I joke. "Well, whatever. Who cares? "It's decided then. Let's celebrate! You guys already have two of my beers, I see."

"Yeah, sorry about that," Colt says. "We kind of helped ourselves."

"Hey, what's mine is yours. And I don't need any more alcohol right now, trust me. I'm trying to keep that under control. It's time to turn shit around. Hold up." I run to the fridge and grab a cold bottle of water and hold it up. "Raise your glasses, gentleman."

"We don't have glasses."

"Raise your bottles then," I say. "To the Wordsmiths!"

"To the Wordsmiths!"

"Now," I ask after we've toasted. "The only real question is where are you savages taking me out to celebrate?"

"Oh, is that how it works now?" Colt asks.

"Well it's only fair. I came up with the name."

"The man's got a point, Colt."

"Yeah," he agrees. "I guess so."

We all laugh. It's the best I've felt in a long time.

3

EVERLEIGH

THREE MONTHS AGO

"Check out his WIP!" I'm being my usual over enthusiastic self, and Rowan just gives me that 'calm down' look she's used to throwing my way.

"His what?" she asks.

Rowan's new to the indie book world, so she doesn't know the terminology just yet. I use phrases around her like 'release blitz' and 'WIP' and she looks at me like I'm speaking Greek. I'm kind of like her personal romance tutor. "His WIP," I repeat. "His *work in progress*. It's the book he's working on now but isn't finished with yet."

"He's posting things from an unpublished book. Who does that?"

She really is a newbie. "Everybody does that, Ro. You're old school. And you're a year younger than me, too! Don't worry, I'll teach you the crazy ways of the indie romance world."

"I can't wait," she says, looking at me like I'm more than a little bit nuts. "So?"

"What?"

"Tell me about his WIP. Did I say it right?"

"Perfect," I tell her. "You're learning. Come check it out, it's really juicy."

We're sitting in the corner booth at the Starbucks where Ro and I sometimes meet to catch up. I work a lot. I'm the owner of a bakery my grandparents opened generations ago in Queens, New York. They passed it to my parents, and recently they passed it to me. It's a crazy amount of work, even with a full staff, so I don't get to see my girls as much as I used to. But I still make an effort to have some girl time. I turn my laptop so that she can see my screen.

The place is alive with the sounds of the under-caffeinated masses. The back of my computer is facing the line of people jammed inside waiting to order their macchiatos and lattes. They have no idea what I'm looking at. I wonder, what the hell did romance readers do before tablets and laptops? It's not like women used to walk around carrying paperbacks with half naked, glistening dudes on the cover. I'm happy that my love of smut correlated with some pretty major technological changes. It helps keep my little hobby private, something I only share with other people in the community and those who know me best. People like Ro and my other best friend, Harley.

She squeezes in next to me so that we're shoulder to shoulder in the booth. She pretends not to be interested in this stuff, but I can see the look in her eyes when she catches a glance at my screen. Her face lights up when she reads a few lines. "Oh, my."

"Right? It's fucking hot. I'm going to one-click this as soon as it's available."

"One click?"

"Jesus, Ro, what decade are you living in? You sound like

an old lady. I can't believe that you still only buy actual books."

"I like the feel and smell of real books. I'm sorry, but a Kindle just can't replace that."

"They're not mutually exclusive," I tell her. "I do both and so can you."

"That's true. So how did you find his WIP?" She says the last part like she's really proud of herself, like a kid who just learned a new word.

"Look," I say, turning the screen so she can see it clearly. "I'm a member of his reader's group, The *Knight Riders*. That's where he posted it. Only a few paragraphs."

"Please tell me that's not really the name of his group?"

"It is," I say, grinning. "He's Michael Knight. Get it?"

"You're so corny, Everleigh. You might be the only one who loves that name." We both laugh. "I'm not in any reader groups, how do they work? What happens in them?"

I've never really thought about it in those terms. "Nothing happens, exactly. But I keep my notifications on so that I get to see all of his posts. Like this one. Authors post excerpts from their works in progress sometimes, it's pretty common. It keeps readers engaged until their next book comes out."

"Is it long?"

"His WIP?" I ask coyly. "I bet it's super long. Thick, too."

"Everleigh!"

"What? It is. Look, it's a long post. God, what did you think I meant, Ro?"

"Lemme see this long WIP, then."

Ro cuddles up to me again as I click on Michael's latest post. I know that she's into this stuff, but she pretends not to be. She's way too focused on the words she's reading to not be interested, but she tries to hide her inner freak a little too hard.

The WIP is the first page of Michael's newest book. His last one was called *Into Your Eyes,* and it's easily the best thing I've ever read. It became my favorite book the second I finished it. It's about a woman who escapes a bad relationship and ends up meeting the man of her dreams. But it's more than that. It's more than just another forgettable romance novel. The main character is an empowered woman, someone who finds herself along the journey that she goes through in the book. She's someone I admire, as corny as that may sound.

I was surprised to see this post because since then Michael hasn't been on social media as much as he used to be. This many months without much activity is rare for an indie author. I'm not a stalker or anything, I'm just a real fan of his work, and I love following authors and seeing what they're working on.

As crazy as it sounds, I probably read twenty books a month, sometimes even more if I have a lot of free time. Romance is escapism, fantasy, something to take me out of my life and give me something to look forward to reading each night. Some people binge Netflix shows for entertainment. My version of that is scrolling through an entire five book series in a week on my Kindle. I devour them, and I'm insatiable.

My other best friend, Harley, is just like me. Scratch that, she's way worse than me. That girl can tear through two books a night if she's into an author, and she's into a lot of them. And she has no qualms about telling everyone she knows that she loves a good piece of smut now and then. Me? I'm a little more selective, and I'm a little more secretive. I feel like people can be really judgmental, and the last thing I need judged is my choice of reading materials. So I mostly keep my love of all things romance to myself, my girls, and my indie book community that I talk to on social media. Ro is the most conservative one of our little group, but low key I think she's the biggest freak.

"Wow," she says a few seconds later as she reaches over my arm and hits the down arrow to see the next part of Michael's WIP.

"What?" I ask. "I didn't get to read it yet since you were hogging the screen. Is it good?"

"It's not just good. It's. . .it's fucking hot! Holy shit. And I wasn't hogging. Who's this guy again?"

"Michael," I tell her. "That's Michael Knight. I read all of his books like a month after I discovered him on Facebook. They're really good. He knows how to write a sex scene, let me tell you."

"You don't have to tell me," she answers. "I'm reading right now. I'm getting all hot and bothered."

"Yeah, tell me about it. That's what a good romance does. Good story, funny characters, and hot fucking sex that makes you all. . .tingly."

"I see that. How do you just read this in a room by yourself and not wanna reenact every page?"

"Listen to you," I joke, seeing the intensity in her face as she stares at my screen. "I think you might need to pick up a good book to read. I know a few great authors."

"I'm not paying for this stuff. Do you have any actual books I can check out?"

"I have a few paperbacks, but I'm not giving them to you."

"What?" she asks, looking away from the screen finally. "How come?"

"'Cause they're signed copies, and those are just for the bookshelf. I don't actually read those. Just bite the bullet and splurge $2.99 and get one. No one will be able to see, don't worry. You can read it on your phone or tablet and I can make some good recommendations if you tell me what you'd like."

"All right," she says. "I think I might have to. And how do I know what I like if I've never read it?"

"Well, what kind of stuff would get you reaching for the vibrator?"

"Everleigh!"

"Stop, don't pretend to be such a prude. I bought it for you, so I know you own one. Unless you threw it out."

"Of course I didn't throw it out," she says. "And you could have really warned me that was in the box when we were all opening my birthday gifts in front of my family."

"What fun would that have been?" I laugh. "I know how conservative your parents are. I wish I could have taken a picture of their faces. I don't even think your mom knew what it was. Unless she's like you and just pretending to be a prude."

"She's not pretending, trust me. And I told her it was a shoulder massager from Sharper Image."

I start laughing hysterically. "And she bought that?"

"Yeah. Or at least she pretended to so the situation wouldn't be awkward. I'm fine with whichever one of those it was."

Rowan smiles ear to ear, and I start to giggle. "Glad to have you join our little romance sisterhood. Harley and I were starting to feel like the weirdos."

"You are the weirdos," she says. "But maybe I wanna be one, too. To answer your question, I guess just give me something not too out there. One of your top ten favorites."

"That's easy. And here." I say, handing her my laptop. "You might as well finish what you were reading."

"Okay," she jokes. "If you insist."

As I put my computer on her lap my phone goes off.

Jeremey likes when I leave the ringer on because he says it's easier to get to me. I don't know why I listen to him, but he gets annoyed when I don't answer his calls or texts right away. "I'll be right back." Ro's not even paying attention as I get up and step outside. She's falling quickly down the romance rabbit hole and I love every minute of it. "Hey," I say. He already sounds angry. "I answered as fast as I could, relax. Rowan and I are just out getting coffee, like we always do."

He does his usual thing. He tells me I'm not a good girlfriend. Tells me that I make him feel like I don't love him. Tells me he doesn't know what he's doing wasting his time with an ungrateful girl like me. I don't know why I even listen. I've been listening to his bullshit for too long. He used to be a totally different man when I met him, but once we were in a real relationship he changed into this guy. The needy, clingy, verbally abusive person I hear every time I bother to answer the phone. I think that's the first time I've let myself think of that word when I think of him, but I know it's the right one. He's abusive. He's never touched me or anything like that, but there are different types of abusive, and his weapon is his mouth.

"Listen, listen, you need to calm down. I answered as soon as I could and. . ." He goes on some more, his voice raising past where it should to the point that I need to hold the phone away from my ear. Somewhere in his rant something changes in me. I don't know what it is, but, something about his tone just gets to me. I can see Rowan inside. She knows that Jeremy can be kind of an asshole. She's finished reading and put my computer down. She's looking at me like a concerned mom would look at her kid after they fell on the playground. My face is tense, I can feel it. She stands up to come outside and I put my finger up to tell her to stay and she sits back down. But she never takes her eyes off of me. I love that she wants to take care of me, but today I don't need her to.

I don't know what comes over me, but I don't scream or yell, I just pull my phone away from my ear and hang up. I'm done taking his shit, and I'm not going to be told that I'm a bad person any more. I never should have listened to that man. I put my phone on silent before going back inside because I know he's going to call back and probably text me a million times, but I don't have time for this shit. I walk back inside, pushing through the lunch crowd, and sit back down.

"What was that?" Ro asks. She still looks concerned, but I try to put her at ease right away.

"Usual bullshit," I tell her.

"Jeremey?"

"Yeah, who else?"

"It's time to leave that fucker behind. How many times have I told you?"

"I know," I say, cutting her off before she makes the speech that she's made to me a thousand times before. "I think we're done."

"Wait," she says, looking surprised that I'm agreeing with her instead of defending him for once. "Like, done done? You're leaving him?"

I think about it for a second. Hearing those words makes it seem a little more real than just hanging up my phone because I was sick of what he was saying. But the thought of breaking up with him doesn't upset me at all, and that tells me that it's probably the right move. "Yeah," I say, looking her square in the eye. "I'm leaving him. I've had enough."

This seems like it's coming out of nowhere, I realize. But far from it. This has been building up for months, and sometimes things just happen that way. A long build up and then a spark that sets off the explosion. For me, that phone call was the spark.

"Does he know?" Ro asks. "Did you tell him that?"

"No," I tell her. "But he'll find out soon enough. He's away on a business trip for a few days. Do you wanna come help me get my stuff from his place?"

"That's the best question I think you've ever asked me." She leans over and gives me a big hug. A best friend hug. A hug like she's proud of me. Hell, I'm proud of myself. I don't need him, and I know for sure that he doesn't deserve me. "I'd love to," she continues. "But can I ask what changed?"

"What do you mean?"

"I've been telling you to leave that jerk for months now, and Harley's been telling you to leave for longer than I have. So what changed in a thirty second phone call? Did he say something?"

"No," I tell her. "Nothing I haven't heard a million times."

"Then what?"

"If I tell you, you're going to either think I'm joking or think I'm stupid. Either way it's a lose-lose."

"Everleigh, you know the last thing I think you are is stupid. I don't care what you say right now, I'm proud of you for what you did outside, whatever your inspiration was."

"It was one of Michael's books, okay?" I feel dumb saying it, but it's true. I look down like I'm embarrassed, but then look right back up. "His last one."

Ro smiles at me. "Why would you think I'd judge you for that?"

"Come on, I know you think I'm just reading stupid books that are basically soft-core porn."

"First, it doesn't matter what I think about what you read. And I'm about to have some of that soft-core porn on my phone, so who am I to judge? I'm your best friend and I just want you to be happy, no matter what. If this book helps you, that's all that matters."

I give her a hug this time. "Thank you, you're the best." I squeeze her tight. I really am happy that her and Harley are in my life. I don't know what I'd do without them.

"So what's that book about, anyhow?"

"*Into Your Eyes*?"

"Yeah. If that's the one that made you brave."

"What isn't it about?" I start to gush inside just thinking about it. "I love that book. And I'm not just using that word in the way I say that I love strawberry ice cream. I really do LOVE that book!"

"Wow," Ro says, raising an eyebrow. "You don't love many things more than you love strawberry ice cream."

"I know," I joke. "Not only did it make me cry when I read it, but it taught me something. The main character is this woman who's stuck in one bad relationship after another-"

"Sounds familiar already," she interrupts.

"Tell me about it. Anyway, this woman finally finds her voice and builds the courage to leave her abusive husband. Jeremey's not as bad as the guy in the book, but it's not about the guys, it's about the strength and courage that the woman showed. It inspired me. For some reason that story popped into my head when he was berating me on the phone before. I don't know what came over me."

"Courage," Ro says. "Courage came over you. And good for you. Jeremey's a fucking tool, and you deserve better. A lot better."

Ro's the best. Between her and Harley I have the two greatest friends a girl could ever ask for. They're there for me and I'm there for them, through thick and thin, no matter what. And it's moments like this that make me appreciate them even more.

"This is going to sound corny," I say, looking down again because that's what I do when I think what I'm saying is stupid but I want to say it anyhow. "But I wish. . ."

"What?" she asks after I stop mid-sentence.

"I wish that I could tell Michael how much his words mean to me. I mean, like, in person, not just in some corny social media post."

"Well, funny you should say that."

"What do you mean?" I ask.

"How do I know about this and you don't?" she answers.

"Know about what? What are you talking about?"

"I have been monopolizing your computer, so I get it, but look at what he just posted."

"Lemme see." Ro hands me my computer back and I open it up to take a look. "Holy shit!" I hardly believe what I'm reading as I look down. It's a post by Michael, and there are two other writers tagged in it—Grayson Blackman and Colton Chase, two of my other favorite authors, only I don't love their stuff nearly as much as Michael's.

ANNOUNCEMENT

Colton, Grayson and I are pleased to announce that we're joining forces and forming our own all male romance and erotica readers group—The Wordsmiths! Now you can still belong to all of our individual reader groups, but we'd really love if you could all join our newly formed group as well. And we'll be hosting a signing this summer for just our readers. Details and dates TBA.

I can hardly believe my eyes as I read. "I'm joining, hold

on. You join too. We can say that we were some of the first members of their group when they're famous."

"You're nuts," Ro says to me, but I see her pulling out her phone to join up. "But why not, right?"

"Don't hate," I tell her. "Just give into it a little. You like this stuff."

"How can I like it when I've never read it?"

"Okay," I say, conceding her point. "Maybe you don't like it, but you sure don't hate it either. I think you're fascinated by all of it."

"I find it interesting, sure."

I've known Rowan long enough to read her. She's been hesitant ever since college. Secretly she's a freak, but in the open she still feels like she has to put on this front of the good girl—the chaste one—the one who has to resist all things sexual for everyone else's benefit. But I know my best friends, both of them. Harley's a whole different type of puzzle, but Rowan is easy. She was raised to be the prude, but she's really a closet sex kitten. My job is just to help her self-actualize and let go once in a while. "It is interesting," I say. "You should join up. It's not some fringe thing. Look, they probably have 10,000 people between their three groups. That's a lot of people. You'd just be one more."

"Have I ever told you how convincing you can be sometimes?"

"You don't have to tell me, I know already." I'm smiling, but it isn't because I won our little exchange, it's because I'm happy to see her let go a little bit. Plus now both of my best friends will be smut readers like me. Yay. "Wait, there's more." We both look down and see that there's another post in our notifications. I click on it.

"I want to go to this event. I want all of us to go. You, me and Harley together."

"An event?" Ro asks. "What are those, exactly?"

"Like a signing," I explain. "You go there, they sign books, we all take some pictures. Like a meet and greet, get it?"

"Ahh, now it makes sense."

"We're going. All three of us."

"Fine," she says right after I'm done. I'm all ready to make a speech about how I need her to come and support my unhealthy smut habit, but then she just gives in before I can make it.

"Oh," I say. "That was easier than I thought."

"Yeah, well, sometimes I can be a surprise."

"You sure can."

I'm beyond excited to get tickets to this event. Maybe it's dumb. Maybe there's a fine line between being a loyal reader and being a straight up groupie. I hope I fall into the first category and not the second, but the fact of the matter is that my heart beats a little faster at the idea of getting to meet Michael. He's not just an author whose books I like—he's someone whose words speak to me in ways no words have before. People hate on the type of books that he writes, as if nothing meaningful can exist in a book that has sex in it. But I know the truth.

Michael can move emotions like the wind can move grains of sand. There seems to be no effort in their power, and even though I'm not crazy and the book is not written for me, *Into Your Eyes* made me feel like he could see inside me, and it changed the way that I see myself. It might sound dumb to be changed by a romance novel, but I was inspired by the main character in that book. I always loved his writing, but the story of that one hit close to home. I can't wait to meet him and tell him everything that it's meant to me.

On top of that he's really, really hot. That shouldn't

matter, right? His words should be enough—and they are—they're more than enough, but it doesn't hurt that the man looks like he's never missed a session at the gym, is over six feet tall, and is just a beautiful man. Yeah. . .that doesn't hurt at all.

I can't wait to have him sign my books.

But, really, I can't wait to just stand in front of him and look up into those beautiful eyes.

4

KNIGHT

Present Day

"This place is sick!"

For such a good writer, Grayson doesn't always have the most eloquent vocabulary, but he's absolutely right in this. The place is *sick*. We just spent a little over four hours driving from New York to Pennsylvania, and as soon as we got close to the place I knew the guys were right in suggesting this whole thing to me. The truth is that when I first heard the idea I was a little skeptical, even though I jumped on board right away. I didn't want to be the one who said no, but I definitely had my reservations. It sounded cool enough in theory, and I certainly wasn't against the idea of a signing for just us, but I had my doubts as to whether or not it would make a difference for any of our careers. Seeing this place now has me thinking that maybe it will.

"Nice town," I say as we get out of the car right in front of our hotel. "Super quaint."

"Did you just say 'quaint', Mike?" Colton's looking at me sideways and grinning. "I think you did."

"I sure did, asshole. And what's wrong with that, it's

fucking quaint, what else do you want me to call it? That's the right word. I'm sorry you don't know it."

"Oh, I know it," he jokes. "I just don't say shit like 'quaint' outside of a book."

"You know what?" Grayson asks. "I don't think I've ever used the word quaint in any of my books. I think I need to get on that."

"How about cock?" Colton asks.

"You mean the fact that you like it? We know that already," I joke

"Shut up," Colt says. "I mean the word. Give me an estimate for the number of times it comes up in your books. Rough estimate."

"Probably 36 times per chapter," Gray says. "Eh. Maybe I'm exaggerating. More like 25 times or so."

"I'd say that's conservative." I'm joking around just like the rest of them, but deep down talking about writing is still a sore subject for me. My last book, *Into Your Eyes,* did alright —definitely the best written of all my four books, but I didn't have anywhere near the financial or critical success that I wanted it to. It had a good push over the first few days after my launch party, mostly do to the loyal readers I'd made on social media with my first three books, but by Friday of release week it's rank in the romance category on Amazon was plummeting faster than an anchor dropped in the ocean.

I'd started my new book right before the incident with Jenny. I was so confident in the story that I'd even posted a short excerpt as my WIP—work in progress—on my Facebook author page, and I'd gotten over 500 likes, which is insane for a few paragraphs. But the sad fact is I haven't done much since I posted that. The term 'writer's block' doesn't even begin to describe the difficulty I've had writing. I don't talk to the other guys about it that much because I don't want them to judge me, but I'm still messed up about my ex. Ever since she left I haven't gotten much down on paper, and my sales have started to slump big time. 'Publish or Perish' isn't just a truth in the academic world, it's true of Amazon's algorithms also. I need to get something finished and up on my author page. Maybe this event will turn things around for me.

"Now comes the fun part where we carry all of our heavy shit to the elevator." Colton throws his arms up in a bicep flex that looks like he's doing a bad Hulk Hogan impersonation from the 1980's.

"Ah, the life of an indie author."

"Some of us have more pre-orders than others," I tell him. I love messing around with Colton, and the feeling's mutual. He's like the younger brother whose job it is for me to play fight with. And Grayson's like the older brother who keeps the group in line.

"I may have fewer pre-orders than you," he answers. "But I'm gonna sell the fuck out of the extra copies of my new book. It's almost in the top 20 in its category."

"Oh, shit man, congrats." Grayson jumps in and gives Colton a fist bump. I do the same and congratulate him. I know that I shouldn't be jealous of anyone's success, let alone these guys, but it's hard to accept your shitty sales when the guys you're closest to are killing it with their books. But, then again, they've been writing and publishing while I've been staring at the TV and wondering what the hell happened to my life.

"Oh my God!" I hear as I'm reaching into the back of Grayson's SUV to grab a box of my books. I pull my head out from the truck, box in hand, and see three women standing on the steps of the hotel with their phones out, pointed at us. "Is that you?" The woman looks about forty years old, and she's standing with three of her friends. The one who's talking isn't looking at me, she's looking at Colt. "It is, isn't it! Colton Chase!"

"Hey ladies, how are you doing? Are you here for us?" Colt's all smiles as the women approach. He's great with fans.

"We sure are! Drove halfway across the country to see you guys!"

"Well aren't we the luckiest authors in the world." He's smiling and doing his PR thing. Colton's the hottest of us right now, Gray and I are just riding his coattails. He released a book a week ago in anticipation of this signing, strategically timed so that he could sell signed copies and get a big push from the event. What he thought was just going to be a few extra bucks from paperback sales became an unexpected ebook hit on Amazon. It's been shooting up the rankings for the past few days, and now he's within range of getting a decent author rank on Amazon. Besides that, he's just everywhere on social media.

I hand the box of books I'm holding to Gray, who loads it onto a cart they have outside, and then I grab a different one. Colton is in mid-selfie with all four of the women while we're doing some heavy lifting. He's already good at being the face of the group and promoting himself all at the same time. I've gotta hand it to the kid—he's doing everything right and killing the game. Grayson had a few early successes but hasn't been selling so well since, and I'm still trying to build a library of books to get to that level. I'm still waiting for it—the one. That book that will make my career turn the corner.

"It's okay, we've got these, you go ahead and take your pics, Colt!" Grayson's fake yelling, and Colton finishes his selfies and the ladies come over to us.

"We really want pictures with all of you guys," the second woman says. "Do you mind?"

"Of course not," I tell her. I put the box on the ground next to the car and take a few selfies. It feels good. It feels like I have a career again. Grayson photo bombs my picture with the women and makes some crazy faces, and a few minutes later we have some highly satisfied fans who are on their way to explore the town around us. I'm glad they're already having fun.

"Don't forgot to post on social media—use the hashtag #wordsmiths, okay?"

"You got it," one of the women says before walking away.

The ladies go off to explore the town and we finishing lugging out stuff inside and check in. It takes a few minutes but eventually we get all of our books inside to the room where the signing is going to take place tomorrow afternoon. Even though there are only three of us, we had a lot of pre-orders. There are over ten boxes of books between us—granted, most of them are Colton's—but even so, the turnout was good. The hotel's nice enough to let us use a conference room they have on the ground floor. It's small compared to the spaces you usually see at signings, but for the three of us and a few hundred fans it's the perfect size. Despite all of my usual negativity, I'm really psyched for tomorrow.

After we load our books into the room we meet back up in the lobby. There are readers everywhere. I can tell some of them recognize us but are too shy to say anything yet, and others still just stare and take pictures. A few people wave or introduce themselves, but mostly keep their distance out of respect. To our right is the hotel bar. It's pretty small, but it's crammed with readers. I look over and see some women whispering to one another and waving. Colton seizes the opportunity. "Let's go," he says.

"Dude, I'm not drinking at four in the afternoon."

"We don't have to drink," he said. "Let's just say hello. You guys have to work on your PR game. Come on."

Colt leads the way, but Gray and I are right behind him. He's the most outgoing of the group—the one most likely to just start talking to strangers. I've known Colt a while and he's like that with everyone. I'm a little more reserved, and so is Gray. But we know that this is what we wanted—a captive audience of women we knew would already love our work and want to read more of it, so what are we complaining about? "He's right," Gray says to me as we walk just behind Colt. "This is part of the gig. Hell, this is the gig."

"I know," I say, looking at the group of women we're approaching. "I'm just tired from the drive is all."

"Me, too. But let's go meet our adoring fans. We can hide out in our rooms and get rest afterwards."

"Good idea, on both counts!"

We walk into the room and you'd think we were Justin Bieber based on the reaction we get. Women are waving, taking out their phones, and smiling ear to ear like we all just told them the funniest joke in the world. I'm a little overwhelmed by the attention. I wave and say hi and just kind of stand back. As I look around I actually recognize some of the faces from the women in my reader's group and I wave to them.

I haven't done a lot of signings, but when I have I've been just another author in a giant room filled with other authors. No one special. And I've never had a table that fans are gathered around in masses just to see me, but this is different. It's just us three brothers, and it's just our readers and fans. It's at this moment, as I'm staring into the smiling faces of these women who are looking at us like we're the damn Beatles stepping off that plane, that I realize the brilliance of this event. We have a captive audience, and we're not competing with one another, we're combining our forces to bring readers three times the experience that any one of us could bring individually. It's a great idea, and I'm finally starting to fully embrace it.

I walk in, shake some hands, give some hugs, and take a few pictures. I'm honestly not much of a drinker, but I order one just because, and take little sips here and there. I'm talking to a woman from my own reader group who I recognize. She's the best, always leaving positive comments on my posts, and sharing anything I put on there about my books or whatever else. It's a cool experience to sit and talk with her and some of the other women. A few minutes later I'm halfway done with my drink and I feel an arm wrap around my shoulder. "Hey Fuck-face." Colton is standing on my left, looking like he's had more than just half a drink.

I can smell the booze on his breath, but I know him well enough to know he can handle his alcohol. He's fun when he's had a few. "Hey," I say back. I lean my head over and yell into his ear. "Great fuckin' idea, man, really."

"See, don't ever doubt me. And we're just getting started! Let me get you another drink."

"I'm not even done with this one," I tell him, but he's insisting, so I tell him to get me another vodka even though there's no way I'm drinking that shit right now. He takes a picture that the women in my reader group ask him to take of all of us, and I excuse myself to make the rounds with some of the other readers.

As I as make my way to the other end of the bar I see Grayson talking to some of the women in his group also. Everyone has smiles on their faces. I'm so focused on everything to my left and right that I'm not really looking where I'm going. I feel the bump against my right shoulder as I move down the bar.

"Oh, I'm so sorry," I hear. As I'm turning my head from the impact I'm not paying attention at first, I just feel bad that I walked into somebody.

"It's okay I'm s. . ." I stop talking when I see her. I stare for a second in mid sentence and she returns my gaze. "I'm the one who should be apologizing," I say to her to break the momentary silence. "Are you alright?"

"I'm great," she says. "But you're big, I'm surprised you didn't knock me over."

"Then I would've felt awful," I tell her, still studying her beautiful face but trying to be less obvious about it. "I'm Knight." I extend my hand like we're at a business meeting or something, and I feel stupid. She reaches out and shakes.

"I know who you are, Michael." I don't know what it is, but the fact that she's using my real name, and that she did so on her own really turns me on. There's something sensual in her voice, and something quietly commanding in her calling me by a different name than I introduced myself by. "You're my favorite author."

She's smiling at me and looking away every few seconds like she's uncomfortable. I hope I didn't make this awkward for her. The woman is sex—plain and simple. She's unassuming at first because she doesn't act the way you expect someone as hot as her to behave. There's zero arrogance to be detected, and no assumption that every guy in the room should be trying to fuck her. I can read that vibe a mile away and this girl doesn't have an ounce of it.

There's something contradictory about her that I can see in the contrast of her expressions, which range between innocent and seductive. And those eyes. They're the most beautiful shade of green I've ever seen—unusual as eyes went. She must be used to guys complimenting them and staring at her, but I can't help it. I feel my cock press against the front of my pants as my heart starts beating faster than normal. I'm not used to being so turned on just by the sight of a girl, but she seems to have that effect on me.

"What's your name?" I ask her.

"Oh, I'm sorry," she says. "I'm Everleigh. Nice to meet you, Michael."

"The pleasure is all mine. Are you in my group?"

"I am," she answers, looking me right in the eyes. "Have you ever been about to say something and then stopped yourself because you realize how crazy it sounds in your head?"

"That's basically my life, so yes. Why? What were you going to say?"

"I was about to say 'I know who you are, I'm your number one fan', until I remembered that's what Cathy Bates says in Misery before kidnapping the author and torturing him for an entire book." I don't know why but I start laughing so deeply and loudly that people start looking at us. I have a deep belly laugh, and when I get going you can hear me from a mile away.

"What?" she asks.

"I'm sorry, but I have a really dark sense of humor and that visual cracked me up. I was picturing myself tied to a bed and you about to break my legs with a sledgehammer so I don't leave your house, like in the book. Plus I love me some Stephen King. I grew up reading him."

"Me, too," she says, energized by the fact that I wasn't laughing at her and that I mentioned the master of horror's name. "I've read almost every book he's written. What's your favorite Stephen King story?"

"*IT*. Easy question. No comparison. It's his masterpiece."

"Oh, jeeze," she says, looking down and grinning.

"What?"

"Would you hate me if I told you that I never read it?"

"What? Oh my God!" I'm smiling but truly shocked also. "What self-respecting Stephen King fan hasn't read *IT*? I'm sorry, I may have to walk away right now."

"Fine," she jokes. "Walk away. But I don't think you really want to."

She looks at me and I catch the slightest glimmer of. . .of I don't know what, but it's definitely something. I've always been good at catching micro expressions people make; little gestures that most people don't even notice. Maybe being extra observant is part of being a good writer, but when she said that to me just now there was a glimmer in her eye—something flirtatious.

"Oh yeah," I joke. "And why's that?"

She looks right at me, and the micro expression becomes a macro one. It's brief but it's intense, a combination of look and voice that just shoots right inside me. "Because something tells me that you're enjoying our conversation." It's forward without being forward, and I get the message loud and clear.

"I am. I really am."

I catch myself staring again as she looks away. I steal a glance and try to take her in before she looks back at me. She's a rare combination—traditionally beautiful and sexy at the same time. Part of me just wants to look at her, and the other part of me—the part that's winning right now, wants to grab her and . . .

"Are you excited?"

"What?" I ask, thinking that she can see the mild stiffening of my cock as I stare at her.

"About the signing," she says. "Are you excited about it?"

"Oh, right, the signing. Yeah, we're all psyched about it. How about you?"

"Absolutely. I've been excited about it since I saw the announcement on your Facebook page. I was. . .I was going through a rough time and it brought a little light to my day."

"Fuck, I'm sorry about that, whatever it was. Is everything better now?"

"Yeah," she says. "Much better, thanks for asking. Not that you want to hear about it."

"No," I say, genuinely interested in what's going on with her. "I do. If you want to tell me, of course."

"I was going through a breakup is all. Bad relationship. Bad choices. Kind of like Ava, you know?"

I smile. Ava is the main female character from my last book, a standalone called *Into Your Eyes*. It's about a woman who turns her life around and finds herself through meeting the love of her life. It's the last story that I saw through from beginning to end before my own breakup. "That's amazing to hear. Sometimes we write books and don't get to hear about their impacts on people, if they even have any impacts. I'm glad that Ava touched you as a character."

"More than touched me," Everleigh says. "Inspired. Made me look at my own life and my own bullshit. Made me leave a bad situation when I otherwise might have stayed longer. Thank you for that."

"You're welcome. You're the first person who's said anything like that to me, you know."

"I find that hard to believe."

"It's true. Makes me want to write another one."

"Oh, you're not writing anything? I thought I saw a post a while back where you posted some of what you were working on. I assumed you were done."

Her words unintentionally hit me like a punch to the gut. I know that she's just asking an honest question, but it hits on an insecurity that I've never been directly confronted with before by another person. Usually I beat myself up about my recent inability to finish a book, but to hear someone else—and a reader no less—say that makes me realize that I need to get my ass going already.

"It's been a rough time. I'll tell you the honest truth. I haven't done a lot more with that since you saw that post. I've had some issues myself."

"Like writer's block?" she asks. "I've heard that can be horrible."

"Sort of. But. . ." I stop because I'm not sure how much I want to tell her about Jenny. I just met this woman a few minutes ago and I don't know how far down the lesbian-cheating-ex rabbit hole I want to go just yet. But she was straight forward with me when she didn't have to be. So I take a deep breath and just go for it. "Similar thing as you, actually. My wife and I got a divorce and I haven't written much since then. I know one should have nothing to do with the other, but I've been blocked, like you said."

She looks at me in a way I don't expect—with compassion in her eyes. "I'm so sorry to hear that. I totally get why that would keep you from being creative. I'm not a writer or anything, but I'd think that you have to be in the right headspace to do something creative and time consuming like writing a novel."

"Thanks," I say. "That's true. But still, that was a year ago, and I'm running out of excuses. I think maybe it's time to get back to it."

"Maybe something this weekend will inspire you."

She's making that face again. It's subtle, but it's there, and I can't get enough. "I'm hoping so."

I feel a hard pat on my back from behind. It's Colt. He leans into my ear from behind. "They're gonna want us to come back later and have a few drinks. Me and Gray are gonna go unpack and shower before we come back. You coming up?"

"Yeah," I tell him. "In a minute."

"Cool, see you up there."

I turn back to Everleigh, who's looking gorgeous as ever, and I feel bad that I have to continue our conversation later on. "I hate to cut this short, but I need to go get my shit together. Unpack my books, take a shower, all that stuff. Are you going to be around in a little?"

"Absolutely. I'm here with my friends Rowan and Harley, only Harley's not here yet. We'll be in and out of the bar. Eventually we'll probably go out and explore the town a little, get something to eat so we're not on a pure alcohol diet."

"I've been on that diet before, it's not that bad. Send me a private message or something and let me know where you guys are in a few hours, if you want."

"How about I just give you my number and you text me?"

"That works, too." I didn't want to ask for her number outright. I didn't know if she would feel comfortable giving it to a guy she just met, but I was wrong. Maybe she's feeling what I'm feeling.

"Here you go." She takes my phone, types in her number, and saves it.

"Until later, then, Everleigh."

"Until later."

5

KNIGHT

I'm already fantasizing about Everleigh by the time I hit my room. It was a quick elevator ride up, but more than enough time to let me imagine her naked in all sorts of compromising positions. Like I said—she is sex embodied. Gray and Colt are sharing a room, but I opted to go solo. I like my space, and if I'm going to write any new words I'm going to need total silence. That'll be hard to achieve in this environment, but I'm going to try to steal a few minutes of me time before the responsibilities of the signing take over. I know the guys are going to unpack and then head back down to the bar. There are a bunch of readers hanging out down there waiting for us to join in the fun. I don't know if I'm even going to go. I decide to text them.

Me: Hey. Are you guys going down?

Gray: Yeah, in a little. It's early still, and those women aren't going anywhere, trust me. Gotta finishing unpacking first. Colt still has a few more boxes of shit to grab from the car. You?

Me: I'm not sure. I'm exhausted.

Gray: You should come down, dude. The women love

your ugly ass for some reason. Did you hear some of them whisper when you walked in before to say hi? "Michael Knight—OH MY GOD!" They'd be disappointed if you didn't at least make an appearance.

Me: I'll go. I just need a little while to refresh from the drive. Maybe take a shower or something. Then I wanna hit the gym.

Gray: You're so weird. Who showers and then hits the gym. Fuck, I don't even know if they have a gym.

Me: They do. I checked.

Gray: Of course you checked. How long will that be?

Me: I don't know. At least a half hour, then another to take a shower.

Gray: When did you become such a gym rat?

Me: When I realized it helped lift me out of my depression when I stress my body.

Gray: Did you mean that as a pun?

Me: Oh. No! But it works. It's a non-negotiable. We don't have to all be together the whole time. You two go, I'll be there eventually, don't worry.

Gray: Whatever works man. I'll text when we're getting close to going down.

Me: Sounds good, bro. Thanks.

I put my phone down and step inside the bathroom to take a shower. The hot water crashes against my skin, and the steam is so thick that I can barely see in front of me. I take a few deep breaths to let it into my lungs, then I put my arms against the wall and lean forward. The water drips furiously across my neck and down past my face, slamming into the shower floor while I close my eyes and breathe deeply.

It's there, in the solitude of the shower, as the hot water massages my tired back, that I make a decision—I'm going to move on. I'm done moping around, feeling sorry for myself, and complaining. In fact, I'm going to do my best to not even think about Jenny anymore. I'm not going to dwell on anything negative. Instead, I'm going to use this weekend for what it is—an opportunity to have a good time, move my career forward, and hopefully get some words written if I have time with everything else.

I open my eyes and see the barrage of water hitting my toes and circling the drain before disappearing. The sound is intense around my ears, and I vow that when I lift my head up, I'll be a new man and a new author—the new Michael Knight.

I like to air dry, so I run a towel over my wet hair really quickly and then wrap another one around my waist. My laptop is sitting in my bag, and I reach for it right away. I'm naked as the day I was born and still a little wet all over, but I'm feeling that twinge of writing inspiration and I don't want the moment to pass.

I take my computer out of my bag and open up the file for my latest book—the one I've been writing for about a year now—the one that has no title and very few words. Actually, saying I've been writing it for a year is a little misleading. It would be more accurate to say that I started it a year ago, and right now it's less of a book and more of a collection of random scenes with not much of a plot glueing them together. When the file opens I scroll down to the bottom, and I remember that I'm in the middle of a sex scene. The main character—who still has no name—and the female character are about to get into it. I read the words I've written so far.

She turned to him with that look in her eye—the one that let him know it was time. There was absolutely no mistaking the intention in her look, and he didn't have time to misinterpret anyhow. She pounced on him like a cougar— practically leaping across the room and attaching her body to his, making them one. Their lips smashed together passionately, hardening his cock instantly and making her so wet that she could feel the drip between her legs. There was only one thing that was going to bring relief to both of their aches—and they each knew what it was. . .

I stop reading when I realize that I'm hard.

It happens all the time. Sounds strange to turn yourself on with your own writing, but when you have sex on the brain all the time it kind of comes with the territory. I take my fingers off the keyboard and look down. I reach down and pull my cock upwards, only I don't let go right away. In fact, I decide that I'm not letting go at all.

The scene in my book may have made me hard, but what's keeping me at attention is her. . .Everleigh. Her name is as beautiful as she is, only she's more than just beautiful, she's fucking hot. She was wearing a blue dress that showed me just enough to keep me curious. On her bare neck she wore a small silver locket, which drew my attention to the smoothness of her skin.

I start thinking about our meeting at the bar a few minutes ago, only I'm writing my own continuation of it in my head. I close my eyes, my right hand still tight around my now throbbing cock, and I clench both my fist and my eyes as the vision of her flows through my mind.

We shake hands again, introducing ourselves to one another, only when our hands separate they don't go back to our sides like happened in real life. No. They go elsewhere, where hands are meant to explore. Mine start on her shoulders and hers start on my face. She reaches up and places them on either cheek, as mine hold onto the outside of her shoulders. I feel the slight pull from her, and I don't resist at all, I just lean over and let our faces get as close as two faces can be without touching.

I think that she's going to kiss me, but she stops the momentum of my head just before our lips touch. My mouth opens in anticipation of the kiss, and so does hers, and I feel her sweet breath inside of me, filling my mouth with her essence before we actually touch.

I squeeze her shoulders, and as soon as she feels that pressure she jerks my face another inch downwards, and our mouths finally meet—our lips pressed deeply into one another. My hands start to wander lower on her body, framing the outside of her breasts, her waist, her hips, until I stop just above her knees. I let my hands linger there a little longer because her body feels amazing, but only for a second or two. After that they move further down, to the hem of her dress, and I grip onto it with my fingers. She's still kissing me, and her hands have started to wander all over my chest—the palms of her hands framing my pecks and abs, moving up and down with no small amount of pressure.

When her hands stop I make my move, yanking her dress upwards until it rolls gently past her hips and ass, and I hold the fabric at her waist. She starts to moan—a sound that makes me even harder than I thought I could get, and my dick is screaming to be let free of my pants, only it's not time yet. Her hands are still hovering around my pecs, and as soon as I pull her dress up she digs her fingers into me, as though she's trying to hold me in place as we kiss. I'm not going anywhere. As I lift the fabric a little more north, the backs of my hands graze against her naked hips, and their smoothness sends a tingle through my arms.

She's not wearing any underwear, and as soon as I feel that I let my right hand circle behind her, to her smooth bare ass, and I grab onto it. She gasps when I grab her, something I do firmly and suddenly to surprise her. I pull her even closer to me, until she has to come off of her stool and stand against me. Our bodies touch fully for the first time, and I can feel the softness of her form in contrast to the hardness of mine. I pull her in, still holding onto her juicy ass, and shove my body into her as our lips smash together again.

Her hands start to go to work, only she's not waiting for anything—there's nothing methodical or calculated in her touch—she reaches straight down like she knows exactly what she wants, and grabs onto my manhood. My pants are still on, but she finds a way to wrap her fingers around my bulge and hold on tight, squeezing me to the point of blending pain and pleasure. I let go of her ass and grip the gathered fabric of her dress behind her body with just my right hand, and with my left I scoop under her right knee. I know she's not expecting it, but I lift her leg up and put it on the bar, and it moves so easily that I'm amazed. She's flexible as hell, and her leg just sits up on the bar at a 45 degree angle like it's nothing.

I separate from her and leave her leg there. She's looking at me like she wants me as bad as I want her, and all I do is reach for my belt. With a few jerks it pulls free, and I pull my pants and underwear down then step out of them. Now there's nothing between us except opportunity. The music is pumping in the background, only there's no one else here but us. No one to watch or interrupt us, and no silly words to get in the way of what's about to happen. I step into her—her pink, clean shaven pussy fully exposed, waiting for my throbbing cock to do its job. I lean in to kiss her again, and she reaches around the back of my neck to hold onto me.

As we kiss I reach down and hold on to myself. I'm ready. I'm so fucking ready. I've never been this turned on in my entire life, and I hold onto the base of my shaft and aim towards her. I do it slowly so that I can feel every moment—experience every sensation her body has to offer. I stop right on the outside of her lips, the head of my cock begging to be let inside. I move myself in circles around the outside, teasing the head just inside of her, rubbing up and down on her clit. I feel like I'm going to come if I keep going. She's too hot and this is too new, so I stop the tease even though she's moaning in pleasure.

"Fuck me, Michael," she whispers to me.

I position myself just right, and as I start to push forward, I feel myself sliding inside of her, and then. . .

"Yo, asshole, what are you doing!" It's Colton! He's knocking on my room door and yelling. Fuck!

"Hold on, man, I just got out of the shower. Text me or something I'm not even dressed."

"Stop touching yourself and let's get going. I'm hitting up the bar now, there are a bunch of fans down there now posting on social media. Our audience awaits. You coming?"

It's an ironic choice of words on his part. If only he knew that I almost had, all over my hand and who-knows what else. My erection is starting to go down since he startled me, but my cock is still inside of my clenched fist. "Yeah, man, I told Grayson I'm just gonna chill for a while and then I'll be down. You go ahead."

"You two are such old ladies. All right, I'll hold down the fort. I'll be our representative until you guys get your asses down to do some shots with the ladies."

"All right, man, meet you down there in a little."

I hear his footsteps as he walks away. My heart is still racing. He startled me out of my fantasy, but it was the imagery running through my head that's made me feel like I'm having a damn heart attack. My laptop is still open to that same paragraph. I take my left hand and close it, then clean myself up with the towel I still have wrapped around my waist.

I guess my imagination got the best of me. The wonders of being a writer. But God, did it feel real. She felt real. Everleigh. I wonder if she's still down at the bar?

Maybe I need to stop fantasizing and go find out for myself.

6

EVERLEIGH

"WHERE'S HARLEY?" I ASK WHILE TEXTING HER FOR LIKE the seventeenth time. "I'm gonna kill that girl, I swear."

"Oh, come on, you can't tell me you're surprised that our best friend is late. she's late for a living. I think she has a degree in lateness."

"I know," I say, staring at my phone and waiting for her to text back. "But for this? I really thought she'd leave enough time. I even told her 5 o'clock expecting that she'd be late. But radio silence so far."

"She'll be here," Ro says calmly. "She always gets where she's going, she's just on her own Harley schedule. It's part of what we love about her. And she may just not have a signal. My phone was going in and out on the trip."

"I guess." I'm not really annoyed. Rowan is right, I should expect this of her. Harley's a free spirit, which is a nice way of saying that she can be flaky sometimes. On the good side she's a super independent woman, which I respect the hell out of, but the flip side of that independence can sometimes be a lack of care for other people's time. I should probably relax, though, it's not like Ro and I are doing anything important. "I just wish the whole crew was here, that's all."

"What am I, chopped liver?" Ro asks.

"No, of course not," I reassure her. "At worst you're just regular liver. The non-chopped kind."

"Gee, thanks."

"Ladies!" From behind me I hear a man's voice, but I don't recognize it at all. When I turn around I see a familiar face. It's familiar only because of Facebook. His name is KL Steiner. That's his pen name, anyhow, I have no idea what his real name is. KL is another male romance author who definitely isn't in the group, and I'm taken aback the second I recognize him. *What is he doing here?* Rowan just stares, wondering who this strange guy is who's approaching us, and I don't have the time to explain before he's hovering over us.

"Hey," I say, not knowing how else to respond.

"Hey," he says back.

I can tell right away that he's awkward as hell. I've known of KL Steiner for a few years now, but I've never read any of his books. He's too taboo even for me. He's an erotica author, which is a little different than a romance author. Erotica uses sex to drive the plot, whereas in romance books there is a plot that also has some hot sex in it—hopefully. KL is one of those erotica authors who uses the most shocking scenarios and extreme sex scenes.

His fans are loyal—rabid, even. If any reader says anything bad about KL on social media, or even leaves a bad review on Amazon or Goodreads, his fans will gang up on her like a pack of wolves. His readers create drama all over the indie community. Personally, I don't care what turns people on, but his shtick as a male author has always turned me off. That, and the fact that his writing isn't very good.

And now I get to look at his ugly face in person, in a place I never thought I'd see it.

"Are you ladies here for the signing?" he asks.

What a dumb question. Everyone is here for the signing. "Yeah," I tell him, trying to be polite but also sending the get-away-from-me signal at the same time. "We're here to see all three guys, but especially Michael Knight." I know this is going to trigger him, which is why I say it. The indie book world is a great place, but it can also be a petty place. Online bullying, shaming, authors being rude to their readers—there are all sorts of things that turn readers off and make them abandon an author. Those kind of incidents aren't common, but they do happen. But there's a reason this whole thing about KL approaching us is really fishy to me.

KL wanted to be one of the Wordsmiths. Badly.

I know this because he posted all about it in his private reader's group. He went on a small rant in one of those posts where you have to click 'read more' at the bottom. I read more, and so did all of the 2,000 people in his group, and who knows who else. It was one of those backfire moments because I think he was going for sympathy—like he was some slighted party who'd been left out of the cool kids club, but instead it read like he was a petty, jealous ex on an epic, post breakup-rant. His reader group, which I joined just to watch the train wreck, went down by about 200 people after that little event. I never thought he'd show up here. He hates the guys. This should be interesting.

"Oh, yeah, Michael," he says, sounding exactly like the bitter ex I just described. "He's. . .he's an interesting one for sure."

"He's great," Ro says, jumping in to the conversation to back me up. She's great at reading situations like this without us having to speak a word to each other. "He's my favorite of the three."

"Really?" He can't help but sound jealous when he asks that question. This whole thing is getting weird. I mean, what the hell is he doing here? Is he crashing another author's signing or something? Did he buy a ticket? I'm not going to ask him any of these questions because then he'll just keep on talking to me, and that's the last thing I want, even though he doesn't seem to be reading my body language at all.

"What is 'interesting' supposed to mean? Are you surprised that I'm here for Michael?" He seems taken aback by the question.

"Well, honestly, a little bit."

"Oh, really?" I ask, putting my drink down and making my voice a little confrontational. "Why's that? You know what, you can answer that question second. What are you even doing here?"

"Research," he says. "I'm doing a little research."

"On what?" Rowan jumps into the conversation. "What kind of research?"

"I want to see exactly what readers see in this little group they've formed," he says. "That, and to connect with readers like you." The last part makes the hair on the back of my neck stand up, and it sounds like some rehearsed bullshit. I think I'm imagining it at first, but it also kind of sounds flirtatious, in that creepy way that he seems to say everything. When I look up at him I see the look in his eyes and know that my intuition is right. "Beautiful readers like yourself, that is." *Is this fucking guy serious?* Not only is he bad at reading my body language, but he's also terrible at talking to women. Ironic considering the kind of books he writes.

"And you think showing up unannounced and uninvited

to this event and asking women why they read the Wordsmiths' work is appropriate?"

"I'm not here for the event. It just so happens that I'm passing through on the way to a different signing tomorrow. This is on the way, and last I checked the hotel bar isn't a private room. I'm just hanging out."

"Right," Rowan says. "Very smooth."

He makes a face like he was just sucking on a lemon, but he doesn't move. You'd think at this point he'd get the idea that we didn't want to talk to him. "Let me help you with your research, okay? And then you're going to walk away and leave me and my friend to our drinks. You ready?" He nods. "Great," I begin, sounding as sarcastic as I can. "The guys are great writers. I buy everything they write, and Michael in particular. I love his writing. It makes me happy."

What happens next is a little surreal. He rolls his eyes at me. Literally. It takes a moment before I realize what I'm seeing. This professional author, this petty little man who's stalking the event, is standing in front of me, rolling his eyes at what I just said. My blood starts to boil, but I don't want to cause a scene. I'm about to tell him exactly what I think about him when my phone vibrates on the bar. Thinking it's finally Harley, I ignore this asshole as he stands over us and check my phone. Only it isn't Harley. When I see what's on the screen I really wish it was.

Ro sees the look on my face. "What is it? Is that her, finally?" I keep looking down at my phone, and I know my face changes immediately. If it looks anything like what I'm feeling as I read the text on my phone then I must look horrifying. "Everleigh?" she asks again, sounding more urgent. This time I look up. "What is it? Who texted you?"

I don't say anything at first, I just stand up and excuse myself. "I'm sorry Ro, I need a favor."

"What is it?"

"I need some fresh air. I promise I'll tell you what it is, but for right now I need you to not ask me and just let me go. I promise I'm okay." That last part is a lie, but the first two things I really do need her to do.

"Go," she says. "If Harley gets here I'll text you. Just keep me in the loop, okay? Don't go missing."

"Thank you."

I get up abruptly and gently bump KL out of my way. Outside the air is warm, and the streets are alive with activity. I should be happy. I shouldn't feel alone, but I do. I realize that I separated myself from Ro and the other readers, but I need some time to myself. I think I'll walk around and find someplace where I can sit and think.

And eat. I'm starving.

7

KNIGHT

For a hotel that isn't that big, they have a hell of a gym. Top notch. And I should know, I'm usually a gym rat when I'm not writing. Keeping in shape keeps me sane and helps me deal with some of the issues I've had. It's not a cure, but it's a little something that helps me cope. There's something meditative to me about pushing my body to the absolute limits of what it's capable of. I started hitting the gym after Jenny left, when I was in the darkest time of my life. Even though I couldn't write much and I was in a terrible headspace, working out was the one thing that brought me back from the brink of depression. I didn't need therapy or pills, I needed to push my body to its psychical limitations as often as I could. I still try to do it every day. I'm not planning on going that hard tonight—a light sweat with some cardio will do—but on a normal basis I like to make my workouts as uncomfortable as possible.

I'm listening to music on my phone—heavy shit mostly. Some metal and hard rock that gets me going when my body wants to quit. I start thinking about Everleigh again. How hot she looked, how easy it was to talk to her, how much she loved my work. The truth is that girl's been in my head since I laid eyes on her only a couple of hours ago. I'm sure Grayson and Colton are down at the bar doing shots and taking selfies as I sweat my balls off in here. I don't want to miss Everleigh or for her to think I'm rude, so I decide to shoot her a text and let her know I'll be a little late.

Less than a minute after I send the text I see that she's writing me back.

Everleigh: Hey. No worries. I should probably get my fat ass on a treadmill too, but can't now. I'm not even at the bar. I stepped out to get food by myself.

By herself? Why is she by herself? Maybe I'm being selfish, or reading too much into her text, but it doesn't make too much sense to me as to why she'd be at some restaurant alone. I hope nothing's wrong. I stop the treadmill and text her back.

Me: Want some company?

I wait a few seconds until I see her response.

Everleigh: Sure. That would be nice.

She texts me the address, some quaint little place that's only a few blocks away from the hotel. There I go using that word again. If only Colt could hear me. It's true though, there's no better word for it. It's a town full of quaint little places. As we were driving through on the way here all I could notice was the complete lack of chain stores and franchised restaurants. No Dunkin' Donuts, no McDonald's, no Subway, and no damn Walmart. None of it. Every little shop and restaurant is unique. It's a town of small businesses, which is probably why I feel so comfortable here. It's a place where regular people are just trying to start a career and make a living. It's the perfect place for indie authors.

My body's still warm from the workout, and I try to keep my pace somewhere between a stroll and a jog so that I can cool down a little and get my heart rate back to normal by the time I get there. It's only a few blocks, so it takes just a couple of minutes to walk there. *Jameson's Burgers and Fries* sounds like my kind of place—nothing too fancy, food so good you can smell it from the street, a line out the door, and great looking food. I'm sold. But I'm not here for the fries, I'm here to make sure Everleigh is okay.

Grayson and Colton keep texting me asking me how long I'm going to be before I get to the bar, and I text them back that I'm not sure, that I had to run out for a few, and that they should mingle without me. I really should be there. The allure of this whole thing for readers is that they get all three of us at once, but right now I'm not worried about advancing my career or selling some books, I just want to make sure Everleigh is okay and see her one more time. I text her.

Me:Where are you?

She writes that she's in the back, at a table for two, minus the second person. I'm here to fix that. I make my way through the masses of hungry people waiting in the front and tell the hostess that I'm meeting a friend. I see Everleigh across the crowded dining room and wave. She waves back and forces a smile, and I can tell even at this distance that she's not happy.

"You have balls," I say, standing over her. "I could never eat alone. I'd feel weird about it."

"It's not so bad," she answers. "I have my phone. I don't know what the hell people did before these things. Back then you'd look like a weirdo just sitting alone, staring around a room. At least now you have entertainment and can block the world out."

"Why would you want to do that?" I ask. She looks up and her eyes appear bloodshot. Her face has a mild strain to it, and the energy she has now is totally different than the vibes I was getting at the bar. "Who am I to ask that, right? This coming from the guy who basically didn't leave his house for two months after his wife left him."

"Do you always talk about yourself not in the first person?"

"What do you mean?" I joke. "Do you not like how Michael Knight is speaking right now?" I get a smile from her. It's a small one but it's genuine, and her face changes completely.

"Are you gonna sit down or just hover over me?"

I pull out the second chair and sit across from her. She puts her phone down, face up, on the table and looks right at me. She isn't speaking, but she looks like she wants to be spoken to. "Should I ask what's wrong?"

"Why do you think something's wrong?"

"Oh, I don't know," I say. "Maybe because this amazing woman who told me that she was going to be with her friends all night is sitting alone in the back of a burger place, staring at her phone and looking all sad. That was my first clue."

"You think I look sad?"

"I think you look very different than you looked before. I know we just met, but you can tell, you know. It might help to get whatever it is off your chest."

She looks around after I say this to her, like she's considering whether or not to be honest with me, or even how much she wants to reveal about whatever is bothering her. I did the same thing earlier when we talked about Jenny leaving. Why are we so guarded around new people, especially of the opposite sex? I'm as guilty of being a little guarded as anyone, especially after what happened with Jenny, but maybe we just need to find the right person to open up to.

"Remember before when I was telling you about the bad time in my life a few months back?"

"Yeah," I answer. "When you were reading *Into Your Eyes*?"

"Right. That's when I left my ex. But he. . .let's just say that he didn't agree with my decision."

"Oh, Jesus."

"Yeah," she says, looking down. "Jeremey's a little bit of a control freak, and he's used to getting what he wants. I had a girl on social media reach out to me that used to date him that I was mutual friends with on Facebook. She told me all kinds of shit—some of it was familiar, like trying to control everything I did and everyone I saw. But some of it was a little darker, like he hit her once or twice. That's when she left him just like I did."

"Fuck." I don't know what else to say. I'm a little alarmed by her story, but I don't say much. Instead I just let her vent because she clearly needs to get some of this off her chest. "Did he ever?"

"No, never," she reassures me. "I'd never let a man hit me. I'm not a victim like that. But I did let him talk to me in demeaning ways and try to control what I do. I don't know why the hell I let that go on as long as I did. Anyway, he keeps leaving me these creepy texts, saying how we'll be together again, and what a mistake I made. I just keep trying to move on and he keeps contacting me. I blocked his number but he must be getting new phones or burner phones and texting me. It just upset me, is all, so I left to get a breather." She takes a deep breath when she's done explaining. I'm glad it's nothing major, at least not at the moment, but more than that I'm glad that she felt comfortable confiding in me. We just met, but I can feel the connection between us.

"I guess I just have bad luck with guys," she continues.

"Just before some guy tried hitting on me at the bar. Some author."

"Author? Who? Was it Gray or Colt?"

"No, no," she says. "Not the guys. Some creep. . .I'm honestly not even sure he's really an author. Probably just some hotel guest pretending to be an author to get laid. Anyhow, I blew him off."

"Hey," I say, reaching across the table and taking her hand. "It's okay. All of it. Forget about the creep and forget about the ex. You're not with him now. You left. You moved on. You realized that it was wrong and that he was wrong, and here you are, eating burgers alone with a B-level indie romance author. Life is good!"

I get another smile from my sarcasm. It's what I was going for. I love it when she smiles. She's gorgeous regardless, but when her cheeks raise up her eyes take on this lightness, and her face becomes even hotter than it normally is. I'm listening to every word she's saying, trying to be supportive and say the right things back to her, but in another part of my brain all I can think about is how much I want her. There's this raw attraction that I felt when I saw her at the bar, and it's there again. Whenever I'm in her presence my arms just want to reach out and grab a hold of her by the waist and pull her into me.

"Hey, don't call yourself that," she says. "You're A-level to me. You're why I'm here, remember?"

"What do you want me to write in the books you brought?"

"Umm. . .sign them to Everleigh, your number one fan!"

"I sure won't," I joke. "No way in hell. But I'll think of something cool."

"I'll take you up on that." What happens next shocks me a little. I don't know why, it's nothing major, but this time she's the one who reaches across and grabs my hand. I look down and then back up to her eyes, and her expression is back to the one I remember from the bar—she's got that something in her eyes that let's me know that she's interested in me as more than just her favorite author. We just met, but there's something there, and I think we're both feeling it. "Thanks for listening. I'm okay. I'm really excited about tomorrow, and I appreciate you leaving your adoring fans to come sit and listen to me vent in some burger joint. It means a lot."

"I think most of the fans are for Colton, honestly. Gray's got his hardcores as well. I'm just happy anyone wants to read my books and have me sign them. But to tell you the truth, there's no place I'd rather be right now than here with you. They can have the shots and selfies. I'm happy right here with you." The place is packed, and the buzz of hungry people laughing and talking, coupled with the music that's getting louder is making me want to get out of here. It's a cool joint, and the food smells amazing, but it's not food that's on my mind right now.

"I have an idea," Everleigh says to me, still holding onto my hand, only now she's caressing it with her thumb in a tender way, her eyes never looking away from mine as she speaks.

"Oh yeah?" I inquire. "What's that?" She's definitely peaked my interest.

8

EVERLEIGH

I SURPRISE MYSELF BY WHAT I'M ABOUT TO SAY. I DON'T
know what the hell I'm doing, but I've known that I wanted
him since we bumped shoulders at the bar today. I've always
loved Michael's books and I admire him as an author, but
seeing those eyes and that face changed everything for me. It
became real. I didn't expect to feel this way, but it's real and
I'm not going to fight it.

"There's a back door that leads to an alleyway which I
saw someone go out of earlier," I tell him. "It's probably
pretty abandoned back there. Know what I mean?"

He hesitates for a second, but only for a second.

"I know exactly what you mean," he said. "Lead
the way."

I flag down the waitress and ask for a check. I throw some
cash on the table and take him by the hand out the door,
trying to be inconspicuous as I do. We step outside in the
alley, the darkness keeping us safe for now.

I don't want to say any more words to him. Tomorrow
there can be words. Today I just want him, and I'm not
holding back anymore.

9

KNIGHT

THERE ARE SOME WOMEN WHO ARE PUT ON THIS EARTH TO remind you that you're a man—women who seem to embody every quality that your body is looking for in another person. Everleigh is one of those women, and right now her mouth tastes like the answer to life, and the smell of her hair is the only reason I can think of to take in breath. She's pressed against me, awakening every nerve ending in my body all at once.

There we are, making out against some random person's car parked in the alleyway. I'm pushing into her, pressing her back up against the passenger side window, but right now I have no care for where we are. I run my hands through her hair and grab a bunch of it in the back and pull her head away from me. She pushes back, wanting more of me, but I hold her in place so that our mouths are only an inch apart, and we breathe into each other, our bodies anticipating the next moment of contact. I don't let go of her hair. Instead I pull her towards me and our lips meet, our tongues smashing together.

We're moving fast but the moment seems to be in slow motion, like I'm watching a movie from outside of my own body. At the same time my senses are on overload: the feeling of her hair, the smell of her sweet breath, the taste of her mouth, and the sensation of her breasts pressed up against me under her dress make me want to fuck her right here in the alleyway.

When our mouths separate for a second I kiss her neck hard, and she leans in and whispers, "You feel so fucking good right now." I'm so turned on that I almost forget where we are. I should be using my head more. Anyone could walk back here and catch us, and then this whole weekend could end up with a headline in a local paper reading 'indie romance author arrested for indecent exposure.' That would be a bad look all around, but I just can't help myself. I don't care about any of that. Fuck the consequences. Fuck anyone seeing us. And fuck this guy's car. I feel alive for the first time in a long time, there with Everleigh in that alley, our bodies aching for one another, and no other care in the world.

I kiss her neck even harder, burrowing my face against her soft skin. She moans, and I can feel her nails digging into my back on top of my shirt. "We need to go somewhere now."

"Okay," I say, snapping back into reality for a second. My dick is so hard that it hurts. Like a fighter who only feels his bruises after the fight's over, it's not until I separate from Everleigh's body that I feel the hardness pressing into the front of my pants. My body is warm, with little beads of sweat forming on my forehead, and my core temperature is through the roof. I can tell that she's feeling the same. Her cheeks are flushed red, making her face even more beautiful, and the fact that we have unfinished business gets my heart racing in anticipation of what's going to happen next. "Come on."

I take her by the hand and we leave the alley. By some

miracle no one sees us, or if they do they just keep on walking and pretend they didn't just witness an intense make-out session happening behind *Jameson's Burgers and Fries*. Either way I don't care. She's holding onto my hand tightly as I lead her back across the path we took to get there in the first place. We pass by a lot of people on the street, some of them are surely readers here for our event, but I'm so turned on and in the moment that I pay no mind.

When we get back to the hotel she stops at the front door. "Wait." She's looking inside at the crowd gathered in the lobby and near the bar. "If we go in there holding hands and get in the elevator together there'll be posts all over social media before we're finished. Some of these women can be like girls in high school. They love gossip, and an author sleeping with a reader is a bad look for any of you guys."

She's right. I'm busy being a horny male whose only thoughts are of fucking this woman silly in my still unpacked hotel bedroom. Meanwhile I'm not remembering the context of where we actually are. But now that she's snapped me out of my sex zombie state I start to notice how many people are around. Male romance authors have a lot of stigmas surrounding them, like I said. One of those stigmas is that we write shitty books for the sole purpose of sleeping with fans. Like we're the literary version of Motley Crew—writing bad songs and going on tour basically to do drugs and get laid. There are certain authors with that reputation, justified or otherwise, but I'm not one of them.

That reputation is career cancer. Once people think that of you then it becomes a thing behind the scenes—whispers and rumors that you're just out there to bang women, not to be a real author. Me? I could care less about that other shit, I'm here to write great stories and bring them to readers who'll appreciate them. But I know how bad this looks from the outside.

"You're right," I say, letting go of her hand and trying to hide my enormous erection by hanging my hands in front of my crotch. I don't think it's working, but it's starting to go down slightly. "I really want to finish what we started."

"Me, too," she answers. "More than you know. But not now. It's too early in the night and too risky, people are everywhere. I can meet you up in your room later. Unless you're bunking with one of the guys?"

"No," I tell her. "I dodged that bullet. I'm more of a loner when it comes to things like this. Don't play well with others. I need my own space to write and walk around naked."

"Really? You walk around naked?"

"All the time. But it's kind of an alone activity, know what I mean?"

"Not for long." Everleigh looks around the room and then reaches down and squeezes my dick so quickly that no one sees. The last few seconds of trying to kill my erection goes to total shit, and I'm right back at attention.

"I'll be up there. Gonna text Colt and Gray that I'm not feeling good and that I'm gonna hang out in my room for the rest of the night. They'll be pissed, probably, but I have all day tomorrow to entertain readers. Can you slip away before too long?"

"I'll see what I can do. Keep your phone handy and keep that cock ready."

"For you it's always ready," I tell her, smiling a devious smile. "Go mingle, I'll be up thinking about you."

Everleigh walks away towards the bar, and I can't help but stare at her ass as she does. It shifts side to side as she moves, and my dirty mind can't help but think of a thousand different positions I want to get her in. She's the hottest girl

I've met in forever, and I also really like her a lot. I told her things that only Gray and Colt know—about Jenny, about my writer's block, all of it. And she opened up to me. I don't care what happens tomorrow, tonight makes this whole trip worth it, and watching her ass shake its way to the bar, I can't wait for the next few hours to pass by.

10

EVERLEIGH

WHAT THE HELL AM I DOING?

I just made out with Michael Knight in an alleyway, and if there hadn't been a million readers in the lobby, I would have slept with him for sure. He still thinks I'm going to. Don't get me wrong, I still really want to, but now that I have a second to breathe I wonder if that's the right thing to do. I'm in a weird headspace with Jeremey, and I'm a little awestruck at seeing my favorite author in person. Not just seeing him, but getting to know him and having him get to know me.

I told him things today that only Rowan and Harley really know about in detail, and I know he did the same about things in his life. But still, is it wrong to hook up with him so fast? Am I wrong about him? Is he one of those stereotypical male romance authors you hear stories about? The ones who hook up with readers and fans and use their status basically for that reason alone? I don't think he is, but I need to figure out how I want to play the next few hours so that neither one of us are uncomfortable with the situation. I hear a shout from behind me.

"Where are you going lady?"

It's Harley! I was so distracted walking in that I didn't even see them sitting in the lobby. I walk up and give her a hug. "You finally got here. What took you so long?"

"My GPS is shit," she says. That's a typical Harley answer. Brazen, blunt, and very honest. "It took me the most fucked up way."

"And you just listened to the random British voice?" Ro asks, joking around. "Not what I'd expect from my non-conformist best friend. I figured you'd just print out directions and memorize them, knowing you."

She smiles. "It was a French lady, first of all."

"Sorry," Ro says, throwing her hands in the air.

"And you're right, I put too much trust in that stupid thing. But screw it, I'm here now. What are we doing? Besides standing in a hotel lobby, that is."

It's funny how personalities work in groups of friends. The three of us have been friends since high school, and even then we balanced each other out. Rowan's the organizer—the mother hen, the one who keeps the group in line and seems the most conservative on the outside even though she's not. Harley's on the other end of the friendship personality spectrum. She's the wild one, the party girl, the one who's the most obviously fun and extroverted, but she still has a solid head on her shoulders. Me? I'm somewhere in the middle. I have my crazy, party-girl moments, but I can also be too mature for my own good.

"You wanna get some food?" I still want to get that dinner we said we'd get together before I stormed off on my own. I haven't gotten a chance to explain that whole thing to Ro, I just kind of left her stranded at the bar.

"Yaaas! I'm starving!"

"Alright, it's decided," Ro says. "Let's go out and explore the town."

"Are you all checked in, Harley?"

"Yeah, just before you got here. Was that...?" She stops and raises an eyebrow at me. I didn't even think about the fact that they could both clearly see Michael and I walk in together from where they were sitting in the lobby. I don't know what to say, so I just stare at her for a second until I see the eyebrow go down and her lips go up into a smile. I know that she knows, and I smile too.

"It was."

"Knight?" she asks. "You and Knight?"

"No," I say hastily. "I mean, yes. Sort of. I don't know."

"Is that where you snuck off to?" Rowan looks at me and I realize that I owe her an explanation. It wasn't my intention to keep any of this secret. They're my best friends and they know everything about me. We've never kept secrets from one another, especially where guys are concerned, and she deserves to know why I left her at the bar.

"Not exactly," I tell her. "I'm sorry I ran off, though, I overreacted to something. Let's go talk."

"And eat," Harley says, jumping in. "Eating is crucial."

"We'll eat, I promise. You can even pick the place."

"Yay."

Before we go I think about Michael. He's upstairs waiting for me, and I don't know what to do. I told him I'd see him later but I feel weird about it. Ro and Harley get their bags and we start walking. Before we're even a few blocks away I get a text. When I look down at my phone I almost cant believe what I'm reading, in a good way. His text reads:

Michael: Not yet. You're the best kisser, maybe ever. I've never been so turned on. But I also really like you, and already you mean more to me than just one amazing evening of sex. Let's wait. What do you think?

I know that some women would take a text like this as some kind of rejection, but it makes me so happy that I read it three times in a row. How many guys who have a woman willing to sleep with them ask to wait because they think it could be something more? None that I know. I understand right away what he means, and after I read it a fourth time I text him back so that he doesn't think I'm angry.

Me: I love that you wrote this. Not yet. Let's wait until next time. Whenever that is.

He texts back a smiley emoji, and I breathe a sigh of relief. Don't get me wrong, in the moment I would have been with him without regrets, but I think it was a blessing in disguise that we had to delay. At the same time I'm going to do my best to stop thinking about Jeremey and just enjoy this weekend for what it's meant to be—a fun time with friends, authors, and other readers. I text Michael one more time to see what his plans are.

Me:Are you coming down?

Michael: I think I'm enjoying my alone time. There's plenty of time for selfies and smiling tomorrow. I want to do something I haven't done in a long time—write. I'm feeling a little inspired. Can't imagine why.

Me: Yeah.Can't imagine where that inspiration came from. Make the scene hot, okay? As hot as it would have been tonight.

Michael: Don't you worry.I'll burn up the page. See you tomorrow at the signing.

Me: You sure will.

I put my phone back in my bag and head out into the night to have dinner with my girls. This weekend is already shaping up to be pretty damn memorable.

11

KNIGHT

I LIKE TO SLEEP NAKED.

I always have. I never understood those guys who sleep in shirts and pants or, God forbid, PJ's. Fuck all that—I like to sleep the way God made me. So the fact that I'm waking up in full clothing explains why I don't feel that rested. That, and the fact that I'm in a weird-ass position on the bed. I usually don't pass out with my computer still on and next to me on the bed, but that seems to be the situation from last night. It's dead now, but I know that I had it on when I finally closed my eyes. I don't remember falling asleep at all, but I remember writing. It's the first time I've written anything of substance in a long time.

I stretch and get my body out of the position it's probably been in for the last six hours. My neck feels like an Olympic wrestler's had me in a headlock for a while, and I have a minor headache to boot. So why am I so happy? Normally waking up in a state like this would make me a very unpleasant person to be around, but I'm in a great mood. First, there's the signing. I'm genuinely happy that I get to meet some readers today. I get to see how happy they are bringing one of my books to the table so that I can write my name and theirs in black sharpie.

But the real reason I'm so happy is just leftover emotions from last night. There are so many layers to such a simple encounter that I don't even know what had more of an effect on me: meeting a hot woman who loves my work and is totally cool, making out with her unexpectedly, or having those two things allow my mind to open up and let words out for the first time in a long time. It's all three, for sure, but that last one in particular.

Writer's block is a term everyone uses, but it doesn't do justice to what it's really like when your brain just can't find the words to express itself. When you have writer's block, your mind becomes a black hole that nothing can escape from, like all of the characters, plots, and stories that tie them together get trapped, and there's no way to see or hear them. You can try to force it—and I have tried—but mostly it produces writing that looks and reads like the crap it is.

My computer still has a little bit of juice left—only a few percent, so I turn it on and look in the left hand corner of the Word document and I see the number 5,000! Five thousand words of my new book in two hours. Once I knew that sleeping with Everleigh was the wrong move, at least last night, I also knew that I wanted to spend my time doing something as enjoyable. Okay, that's bullshit, being with her would have been much more enjoyable, but a close second is writing my new book. Five thousand words isn't a lot when you plan on writing seventy to eighty thousand of them in total, but it's an amazing chunk of material when you've barely cracked one thousand in the past two months combined.

Who knows if it's any good, I'll have to read it later. But for now I'm gonna ride the happy wave right out of this bed, these clothes, and into a hot shower. Standing naked in the middle of a hotel room seems as good a time as any to send a text to Grayson and Colt because, why not? Knowing how hard they were hitting the bars I'm sure they're not up yet. It's 6:30 am. The signing is in a small room, so the person in Colton's reading group who helped organize this whole event set it up so that there will be three different mini-signings that the readers had to buy tickets for. The first was at noon, the second at one o'clock, and the last at three, with an hour in between for us to get food and relax our signing hands a little bit. I have time, but I'm going to use it for something more productive than just setting up my table—even though I have to get that done also. I'm going to finish the chapter I'm working on.

Thirty minutes later I'm stepping out of the shower. The mirror is steamed, and my body is the kind of hot that gets inside of you and stays a while, long after you've left the confines of the steamy bathroom. I needed to shave, so I made it a point to make my face smooth, and without my usual shower mirror I'm hoping that I didn't shred my face something awful. I don't see any little drops of blood, so I think I'm good. I let the remaining water fall off of my naked body as I stand there, using my forearm to try to clear a little space in the mirror where I can see myself. I feel great, and it's all because of her. . .it's all because of Everleigh. I can't wait to see her again.

But first thing's first.

I towel myself off. Once I'm dry I sit back in the lounge chair in the corner of the room with my laptop. I'd let it charge while I was in the shower, so it's only at 30%, but that's all I need. If it dies I'll use my phone. If my phone dies I'll pick up a damn piece of paper and keep on writing. The forum doesn't matter—that's all ancillary. What matters are the thoughts. The impulses. The moments playing out in my mind that I can capture as written word.

That's what I've feared this whole time since I broke up with. . .fuck, I don't even want to think of her name right now. Maybe that's immature of me, but all it's going to do is bring back memories, and that's not the point. But since that whole thing happened I've feared that I've lost those impulses, those moments, those thoughts. Maybe they are just romance novels. I'll take the criticism. Lots of sex, similar plots, cookie cutter characters. Guilty as charged. But what's more important than that is the following—none of that matters. What matters is what Everleigh reminded me of last night. That my stories make differences in people's lives, however small, and however temporary, they matter.

Books are escapism. It doesn't matter what's inside them, does it? No. What matters is how they effect people—how they change hearts and minds when their words are allowed to be committed to paper. Sometimes those words win Pulitzers and National Book Awards. And other times, well, they just turn people the fuck on and allow them to escape to fantasy land for a few hundred pages. People can judge that as they will, I certainly can't stop them, but I don't care about those people's opinions. All I care about is my readers, and it took an amazing woman to remind me of that.

She's also shown me, inadvertently, that my worst fears are just that. The words are there. The thoughts are still inside me when I stop and open my ears enough to truly listen. And even though it's a cliche thing to say, she's inspired me. Maybe that's the wrong word. She hasn't inspired me at all. She's reminded me. Now it's just about taking that memory and writing an amazing fucking book with it.

Here goes.

EVERLEIGH

MY HEAD IS POUNDING.

Fuck.

I must be getting old because I feel like I've been on a bender like Nicholas Cage in Leaving Las Vegas. The truth is that I had a few drinks with my best friends last night, but I guess I'm getting to be a lightweight the closer to thirty I get. Everyone tells me how young I am or how young I look. But trust me, 29 is a far cry from 21, and I'm feeling that near decade of difference right now in both temples. I open one eye first, and then the other, as though waking up in stages might make the pain I'm feeling less. It doesn't work.

Shit, what the hell did I drink? Oh right, I remember now. The shots. All the damn shots.

I'm usually not the type to relive my college days, but being with your best friends on a far off fantasy land trip feels just like when you're away at college. That's where we all met. Our school was in a small town just like this one, and just like this one, there were plenty of places to remind you that you were far away from real life, and all of those places served alcohol.

I reach for my bag, which is lying right on the floor next to the bed. Without even looking I just feel around and grab onto the bottle of Tylenol I always keep in there. I sit myself up and down a few pills with the bottle of water on my nightstand. I can hear the shower going, so I guess Rowan is more functional this morning than I am. Good for her. I don't remember if she drank as much as I must have. I don't remember much, but I'm pretty sure it's safe to assume that Harley isn't up and in the shower right now. I'm sure she's passed out.

I close my eyes while sitting up in bed, as though I have a migraine or something instead of an alcohol induced headache. It doesn't help at all, but once my eyes are closed the first thing that comes into my mind's eye isn't the dinner last night, and it isn't thoughts of the signing that's going to happen in a few hours. When I close my eyes I see Michael Knight. I see him like I saw him last night in the alley—tall, imposing, full of confidence, and looking at me like I was all that he wanted in the world, as though he could see right inside of me. I could open my eyes right now but I force them to stay shut, and the pain in my temples disappears from my conscious mind. As soon as I come back to reality I'll feel it again, I know, like the Coyote realizing that he's about to fall off the cliff only when he looks down.

But not now.

Not yet.

First I want to remember him for a few seconds. I want to remember us, there in the alleyway, feeling dirty and unlike myself, yet loving every second. My heart was pounding, terrified someone would see us, yet wanting him to press me even harder into that car, to lift my body up in his strong arms and place me on the hood. I wanted him to explore every inch of my body while the fear of being seen, coupled with my arousal, made my heart beat race faster than it ever should. That didn't happen. I stopped him in his tracks. I pulled away. I injected rationality and responsibility into a situation that was all about feel and being in the moment. I know it was the right thing to do, especially for him, but that doesn't mean that I wanted to.

I know he would have fucked me right then and there outside of the restaurant. I could feel his hardness against me. I could feel the force in his arms and the passion in his kiss. But he's a man, and I knew that the last thing on his mind in that moment was his career, but I also knew that the last thing he needed while trying to rebuild everything he felt he'd lost was to be seen screwing a reader in an alleyway near his own signing. There would have been no recovering from that. I would have been the anonymous, slut groupie, but it wouldn't have affected my life at all. But for Michael. . .for Michael that would have been it.

So I stopped us and went out with the girls.

But I wanted him.

I still want him. And if I didn't have such care for his career, he'd be waking up next to me right now. I open my eyes as Ro steps out of the bathroom, a wall of steam trailing behind her. Her hair and body are wrapped in two huge towels, and she still has beads of water on her chest just below her neck. "Hey sleepy head," she says, smiling at me like a mom with a sick kid.

"What in the hell did I drink last night?" As I ask her that question the pain comes back in full force, and I feel the pressure in my temples with even more intensity than I had a few minutes ago.

"What didn't you drink is the better question," she answers, starting to towel dry her hair. "And the answer would be a resounding 'nothing.' For real, I felt like we were pledging *Kappa Theta Omega* again."

Kappa. I haven't heard or thought of those three words in years, but they'll always have a special place in my heart. I was kind of the reluctant sorority chick in college. Ro and Harley are a year older than me, and we met at orientation at Ralph Emerson University in New England after I arrived in the summer before my freshman year, wide-eyed and more than a little naive. Rowan and Harley were sophomores at the time, and both of them were members of the *Kappa Theta Omega* sorority. They convinced me to pledge, and before too long we were all just sorority sisters and best friends. Not much has changed between us since then, except now we have jobs and follow our favorite romance authors around the country looking for autographs. My little sister, Hadley, is pledging Kappa right now. It's becoming a family tradition.

"Those days are long gone, but my post drinking headaches definitely feel the same." I'm not kidding when I say that. The reason I never drank much, even in college, was that I get ridiculously painful hangovers that last longer than they do for most people. I did one of those DNA tests a while back and it turns out that I have a high sensitivity to alcohol, so I generally avoided getting blitzed like I was twenty-one all over again.

"I didn't recognize you last night. But it was kind of cool to see you let loose at the same time."

"I'm glad I looked cool. It totally makes this worth it. I think I may throw up, by the way."

"Again?"

"What do you mean again?" I ask.

"I mean I spent half of my night standing behind you in the bathroom with a fistful of your hair. You really don't remember?"

I shake my head. I also tend to black out when I drink, even if I'm not that drunk. I just kind of lose time. "I sure don't, but I believe you. I need to get my shit together, we have a signing to attend."

"Tell me about it," Ro says. "This isn't even my thing. You dragged me here."

"I dragged you here?" I raise my eyebrow at her. Sometimes her fake conservatism annoys me. Especially when I'm already in a bad mood. "Stop telling yourself that. I didn't drag you anywhere. You're here because you want to be here. The sooner you admit it to yourself the better time you'll have. Just give into it, already."

"I can't," she says. "Irish-Catholic guilt. It's hard to shake. You wouldn't get it unless you were raised in a house like mine."

She's right on both counts. I don't understand, and that's entirely because I didn't grow up like she did. My parents were cool people. Educated, liberal, progressive, and generally let me make my own mistakes in life. Rowan was one of six children, the first generation American daughter of immigrants from Dublin, and the story of her childhood read like a modern version of Angela's Ashes. I love her mom and dad, but they're old school Irish Catholic immigrants, and they mastered the art of making her feel guilty about almost everything, so it takes a lot to pull her out of her shell sometimes.

"I know," I tell her. "But, still, don't turn that shit on me. I didn't drag you here."

"I know," she says, sounding guilty. "It's just hard to shake. I feel weird being here to meet a bunch of guys I don't know who write sex books."

"Romance," I correct her. "And a little erotica. Depends on which guy you mean, they're all a little different."

"Now who's convincing themselves of something?"

"What do you mean?

"Oh, come on, Everleigh," she says, sounding a little annoyed herself. "You can call them whatever label makes you feel better, but the fact of the matter is that they're sex books."

"Bullshit!" I say, the pain in my head secondary to the annoyance I'm starting to feel at her judgement, of all people.

"It's the truth. Let me ask you this—if there were no sex in these books do you think that women would read them? You really think that if *Fifty Shades* was just a book about a timid secretary working for a high powered businessman with no S&M that it would have sold a gazillion copies? Come on."

"Even if you're right, so what? Who cares? You go to an action flick to see car chases and gun fights. You go to a comedy club to laugh. So what?"

"And you read sex books to do what, then?"

Check mate. She has a point, even if I don't want to concede her argument just yet. If I'm being as honest as I'm asking her to be, the fact is that romance books are about sex —they just are. Even though I don't think there's anything wrong with that, we live in a conservative country founded by people who viewed sex as a dirty thing to be discussed only in private. A few hundred years later and we're still passing those bullshit beliefs through generations. But Ro is technically correct. If you took the exact same books and removed all the sex, the stories wouldn't hold up. The sex is the glue that binds the stories together in romance—it's the foundation of everything else. But again, I fail to see why that's a problem or something to be ashamed of.

"Sex. . .romance novels give you an escape, just like everything else. They take you to places that you're not in in real life. They let you be with men you'd honestly never have a chance with, if they even existed like they do in the books, which they really don't. And yeah, romance is female porn. I'm not gonna lie. Guys look at YouPorn on their phones and give themselves a good tug. Us women like a little storyline and description in our porn. So what?"

"Fine. You're right."

"Huh?" I almost can't believe my ears. Ro can be as stubborn as she can be conservative at times, so hearing her give in like this is freaking me out a little bit. "I'm sorry, I didn't hear you right. I'm what now?"

"Shut up," she says. "You heard me. You're right, okay? You're right. And how do I know? 'Cause I downloaded one of their books last night and read the whole damn thing in one sitting before I went to bed."

"Wait, you did what?" Now I really don't believe my ears. "I'm gonna need to hear you say that all one more time."

"Last night, in between assisting your vomit sessions and sobering up myself, I took out my phone and downloaded a book. I figured that with you being sick I couldn't just go to sleep until I knew you were okay, so I. . .occupied myself for a while."

"Holy shit," I say, the smile on my face growing as I stare at my friend in amazement. "You're one of us now. You popped your romance cherry. Which book was it?"

"It doesn't matter."

"It sure as hell does!" I say. Just then I hear a knock at our door, followed by Harley's voice.

"What are you talking about?" she yells through the door. "I could hear your voices going all high through the wall."

I'm shocked that she's up and about, but I'm ten times more shocked at what Rowan is saying. Despite the pain in my head, I jump out of bed and rush to the door to let Harley in. She needs to hear this conversation. "Oh. My. God!" I tell her.

"What?"

"Our baby's not a virgin anymore."

"What?" Harley repeats, not having any idea what I'm talking about. I open the door all the way and she comes in and sits on the bed. She doesn't look disheveled or hung over at all, she looks beautiful as always. "What are you saying, now?"

"Oh, God!" Rowan cries, covering her eyes in embarrassment.

"Well, Har, it seems that, unbeknownst to my drunk and passed out self, Rowan took to Amazon to download a romance novel, which she read in a few hours last night."

"No shit!" Harley blurts out. "Which one?"

"And now you're all caught up," I say. "I was just trying to find that very thing out when you started knocking."

"Well?" Harley says, staring at Rowan. "At least tell me which author it was."

"Grayson. It was Grayson. He's a really. . .talented writer."

"Grayson? No shit, huh?" I'm a little shocked, but not really. "Very interesting."

"Why is that interesting?" Rowan asks.

"Because it is," Harley answers before I have the chance. "On a few levels. I like Grayson's books. I'm more of a Colton girl, myself. Maybe I can just relate to his storylines a little more."

"I bet you can," I joke.

"What can I say," she starts. "We all like what we like. I'm into his MMA series. "

"Then we've come to the perfect place, haven't we?"

"You, especially," Ro says, giving me the raised eyebrow.

I don't remember much from last night, but I remember telling them all about Michael and me. I would have felt guilty keeping it from them—we've always told each other everything when it comes to guys and relationships—so this wasn't going to be something I would feel comfortable keeping from them. They didn't judge me when I told them, but they were surprised I'd hook up with a guy that fast. That wasn't like me at all.

"Yeah, it seems so," I say.

"Is it going to be weird seeing him later? Handing him a book to sign when you almost slept together last night?"

"I don't know," I say to Harley. "I guess we'll see."

"Yeah," she answers. "I have an even better question."

"What's that?"

"How much heat is he packing?"

"What?"

"His dick, Ev. His dick. How big is it?"

"I didn't really get to see it. I'm not sure. Don't worry about his dick."

"I'm not worried," she says, looking mischievous. "I'm just curious. I'd like to know if renowned romance author Michael Knight is packing a hammer or not."

"How would I know? We didn't fuck."

"But you felt it, right?" This time it's Rowan chiming in, confirming all of my suspicions about her score on the freak scale.

"Yeah, I felt it. I grabbed hold of it, actually. It was. . .substantial."

"I knew it!" Harley screams. "I knew he had a big one. But is it long or thick? Or both?"

"I think our game of twenty questions about his cock has come to an end, Har."

"Okay, fine. But keep me updated as things progress."

"I'll stop in the middle to text you, including pics."

"That's my girl."

I'm done talking about Michael's cock, but I'm not done thinking about it. I'm not just remembering either. I'm fantasizing. I'm projecting into the future. I'm seeing a reality where we didn't just make out and do some heavy petting, but where our naked bodies are crashing against one another, and he fills me up with that giant cock of his. *Soon*, I think, *it's going to happen very soon.*

KNIGHT

SETTING UP A TABLE AT A SIGNING IS WORK.

Good work, but work, nonetheless.

After grabbing a quick breakfast together at a local diner, Gray, Colt and I get back to the hotel and walk down to the singing room in full Wordsmith solidarity. When we do it looks like a house that someone just moved into, only they haven't unpacked any of their shit yet. Huge brown boxes filled with paperbacks decorate the floor. Next to them are our banners and envelopes holding the swag—free extras like stickers, bookmarks, buttons, and custom pens—that each of us brought with our logos and book covers on them.

One of Grayson's readers, Connie, helped run point on this event with the hotel, and when we get to the signing room she's already there taking inventory and helping unpack Gray's stuff. She lives in the area and has stayed here a bunch of times. She was good enough to help with things like negotiating a reduced bulk rate for rooms, getting us space to actually have the signing in, and a bunch of other logistical matters that, quite frankly, we're too irresponsible and busy to be trusted with. If Colton or I had been in charge of any of that, our readers would be fucked right now, so I'm glad Connie is in charge. She's super responsible and everything she's touched so far has been golden.

"Connie, what time did we say the first reader is going to be walking in the door, again?"

"Noon," she answers, tapping her watch is a not-so-subtle communication of 'hurry the fuck up you lazy and irresponsible male authors.' We all look at each other and start moving our feet a little faster than before. It's 11:15 am, and I realize right away that I should have done this shit last night, but I wasn't about to stop my late night writing streak to unpack some boxes. Nonetheless it would have saved me some morning anxiety, but those are the trade-offs in life.

Fuck it, let's go.

Our tables are spaced out a few feet from each other, with a little bit of space in between to take pictures with readers and generally move around. As I start to do some quick organizing I'm brought back to the reality of being an indie author. It's easy to get caught up in our own little writing bubble. When we got to the place yesterday I felt like the Beatles coming to America or something—everyone knew my name, we were taking pictures with fans in the parking lot, everyone was super nice. In other words, it isn't reality. It's great, but it's easy to forget that we're not *New York Times* bestselling authors who have assistants. No. We unpack our own stuff, we lay out our table, set up our books in just the right way as to entice readers, all of it.

"I hate unpacking boxes and pre-orders!" Colton is already becoming a prima donna. He was the biggest hustler of all of us, in a good way. A year ago at this time, while I was watching sad TV, drinking too much, and empathizing a little too much with Ross from Friends, Colton was doing work, banging out the series—yes, the entire series—

including what's now his Amazon ranked erotica novel. Amazon rank is a huge deal for authors, it gets your book noticed, seen more frequently in searches for similar books, and generally gets you on the road to a successful career. But already minor success is getting to Colt. I love the kid, but I can see his head swelling a little bit. Then again, his cockiness is kind of what I like about him—he's a loyal friend and an overall great human being, maybe he has a right to live this up a little. I just hope it's not getting to him too much.

"Me, too," I agree, lifting my still tape-sealed boxes, hating myself for not devoting even a half hour to this yesterday. "But it's part of the gig. Keeps me humble."

"Fuck being humble," Colton jokes, only he's not joking at all. "Do you do your own plumbing, or paint your own house? We need people doing this shit for us."

"First off, I did paint most of my own house, yes. I used to be an assistant over the summers in high school with a company that painted houses. It was how I made money as a kid." He rolls his eyes at me. "And I agree, this is annoying, but just keep writing those books that climb the rankings and we won't have to. At least you won't, anyhow."

"And what makes you think he's going to hit number 1 before I do?" I turn at the sound of Grayson's voice, who has less work to do because of Connie being Connie and already having most of his shit out, organized in piles, and generally looking ready for the signing. "I'm in that race, boys, don't bet against me."

"I like your competitive side," Colton says. "It's adorable that you think you're getting there first, but you keep that dream going."

Colt's joking. That's what we do with each other. We're sarcastic as fuck, even more competitive with each other than it seems, and give each other shit at every possible opportunity. From the outside it would look and sound like we're brothers who don't really get along, bickering and fucking with each other non-stop. But you have to be inside our little trust circle to see that external stuff for what it is—guys who love each other like brothers just acting like guys.

That said, I can tell Grayson is a little annoyed that he isn't where Colt is in terms of his career. He's been writing the longest of any of us, and he published his first two books before I got my first out, and way before Colton got his out. Gray takes the older brother role in the group, and just like that older brother, I think he feels like he should be the first in line to some kind of material success. Unfortunately for him, this game doesn't work like the British monarchy—power and success isn't passed to the eldest son, it has to be earned and hustled for. So far Colton's winning that race.

"We'll see," Gray says, smiling as he takes out his last few pre-orders.

By the time it's 11:55 we're all practically sweating. I open the window behind us which faces the street that stretches along with west side of the hotel. I can see the restaurant directly across from us, a barber shop on the corner, and a cute little ice cream place just in the distance. I won't say it out loud because I don't want to get shit from Colt, but it's really quaint here. Moms and dads are walking around with their kids, people are going in and out of shops, and the whole place just has a feeling of niceness to it, if that's even a word. I need coffee.

Connie comes over just before the event is about to start with a piece of paper and a pen. "What do you guys want from Starbucks?" she asks, positioning a custom Grayson pen just over her paper. Colton and I look at her in disbelief.

"Are you going?" I ask.

"My husband. He's gonna grab for you guys. We can't have tired, under-caffeinated authors meeting and greeting all those wonderful women out there. It's a bad look. Now what do you want?"

Grayson's order is already down on paper. Maybe I have it wrong about who's the prima donna and who's not. Gray ordered maybe the most pretentious drink ever. I'm trying to read it, but it goes on for three lines on Connie's paper, so I know it has way too many parts for a simple coffee order. I'm not a whole lot better, but the only specifications I have for my drink are about three more shots of espresso than it comes with, and whole milk instead of that 2% shit they default to. Colt's the easiest.

"Black. Venti."

"That's it?" Connie asks.

"Black. Venti."

"Sugar? Cream?" Connie could never assist Colton. Gray's the right author for her. Colt shakes his head before I chime in.

"Connie, what you need to learn is that Colt takes his coffee like he takes his dick. Hot, large, and black. We don't question these things, and we certainly don't judge. Just get the man what he's asking for, okay?" Connie starts laughing hysterically and finally writes down the words black and venti. "And please thank your husband for us, he's the man."

"I know," Connie says, taking the paper. "He's a keeper."

By the time the first reader walks in the room we mostly have our shit together. I finish a little early and I'm still so full of ideas for my new book that I take out the laptop from my room and jot down a few paragraphs real quick. I probably look a little nuts but fuck it, I'm inspired! This laptop is a piece of shit, though. It's one of those cheap ones that doesn't have anything on it at all. The guy at the store looked at me like I was nuts when I bought it. I was half broke, and didn't need anything fancy, anyhow. I had my phone to go online and download shit. The only thing I needed a laptop for was to not have to write all of my ideas by hand on a pad. But, still, when I make it big with this book I'm going to treat myself to a new machine.

All of our tables are set up, and I had a specific Wordsmiths banner made up that I put on the wall behind us. I'm proud of myself for getting it all together. I have my pre-orders ready behind me, extra copies for purchase on the table —neatly stacked of course—my swag all over so that my readers can just take whatever they want, and I have about 100 Sharpies ready to sign. I'm hoping to meet some new readers as well. We all have our own group of fans of our work, but part of the point of this whole thing is to bring us together into one entity, one organization whose reach is wider than any one of us individually.

I even went that extra mile and made some cool little stuff that readers love. There's a character in one of my first books who's a cop, so I went on Amazon and bought fake plastic evidence bags to put that book in. Readers love that kind of stuff.

I'm so caught up in the moment that's about to happen that I forget I'm about to see Everleigh. It'll be the first time since we parted ways in the lobby last night, and I'm excited to see her again. I want to tell her everything—how I wrote for the first time, how she inspired me, how much I enjoyed myself last night, and how much I want to see her again. I realize I can't say all of those things the second she walks in, or even at all in front of other people, but those are just the thoughts going through my head. Then the first reader walks in, and I'm back into author mode.

"You ready, boys?" Grayson yells down the row.

"Ready!" I say.

"Born ready, let's sign some shit," Colt says.

And with that, the ladies come in.

The first session goes smoothly. An hour passes in what feels like five minutes. I don't love crowds of people in general, but this is different. I'm genuinely enjoying being around readers—mine and the other guys'—and I'm happy that my hand is cramping from all the books I'm signing. Grayson took the big brother lead on a few of the things involving the event. He had one of his readers who makes things make some cool shot glasses, blank canvases with our logo, and white mugs that we can all sign. Those things are great because it gets expensive to buy all of these paperbacks from all of us, so those items let readers have a fun experience and get all of our signatures without having to spend too much money.

I have to say, the readers are great. They go from table to table, smiling like it's romance novel Halloween, grabbing books that they pre-ordered, swag by the handful, and some paperbacks from each of us. I sign my books and some of the specially made swag for what seems like a hundred people, and I take more selfies than I ever have in my life. It's a great event.

When there's a lull in the crowd I take a second to look down and reorganize my stuff at the table. I lay out some more swag, straighten up my books, and try to get as organized as possible for the next wave of readers who'll be coming in soon. I'm crouched over, bent under my table taking out some more paperbacks from the box of extras I have stashed under there when I hear my name.

"Oh. My. God. It's Michael Fucking Knight!"

I pull my head up from under the table too fast and smack it against the edge. "Ahh!" I yell as I stand up. When I come to my senses I see Everleigh standing in front of my table, looking as hot as ever.

"Oh, shit," I say without even processing. "Hey."

"Oh, shit, hey," the girl standing next to to her says. She's pretty also, but in a different way than Everleigh. She has a little more of an edge to her. "That's a beautiful sentiment Mr. Knight."

"Just Knight is fine," I tell her. "It's nice to meet you. . ."

"Harley," Everleigh says. "This is one of my best friends, Harley."

"Nice to meet you Just Knight. This whole thing is awesome."

"Thank you. And thanks for being here. And who's this?" I say, motioning to Everleigh's other friend.

"Rowan," she says. "But you can call me Ro. Nice to meet you, Knight."

"The pleasure is all mine. Are you ladies having a good time?"

"Better if I can meet your friend over there." Harley is motioning towards Colt, who's in the middle of taking his 50th selfie of the day.

"You got it. Chase!"

"Yo?" he answers. He looks at me and I wave him over. He puts up his give-me-a-minute index finger and finishes with his readers before coming over. When he finally does, he doesn't look anywhere but at Harley. "Hi, I don't think we've met. I'm. . ."

"Colton Chase," she fills in. "I know. I love your stuff."

"I think I love yours, too," he says.

I want to cringe at his terrible lines, but it's kind of funny to me at the same time. Rowan steps away from the group to go towards Gray's table, which is surrounded by readers, and I step to the side and let Colton talk to Harley. I have selfish motives. I really want to be alone with Everleigh, and this is the best I can do in this scenario.

"How are you? You look great."

"Thanks," she says, blushing a little and looking at me intensely. "So do you. How was the rest of your night?"

There are other readers all around us, plus Gray and Colton, so I don't want to say anything too obvious, and I have no idea what she told her friend, so I keep it close to the vest. "Not nearly as good as it could have been. But I got some writing done, which was nice. How about yours?"

We smile at each other, an understanding existing between us without any more words spoken on the matter. I can't say what I want to say, and neither can she, but there's something in her look that lets me know that later on we'll have plenty of time. And if not, we'll make time. "Same. Could have been better. Apparently I had a few drinks and passed out."

"I've been there plenty of times, trust me."

"Can you sign this one for me?" Everleigh hands me a worn out old copy of *Into Your Eyes*, and as I take it from her hands I notice how messed up it is. It looks like a college textbook at the end of a semester. It's faded, the pages are a little messed up, and it has little sticky notes and annotations inside of it.

"Do you need a new copy? I have a bunch of extras."

"I love my copy," she says. "I know it looks like its seen better days, but I've read it a lot. I used to make little notes and highlight passages that I loved the most. I love this copy, I want you to sign it."

I do what she asks. I've never seen such a read copy of one of my books. It's kind of cool. I know the significance of this book to her, even though no one else does, and seeing it in physical form really touches me. Before I sign the inside cover I flip through the pages a little. I want to see some of her notes. She wasn't kidding yesterday when she told me that this story impacted her life. There's hardly a page without underlined or highlighted passages, and not a single chapter without some parenthetical notes. On one page all she wrote was 'strong woman.' On another it says 'She found strength in her ability to love.' All of them are either direct quotes or rephrased from things that I wrote. I feel honored seeing the care that she put into reading this book.

She didn't just read it—she *experienced* it.

I go back to the front cover and choose the perfect place to sign. Some of my signatures were getting a little sloppy at the end, but with hers I take my time so that it's something she'll really appreciate. I sign *Michael Knight* in the center, then take a moment to write her a little note, and hand it back to her. "I hope you cherish that."

"I already do," she says, smiling at me. "I hope you know that."

I smile back. I don't want her to read the note I wrote her right here, so when she starts to open it I reach across the table and pinch it shut. "Not here," I tell her. "Later. Read it later on."

"Okay." she says, keeping it closed after I remove my hand. "Later."

She walks away from my table and meets up with her friends who are at Colton and Grayson's tables. It's both great and frustrating to see her. It's great because every time I look at her I get excited and turned on like some high school boy because she's so beautiful, but our surroundings won't allow me to do anything about it in the open. I'm patient though, I can wait and figure out a time. I have her number, and I know that we both want to see each other again really badly, so I'm not worried at all. But, still, while watching her walk away I steal a look at her tight ass and feel my cock start to harden. I sit down on my chair as soon as I feel it to avoid anyone else seeing.

I was the one who stopped things yesterday, and we haven't seen each other since, but all that self-control and rationality goes right out the window as I watch her walk away. There's something so base about the way she makes me feel. Not only is she pretty—she's easily the prettiest woman in the room—but there's something so sexual about her without it being too obvious. There's something in my body that just responds to her and wants to be pushed against her whenever I'm in her presence. I couldn't explain it, and it has nothing to do with things we've said to one another, it's just this powerful attraction that I'm not used to feeling for someone right away.

The second signing goes on just like the first one did—packed with happy fans holding tote bags full of paperbacks for us all to sign our names to. The readers migrate from table to table, getting signatures, swiping some swag, taking pictures with one or all of us, and talking to each other. I've always been capable of separating myself from whatever situation I'm in to see it from an outside perspective. It's something that's served me well, especially as a writer. I'm always analyzing situations and describing their detail in my head, whether that detail makes it inside of a book or not. Today I just want to remember, because the whole day feels good. Thinking back now, as sad as it is to say, I can't remember a time in the recent past where I went 48 hours without feeling shitty at least for a few minutes.

The ghosts in my life like to check in with me at least once a day, just to say hi, sometimes to stay a while and chat, but they're always there. Sometimes it's a fear that I'm a failure as an author. Other times it's the image of my ex cheating on me in full technicolor and sound. Or it could be just your run-of-the-mill anxiety about bills and career that everyone suffers from. No matter what the specifics, there really isn't a twenty-four hour cycle that goes by when I don't have at least some of those types of thoughts.

But since the three of us packed up and left New York for this hotel, everything's been great. I've been surrounded by wonderful, respectful fans, readers who can't get enough of our work and who want to know what we're all writing next, and now this amazing woman who I'm really feeling something for. It's been one of the most satisfying and uncomplicated few day in memory, and it's not even over yet.

In between sessions two and three we have lunch, some pizza that Connie had delivered to the hotel for us. When I'm done I look at my watch and see that there are still another twenty minutes before the third and final signing gets going, so I decide to step out of the room for a second to get some air. We've been in here for hours now and I could definitely use a temporary change of scenery. It's risky to take a break in the lobby because there are a bunch of readers out there waiting to get in, but everyone here has been super respectful and nice with giving us space.

"I'll be right back," I tell the guys.

"No problem, see you in a few." Grayson's cleaning up his table and doing a little mini setup for the next wave, and Colton just waves at me since his mouth is still full of pizza, red sauce painted all over the outside of his face.

"Get a napkin, man. Pizza face is a bad look for selfies all over these women's social media."

I take what's left of my venti coffee—which isn't much at this point—and head into the lobby. It's cooler out here, probably because it isn't an enclosed little space and the front doors keep opening and closing. The drop in temperate feels nice, and I didn't even realize how much I needed to step out until I actually did. I take a deep breath, still stuffed from that pizza, and exhale as loudly as I can.

"That's a really deep breath you just took." I stepped out from the far door, away from where the readers are lining up, but I hear the voice to my right. I turn to see Everleigh, standing next to me.

"Too much pizza. I ate like a damn pig."

"You're allowed. This isn't real life, take fun as it comes."

"I'm not sure how to interpret that," I tell her, really not sure if she's speaking in code, or just telling me not to feel guilty for stuffing my face.

"Stop being a writer for a minute, not everything is a metaphor or cloaked subtext. I literally meant enjoy your pizza." She giggles and so do I. She's right, that's a writer's problem if ever there was one. We tend to overanalyze situations and see real life as if it's been plotted out and edited to include all sorts of meaning that isn't there. It comes with the job.

"Sorry, force of habit. And I enjoyed it at the time, but now that I stopped eating I'm paying for it." I take one last chug of coffee, hoping that the little bit of caffeine left at the bottom of my cup might get me out of the carb-induced brain fog I'm feeling.

"I've been there," she says. "But I think I have something that might cheer you up, or at least make you forget about the carb loading."

"That would have to be something mighty powerful," I joke, but then I see her raise her eyebrows and grin deviously, as if to communicate that's exactly what's coming.

"You tell me." She extends her hand and gives me an envelope. It's tan, and only says my name on it. Inside there's a little note that reads, "Later was fine last night. But it's not last night anymore. I want you, and I know you want me. The ball's in your court. I'll be up there after the dinner tonight."

Inside the envelope, behind the note, is her room key card. I look up from what's in my hand to see that same devious grin. She doesn't say anything else and she doesn't need to. Now I know that we're on the same page, and I get to steal another glance of her walking away, my cock turns right to stone.

KNIGHT

THE REST OF THE DAY IS ABOUT AS PERFECT AS IT GETS.

The third signing ends up having the fewest readers but they're all great people. We end up signing more books than we ever thought we would at a single session, and everyone left that room happy and with arms full of our stuff. Grayson, Colton and I all decide to take naps like old men in between the signings and the formal dinner tonight. It's fun doing all that interacting, but it's also exhausting to be social without any break for hours on end, so we're sleeping it off. The dinner tonight is the last hurrah for this event, organized by Connie in the formal dining hall of the hotel.

I pass out for a few hours, and when I wake up it's only an hour and a half before dinner. I have to shower and put my nice clothes on. I wipe the sleep from my eyes and stretch my arms a little. Before dropping my clothes in a heap on the floor and taking a shower I text Everleigh.

Me: What are you wearing later?

I expect to leave my phone to charge and come back after my shower to see how she responds, but I can see that she's already writing back. Her message pops up on my screen instantly.

Everleigh: As little as possible.But if you mean the dinner I'm wearing a black cocktail dress.

Me: How will I know when it's time to use that key?

Everleigh: When I make my exit and leave the girls behind, you'll know. I know you'll have your eyes on me, so when I disappear towards the end, give me five minutes and come find me. Don't text, just come.

I get excited even reading those words. It sounds mysterious, inviting, and I want to run over right now, naked as I am, and fuck her silly. I don't want a plate of filet mignon with asparagus and mashed potatoes, I don't want some shitty cheesecake for dessert. I appreciate the idea of dinner, but right now it's just a nuisance, and distractor from what I really want my main course to be. But it's part of the gig, so I know I have to smile and put my best face forward, even though all I'll be thinking about is Everleigh. I think I'm going to leave the hot water off for this shower. I need my dick to not look like a spear my stomach is wielding before I put on my nice dress pants.

I shower and get dressed, and for some reason I've become that annoying, nerdy writer who has to take his laptop everywhere just in case inspiration hits. When did I become that guy? Oh, yeah, last night. Fuck it, I'll go with it, even though I'll have no time to write. I put the laptop in my backpack, sling it over my shoulder, and head down to eat some overcooked filet mignon.

◇ ◇ ◇

The formal dinner comes and goes. The food is better than decent—somewhere between crappy Sweet 16 and okay wedding food, no dancing required, thank God. I sit there and do my thing, talking it up with my boys and interacting with fans whenever possible, even though they're sitting at their own little tables all over this gigantic room. Even if we walked around for an hour straight, there's no way that we could meet and talk to everyone, so after we finish the food we all just get up and let people come over to us.

Even though I haven't spoken a word to Everleigh since our encounter in the hallway where she slipped me her room key, I made it a point to find her table the second I walked in here. She's sitting with her two friends, of course, and in between talking to all the people who approach me I make it a point to look over and see if she's still there.

About forty-five minutes after dinner ends I look over to her table for like the tenth time, only now she's gone. My heart starts racing a mile a minute, and before I know it I'm scanning the room frantically like a parent looking for their lost kid in a crowd. A few women are standing by me, trying to ask me about my next book and where my inspiration for writing comes from. They're really nice, and the last thing I want to do is be rude, but I'm not even looking at them right now. I just scan as quickly as I can to make sure I'm not crazy. But once I see that she's gone I know it's time to act. I finish up the last bit of conversation so as not to seem rude, and then I excuse myself from the group.

Gray and Colt each have their own following encircling them, but they make eye contact with me as I start to walk out. I can tell when I walk away that they're both a little annoyed with me. Neither says anything, but the looks on their faces scream of 'where the fuck are you going?'

I feel bad, but there's really no choice.

If it's between meeting Everleigh in her hotel room or

throwing a few beers back in a hotel bar, then there's absolutely no choice to be made.

I'm coming.

I put my bag at my feet as the elevator takes me to the fifth floor, and the ding that comes before the opening of the doors sets my heart going a step faster than normal. The truth is that I'm already excited, the rising of the elevator from the first floor to the fifth took me on a journey. When the doors closed I was concerned about what Gray and Colt were thinking, concerned for the readers I felt that I was neglecting, and feelings of guilt that I wasn't doing my part for the group.

But that was four floors ago. Now I'm here. Now the doors are opening. They're not just the doors to the fifth floor of the hotel, they're the last barrier to her. They're the doors to the future, and once they open I walk through them without hesitation, taking giant steps down the hallway to her room, 514. I read the numbers on the door as they increase, each one a little bit closer to her. My heart is pounding in anticipation of what's going to happen. I stop in front of her door and look back to make sure no one sees me, but the hallways are clear. Everyone is down at the bar, taking shots, taking pictures, talking about whatever the hell they're all talking about. And I'm here, where I'm meant to be. Where she invited me. Where she is.

I use the key that she gave me. I insert it, downwards into the hole, and wait. It's only a second of waiting, but in that space the small amount of insecurity that I have comes to the forefront of my mind. What if this whole thing was a mistake? Those thoughts have no time to linger, because I push the door open and there she is.

She's wearing black lingerie, the kind that I'd describe in a scene in my book, only now I don't have the words to describe how she looks accurately, except to say that she's everything I've ever wanted, standing right before me in one small package. Her hair is down, falling along either shoulder, draping down and falling just on top of each breast. She doesn't say a word, and it builds the tension even more between us. But, then again, what words do we need at this point? The expression on her face speaks volumes, communicating all that I need to know at that moment.

She steps back, and I walk into the room. I step across the threshold willingly, and close the door behind me so that we can be truly alone. The room is dim, almost pitch black, save for a small lamp with a low wattage in the corner. It lights the room enough to not be in total darkness, yet creates the effect of a glow that bounces off of Everleigh's face. She doesn't look away from me, not even for a second, and with every step she takes backward, I take a step forward. She stops after three, the edge of the bed tapping against her thigh and halting her momentum.

She doesn't fight the fall.

She collapses backwards onto the bed, her back falling almost angelically against the softness of the comforter. I stop just in front of her body and look down. Her erect nipples are pointing upwards towards the ceiling, while her arms are spread out. It's a position of vulnerability, of submission, allowing me to do to her whatever it is that I want.

I'm rock hard already. I don't remember feeling that happen, it's just there, ready to go, and I give in to the sensations. In fact, I'm giving in to this entire moment. On some level I was fighting it yesterday, and maybe that was the right thing to do. I said that I wanted to wait, that I wanted to get to know her better, and that the last thing I wanted was for sex to ruin what could be. But that late night text from twenty-four hours ago seems an eternity. I don't know that guy right now.

He's levelheaded. Rational. Good at controlling his impulses. That Michael isn't in the room with this beautiful woman who's lying half naked on the bed in front of him. No. That Michael wouldn't be good in this situation.

I'm the real Michael right now.

The one who doesn't care about consequences. I'm the guy who can feel his cement-like cock protruding against the front of his pants more than he can sense the responsible thing to do. I'm the Michael who's about to fuck this woman like she's never been fucked before. The one who isn't worried about ruining the future, but rather the one who knows how to create the most memorable present she's ever known in her life.

I post my hands on either side of her body and hover just above her mouth. I can feel her warm breath against my mouth, and she lifts herself up just slightly to meet my lips, but I pull back. I want her to want me, and I want her to know that I'm in control of when this happens, no matter how bad she wants it. She tries again, lifting her head, and again I pull up just a little bit—maybe a half of an inch—until her kiss just misses me, but I feel her breath against my lips. As she's dropping her head down I follow, kissing her hard and aggressively, and she responds in kind.

Her arms are around me, clawing at my back in a frenzy of passion, all the while I hold her in place with my body. She can move her hands all she likes, but her body stays where I want it—where I can do what I want to it. She uses the only control she has to her fullest ability, digging sharp nails into my back so hard that I can't separate pleasure from pain. I know that she wants me to react, to yell out or to retract so that she knows that she's in control. But I won't. She can pierce my skin and wrap my back up as tightly as her arms will allow, but she's still going nowhere. I keep kissing her, my tongue plunging willingly into her mouth, and she starts to moan, a sign of submission that turns me on even more. The real pain isn't against the raw skin of my back, it's pushing in vain against the front of my jeans.

I feel its frustration at being restrained, and all I want to do is let my cock out, but that would be like bringing your Queen out too early in a game of chess. I have to pace myself. I have to be patient. I have to make her body ache for me as much as mine is aching for her, but that means taking my time and letting her body build up the excitement that I'm already feeling. My mouth leaves her lips and migrates down, ever slightly, to her neck. I can tell right away that her skin is sensitive, because as soon as my warm lips press into her— my mouth slightly open so that I can suck on her—her whole body moves upwards in a small convulsion. It gives away enough for me to know that I've hit a sweet spot, and I put even more pressure on that spot, and on the rest of her neck, moving my body up and down against her as I do. It's a tease for her and I both, but I want to give her only the slightest taste of what's coming.

Her hands are still at work, rubbing and clawing on my back, and she wraps her legs around me from the bottom, squeezing my torso between her thighs. I can feel the warmth and wetness between her legs. It feels like opportunity. It feels like everything my body was made to connect to, and soon my cock will be deeply buried inside that warmth, but not just yet. I'm not ready to rush that part, but we need to lose some of these unnecessary fucking clothes. I'll start.

I sit up and take my shirt off, tossing it next to me on the bed. I'm not vain, but I become very aware of the contours of my own muscles as I feel her hands rubbing against my pecks, and then tracing a path down across my washboard abs. I work hard on my body, and I can tell that it's turning her on. I flex as hard as I can, making my chest into stone, and I allow her hands to explore every facet of it. When she's done rubbing her hands against me I grab both her wrists and pin them down next to her head. We kiss a little bit more in that position, and then I let go, leaving her hands where they are.

I don't know what comes over me, but when I'm turned on I'm not thinking with my brain, I'm feeling with my body and my heart. I reach down and rip her lingerie open down the middle, exposing her white, creamy breasts. Her nipples are rock hard, and her tits are perfect circles, symmetrical in their beauty, and begging to be heid.

I grab on to her left breast with my hand, squeezing her flesh and isolating her nipple so that I can suck on it. She convulses again when I put the full suction of my lips around her nipple, which makes me go even harder. She tries to sit up but I put her back on her back, removing my mouth and putting it to better use. My lips trace a vertical line downwards, passing in between her tits, down over her stomach, and all the way down to just above her. . . I stop. Her panties have to go. I sit up and remove them quickly, yanking at her hips as she lifts up to assist me. Once they're gone I take my place again. My face stops just above her pussy, which is clean shaven and waiting for me to go to work. My tongue hits her first, right above her clit, and I keep my head perfectly still while my warm tongue dances in small circles over the top of her clit. She starts moving around and making sounds, and I love how much pleasure I'm already bringing to her.

This is about her, not me. I want the lead only so that I can control how much I bring to her body and soul. And right now it's working. I work my tongue over the same spot for a while, before lowering my head even more and plunging my tongue inside of her. She gasps as I lick back upwards, hitting her clit with as much force as my tongue can generate, while reaching a finger inside her at the same time. She's so wet that even with only one finger inside her, my entire hand is bathed in a matter of seconds just from being pressed against her dripping pussy. She's dripping because of me, and I'm as hard as I've ever been because of her. I move my finger in and out of her at different speeds, fast or slow depending on how I'm moving my tongue, but I vary it so that she's getting the sensations of fast and slow at the same time no matter what I do.

She's soaking the bed, a combination of her juice and my spit melded together. I work her clit with my tongue until I feel her getting close to coming, and then I immediately stop. The time for teasing is over. I sit up again and undo my pants, clumsily getting them off of my waist and down my legs. My boxer-briefs follow, and I'm standing in front of her naked, but not feeling even the slightest bit uncomfortable. She sits up on the bed, and comes face to face with it, my hardness staring her in the face, only inches from her lips. She reaches out with her hand and grips me, examining my dick with her eyes as she caresses it, as though she's never seen anything quite like it. She never hesitates, however, and even as she stares she's stroking me, working her hand seamlessly from base to tip, applying just the right amount of pressure to drive me insane. I try not to show it on my face but I don't think I'm going to be able to maintain that facade of control for long.

Her hands feel amazing, and she's teasing me without being obvious about it, running her face near my cock and brushing my throbbing head against her lips. She keeps moving, and with every near miss my cock throbs. When it does she squeezes even harder, teasing me and pleasuring me at the same time. I want her mouth, but I want to be inside of her even more than that, so I waste no time. I push her back on the bed and fall over her, keeping my weight elevated once again, but pressing my hard cock against her body. She doesn't wait for me. She reaches underneath with her hand and puts the head right on the outside of her lips, and the sensations of warm and wet are all I can feel. For a second it's too much, and the excitement seems to overwhelm everything. I panic that I'm going to come right there on her leg, so I take a deep breath instead and try to slow down a little.

"What's the matter?" she asks.

I open my eyes and look at her. "I'm so turned on right now and I don't want to. . .I want to go slow for a minute."

"Go slow," she says, caressing the back of my head lovingly with her fingers. "I'm not going anywhere."

She's so understanding, just waiting underneath me without moving, even though she wants me as much as I want her. I take one more deep breath to steady my nerves before I proceed. This time I reach down so that I can control the pace. I hold myself steady and tease her clit, rubbing the head of my cock over it, then up and down over the outside of her lips. I'm feeling good, but not too excited for my own good, so when I rub downwards to the right spot I slip inside of her seamlessly. My cock is a hot knife through butter, pushing inside of her with no effort at all except a gentle thrust foreword with my hips, until I'm so deep that I can feel my pelvis pressed against hers. I stay there, deep in her, not moving an inch. I start kissing her from the top as she starts gyrating her hips from the bottom, moving herself so that I hit all of the right spots.

We keep going for a few minutes. I sit back on my knees and grab her legs, putting them together in front of me and hitting her pussy as hard as I can with some forceful thrusts of my hips. She starts to scream, and I increase my speed, hitting her hard and fast over and over again until I need to slow down a little. I spread her legs back open and leave them hanging in the air. Reaching down I start rubbing her clit in fast, gentle circles while I fuck her, moving in and out of her slowly while I keep the pace of my hands fast. It doesn't take but a few seconds for her to come, and when she does it's an explosion of passion. Her body thrusts underneath me uncontrollably, her hips moving up and down, and her eyes closed so that she can experience the overwhelming sensations. It's only a few seconds, but when it's over her energy is drained and I feel her body relax. I haven't finished yet, but I'm so happy with what just happened that I decide to take a break and pull out.

"Do you want me to finish you?"

"Absolutely," I tell her. "But like you said, I'm in no rush. Just taking a breather and letting you bask in the afterglow a little."

"That was so fucking hot," she says. Her cheeks are flushed red and her hair is all messed up. She has that I-just-got-fucked look to her, and her chest is heaving up and down as she struggles to catch her breath. I lean in and kiss her, then collapse on the bed next to her for now.

In this room she's not just my lover—she's my redemption. Her body isn't a thing to be felt, it's a mystery to be solved, a thing to lose myself in and find myself in simultaneously, and as I experience the splendor of it all, only her name can escape my lips.

"Everleigh," I whisper in her ear as we lay next to each other, naked and sweaty. "Can we just stay here forever?"

15

EVERLEIGH

"THAT'S FINE BY ME," I ANSWER. "BUT YOU'D HAVE TO AT least get your computer so you could do some writing. I'm counting on that next book."

"Holy shit," he says, popping up out of bed like a little kid on Christmas morning. "Let me tell you about it!" He looks funny. He literally jumped out of bed and is standing there, half erect, naked as the day he was born, and he's trying to talk to me seriously. I'm trying to look in his eyes but it's distracting—his body is amazing and he's moving his hands a lot, which of course makes other things move a lot. . .

"Tell me."

"So, it's about this guy, a down-on-your-luck sort, only he used to be this high powered attorney. . ." As he starts to tell me about the plot of his book I feel really happy. Yes, I'm in post I-had-sex-with-Michael-Knight bliss and all that, but that's not why I feel happy. I feel so good because he's genuinely enthusiastic right now. He's frantic, pacing back and forth, waving his hands around, and speaking so fast that I can barely keep up with what the book is even about. But I don't care about the plot, I care that he feels good enough to write anything at all. The rest will work itself out.

He talks for about five minutes, telling me all about the main characters, the setting, how it's going to be part of a three book series, all of it. He's so excited and it's making me excited for him. The sex was great, but honestly, this is even better. And it wasn't just sex for me either. I've never been that girl to just sleep with a guy like that, no matter how attractive I find him. And Michael's about the sexiest man I've ever seen. His body is muscular and tight.

His eyes are light and haunting to look into. He's tall, which never hurts, but more than all those features he knows how to use them—how to stand just over you to make you feel his height without being intimidating or dominant; how to cock his head just slightly to the side and give you that kind of intense eye contact that makes you feel like the only woman in the room. I just stare as he starts to wind down his story, my ears listening to his words and my eyes taking in that amazing body that I just want on top of me again.

"That's basically all I have so far," he says, sounding more out of breath now than when we were having sex. "But I think it's enough of an outline to go on. It's funny, I usually don't do outlines or even think about where a story is going before I start writing it."

"You just write?" I ask.

"Kind of, yeah." He looks up to think about what to say next. "I start with characters in my head, and I try to make them as real as possible, even if I don't include the details in the book. Like how some great actors know details about their characters that don't end up in the movie, they just use them to get into the head of whoever they're playing. It's like that, only the writing version. Once I know who a character is, I kind of know how they're going to behave, so the plot kind of writes itself a little."

"I see, that's really fascinating. I know all writers are different, so are your fellow Wordsmiths the same? What's their deal? I've always wanted to know."

"How much time do you have?" he jokes. "Each one of those guys could take a few days to tell you all about. But if you mean their writing process, I'm not really sure. Believe it or not we've never spoken about that—actual writing—very much. We more talk about author stuff."

"Wait, I'm confused, what do you mean 'author stuff?' Isn't writing the most important part of being an author?"

"Sort of," he answers. "I read a quote once by some gazillionaire who publishes sci-fi novels—some dude you've never heard of but has a rabid fan base of readers—on some promotion website where he said 'it's a writer's job to write, and an author's job to sell and promote their books.' That always stuck with me, and it makes sense. So me and the guys have always discussed author stuff more than we ever have writing stuff."

"I see. That makes sense. I guess it's like the difference between a chef and a cook. People think they're the same thing, but they're actually very different."

"That's a fair comparison. Do you work in the food business?"

"Yes," I tell him. I hadn't mentioned my job to him in our conversations yesterday or today, but now's as good a time as any. "I'm actually a small business owner. I own a bakery that's been in my family for generations now."

He looks at me and raises and eyebrow. "Oh, shit, really! That's great."

"On some days it is. I'm not rich or anything. Not some restaurant mogul. It's just my little place in Queens, New York."

"Wait, wait, wait, hold on. You're in New York?"

"Now I am, yeah. My family's originally from New England—Massachusetts. My sister Hadley goes to school there."

"See, I knew I heard those vowels. That sure as hell doesn't sound like any New York accent I've ever heard, and I'm from there."

"I know," I tell him, trying not to sound too stalkerish.

"How do you. . .oh right, social media. I'm still old school in so many ways, I swear. I forget how much of our personal shit is out there. That's crazy that we're in the same area, though."

"It's a crazy coincidence, right? I've known for a while 'cause you mention that you're from New York. You know how many times I wanted to contact you and just be like 'hey, we're both in the same area, wanna. . .' I don't even know what I would have said, honestly, but thank God I stopped myself. You would've thought I was nuts."

"I don't think you're nuts," he tells me, lying down next to me and stroking my hair gently. "I think it's amazing that we're near each other. We have to get together at some point." There it is. I knew that eventually we'd be having the 'What comes next' discussion, but I let him take the lead.

"I'd love that, Michael," I tell him, looking deeply into his beautiful eyes. "But only if you want to. You don't have to tell me that out of obligation, or because you want me to feel better 'cause we slept together. I only want you to say that if you really want to see me again."

I start to look down as I say the last part, afraid of rejection from him in a way that I didn't really think I would be, but he puts his fingers under my chin and gently angles my head up until we're looking at each other once more. "Listen to me, Everleigh," he begins. "In some ways we know more about each other than two people normally do after 48 hours together. But there's more that we don't know about each other. Here's something you should know about me—I only say things that I mean. I'm a man of conviction, and as uncomfortable as it would be, if I didn't want to see you after this I'd tell you straight out."

Wow. I wasn't expecting that kind of blunt honesty from him, but it's really refreshing. "Most people can't handle that level of honesty face to face. Easier to tell a comforting lie and just ghost the person later on when they try to contact you."

"Cowards," he says. "Cowards act like that, and I'm no coward. But more importantly than all that, I genuinely want to see you again. I'd be sad if this were it."

"I'd be sad, too. I want to see you again."

"Then you will. You'll be seeing a lot of me."

"I already do," I joke, looking right down at his huge cock which, even when he's relaxed, is impressive. I reach down, grazing my hand across his thigh until I hit it, and I wrap my fingers around him like a vice. "See, I see a lot of you right now." He gets instantly hard as I start to stroke him, his eyes rolling back in his head. He lays all the way back so that he's totally flat—the only thing upright is his massive dick in my hand. I stroke slowly but firmly, making him feel every inch of the movement of my hand, squeezing tighter as I roll from the base to the gigantic head. "You never finished before. It's your turn. Let's keep it going so you can come on me."

I roll over onto my knees and wrap my mouth around it, and he lets out a deep moan that just gets me going even more. I'm already turned on by him, but knowing that I'm bringing him that kind of pleasure makes me keep going. He's huge, but I manage to fit all of him inside my warm mouth, stroking the base as I deep throat him. "Oh my fucking God!" he yells, so I just keep going. I stroke faster and faster, gripping him hard and creating a suction around his head that I know will make him come quickly. In a few seconds he warns me, "I'm going to fucking come, don't stop!" I don't. I pull it out of my mouth just as he's exploding, a spray of his hot cum flying all over the bed and my face.

It's his turn to just lay back and be pleasured, and as I stroke a few more times—his cum on my face—I feel great that he exploded so fucking hard. I wipe my face on the sheets and fall back next to him. We're both exhausted, our energy drained from the last few minutes, and now there's just time to feel each other's warmth.

16

KNIGHT

WE NOD OFF, WHICH I ONLY REALIZE ONCE EVERLEIGH WAKES me up, frantic. I have no memory of falling asleep, or even starting to fall asleep, but clearly we did because we're still both naked.

"What's going on?" I ask, still out of it.

"Ro and Harley are coming back soon," she says, sitting down next to me in the bed. "I knew they were planning on having a night out after the dinner, that's why I invited you here. I told them that I had a bad headache, and that if they came back too early to just go into Harley's room while I slept for a few hours, but it's been that long and they just texted asking if I was awake."

"Shit. How long do I have?"

"Probably 15-20 minutes, but I'm making that up, I'm not sure exactly."

"I'll get dressed. But first. . ."

I lean over and kiss her gently. She smells so good. I wish there were time for another run, but there just isn't right now. I jump up after we kiss and start getting dressed as quickly as I can so I can get out of there. We're both quick to get our clothes back on, and Everleigh opens up the room widow to air out the smell of sex that must be lingering in the air.

It takes about a minute, but I get my shirt, pants, and shoes on well enough to not look like a drunk guy getting dressed in the dark. There's only one thing. . .oh fuck.

"Oh, fuck!" I yell.

"What's wrong?"

Fuck. Fuck. Fuck. My laptop! Where is it?

"Did you see me bring a bag in here?" I ask as the anxiety rises in my chest.

"I don't remember seeing a bag. Were you supposed to have one?"

"I had it on me before, but I don't see. . ." I stop right there because I realize where I left it. If I could punch myself in the face I would. "I've gotta run."

"Wait, tell me what's going on," she says as I speed towards her door. There's no time to explain right now, but I'll tell her later when I hopefully find my laptop.

"I'll text you," I tell her as I open the door. "I need to go find something I lost right now."

"Okay, good luck."

I pull the door closed behind me and run out like a crazy person. I was keeping my shit together in front of her, but I'm gonna lose it if that laptop is gone. I turn the corner and hit the OPEN button over and over on the elevator. Those few seconds feel like whole minutes, but eventually I hear the ding and the doors open up, left and right, to a completely empty little box. No laptop. Nothing.

"Fuck."

I get on and hit '1.' When I get to the lobby I run out and go right to the front desk. I must look nuts, because I'm breathing heavily and haven't even bothered to look in a mirror since I woke up next to Everleigh. I wasn't exactly expecting to be seeing other people at the moment. "Excuse me," I say a little too loud, but it gets the attention of the woman behind the counter.

"Yes, sir?"

"I'm Michael Knight, one of the authors here for the event."

"Yes, Mr. Knight, how are you this evening? Is your room meeting your satisfaction?"

"It is, yes," I say, trying to not be rude but get to what I really want to know. "It's not that—see, I lost a bag of mine in your elevator a few hours ago. It's kind of important, has all my stuff in it."

"Oh," the woman says, understanding the severity involved.

"Exactly. I'm panicking a little right now. I looked in the elevator and it's gone, I was just wondering if anyone here turned in a bag."

"Let me check."

"Thank you."

She scurries away into some room in the back and comes out about thirty seconds later with nothing in her hands. "I'm sorry, Mr. Knight, nothing was turned in here. Maybe check the elevator one more time, or ask the readers here if they've seen it. Perhaps one of them found it and just wants to give it back to you personally."

"Thank you for looking." I walk back to my room using the stairs, taking my time as I do. It's not a terrible idea asking the readers, without tipping them off as to what was inside the bag. I take out my phone as I'm walking up the stairs and post in the reader group. I don't go into detail, I just mention that if anyone comes across my 'empty' bag that I left behind that they can send me a private message. We'll see if that helps. I'm not counting on it. I'll say it one more time.

FUCK!

Back in my room I collapse on the bed. There are a bunch of texts from the guys asking where I am from earlier. I ignored them when I was with Everleigh, but now I have to respond. I text them that I didn't feel well again, and that I'm back in the room now. I also text her. I decide to go with the direct, blunt approach.

Me: Hey. I lost my laptop. It had my new stuff on it. The front desk doesn't have it. I'm ready to kill someone.

Everleigh: Oh my God," she writes back. "Michael, I'm so sorry. You can re-write.

Me: Thanks. I'm going to sleep now. I had an incredible night and I'm sorry it had to end like this. It's not you, but I need to just sleep this off and decide what I'm going to do in the morning.

Everleigh:I understand. Goodnight.

Me: Night.

I lay down in bed and close my eyes, fully dressed except for my shoes, which I slip off before collapsing. One last time for good measure, only this time it's not a thought, it's a yell that I let out no matter who the hell is listening.

"FUCK!"

KNIGHT

I'M REMEMBERING THAT THOUGHT I HAD BEFORE, ABOUT HOW amazing it was that I'd gone a full two days without any drama or downturn in my mood. That seems fucking laughable right now. After what may have been the best weekend of my life, a weekend where I met a woman I'm really in to, and had some of the best moments yet in my career, I end up losing my fucking laptop. The first original story I'd started in a year—the book that may have been the one to get me on a list—was saved to its hard drive, and now it's vanished along with my bag. I guess it's my fault for not backing the story up, and for leaving my bag on the elevator floor, but still. Whoever took that bag and didn't return it to the front desk is an unethical piece of shit.

I checked with the staff before the three of us left just to make sure they hadn't gotten anything turned in that was mine. But no. No bag. No laptop. Nothing of mine was returned, and it obviously wasn't on the elevator when I went back, which means that someone took it, saw that it was mine, and kept it for themselves. I hope that it wasn't one of our readers, I really do, but you never know how people will behave. What if I had found a laptop with Stephen King's latest short story on it at some hotel? I wouldn't keep it, that's for sure. I might read it and then give it back but I wouldn't flat out steal it from him!

It's time to go home.

I pack up the rest of my shit and text Everleigh. I want to go see her, but she's rooming with her friends, so that's out. I'd really like to see her one more time before I go. I left in a mood after an amazing evening, and now I'm not even going to get to say a proper goodbye, but it is what it is. If anyone saw us and the rumor-mill got going online that would just be the icing on the shit cake, so I just suck it up and send her the nicest text I can muster as we all get ready to head down to the car.

Me: I had the best time last night. You're amazing, and I don't want this weekend to be the end of things. That would break my heart. Once I get back and get settled I'll text you and maybe I can take you out for real.

She writes back in no time, as though the phone was in her hand when she got my message.

Everleigh: Good morning! And I'd love that. It won't help to say this, but don't let this stop that momentum I saw. Write your story. Write our story if it helps. Whatever gets those amazing fingers hitting the keys of your computer.

Me: Our story isn't written yet," I write back. "But maybe I'll jot down the first few chapters.

Everleigh: Please do. I'll talk to you this week, okay?

Me: You got it.

Even though it doesn't change how I feel entirely, my mood gets a little lighter after that text exchange. She has that effect on me. It's an amazing thing because I know that I lean towards the darker side of things, I always have. Even when I was a kid I was kind of sullen, very intense and serious most days, and always very focused on whatever I was doing. I have a good sense of humor, but it's not my natural state to sit around joking and laughing with people. I've had a few serious relationships in my life, but it's a rare thing that just being around a woman makes me feel less serious, less depressed, less of everything. But even just a message on a screen took a little bit of the edge off the sting of this whole laptop thing. This woman's amazing. Me and the boys pack up what's left of our stuff into the back of the car.

"Did we all sell out?" Colton asks.

"You did," Grayson jokes. "A long time ago when you became a rock star in your mind, but I don't think that's what you're asking."

"No, dick," Colton says, putting the last of his boxes in the back. "Did we all sell all of our extra books? I did."

"I did also," Gray answers.

"I mostly did." I have one box left that has a few copies of Into Your Eyes, and a few envelopes of extra swag, but that's about it. Colton comes over and takes the box from me.

"Feels like there's nothing in here, good for you, man!" He gives me a little punch on the shoulder to try and cheer me up. Colton's a really good guy. Everyone thinks he's this brash asshole, especially other male authors, he has that alpha thing going for him, but he's really the kindest person I've met. His cockiness is only there to sell books and as a mental trick to help make him successful. He's ambitious and driven, for sure, and he has incredible self belief, which can sometimes come across as arrogance if you don't know what you're looking at, but he's one of the most selfless people I know, and definitely a great friend. "You killed it. You see?"

"I guess," I say. I can hear the negative tone in my voice and I don't like it at all.

"No, man, don't guess, that's what happened." Colton

closes the trunk and turns to face me right there in the parking lot, putting both of his hands on my shoulders. "Listen to me, I know what happened last night sucks." If he only knew what else happened last night. "But how much did you actually have written down? New and old material combined?"

I think for a second and do some quick math in my head. "I don't know, about 10,000 words."

"See, it's not that big of a deal. That's what, two days work if you lock yourself in the house? And we all know how much you love to do that. If you were a country, locking yourself in the house would be your national sport. Come on, you can get that shit back."

The number 10,000 may sound like a lot, quantifiably, but it really isn't. Writers think in terms of words, not pages, and Colton is correct that 10,000 isn't nearly as much as it may sound like to a non-writer. Your average romance novel is between fifty to seventy thousand words usually, and he's also right that if I sat down with a pot of coffee and no distractions that I could bang out 10,000 words in two days, easily. Maybe one day if I started early in the morning. But if he's so right, why doesn't it make me feel any better?

"And look," he continues. "It's not like anything can be done with that story. You have a really distinct style of writing, there's no way someone could pirate a few chapters and do anything meaningful with it, so don't even worry about that part of it."

"Yeah, I guess."

"There you go guessing again. Stop that. Don't guess, just trust me, can you do that? For real."

"I trust you," I tell him.

"Good, then trust what I'm saying to you. You know I'm not a cheerleader, and that I don't say shit just to make people feel better about themselves. I mean what I say. You'll get over this, fast. Do you remember the characters?"

"Yes," I answer.

"The plot so far?"

"Yup."

"The basic narrative of what you had written?"

"Absolutely."

"Well then, there you go, shut your whiny ass up and take this."

Grayson, who's been quietly listening to Colt's speech to me this whole time, walks up next to me and hands me his computer. "Here," he says, handing it to me. "I already formatted a Word document for you. It's numbered, spaced correctly, and just waiting for you to be brilliant. We have a four hour drive, get after that shit."

I smile. What else can I do, the kid should be an inspirational speaker. What makes me smile and feel a little better is the sincerity in his eyes. He believes what he's saying, and it makes me want to believe it too, even if that isn't the case just yet. He's right, though, I don't need to believe anything, I just need to get my fingers to hover over those keys, and I know I can make some magic happen. Time to shut up and write.

I think I surprise the hell out of Colton when I step towards him and give him a huge hug right there in the parking lot. We're both big, muscular guys, so the image of a gentle embrace in a parking lot is probably funny if someone is looking, but I don't care. That type of friendship moment deserves a fucking hug.

"Are you gonna fuck me now, too?" he jokes. And with that delicate line Colton is back to his usual brash self.

"But you haven't even sucked my dick yet!"

"And there we have it," Grayson says, putting his hand on both of our shoulders. "Time to go."

"Wait," Colt jokes, turning towards Gray. "If we started banging right here, like all three of us, I think we could hit some lists."

"Yeah," Grayson says. "The arrest list for the local police department. Plus I can do better than you two, anyhow."

"Oh, fuck off," Colton jokes. "You'd be blessed for me to gift you my dick. It would be like Christmas for you."

"Guys, guys!" I yell, only it's not a real yell. "I can't write my masterpiece while we're all standing in a parking lot talking about fucking each other. I'm distractible like that. Can we hit the road, we have a long drive."

"He's right," Colt says. "And anyhow, if we get bored we can always talk about banging each other while we're driving."

"Goals," I joke.

We get in and pull out of the lot. The hotel starts to fade into the horizon as Gray hits the gas, and I turn to take it in one last time. I have pictures, and I'll have my memories, but there's something I want to see in person one more time before it's gone. Some special things happened in that building this weekend, things that will effect me, one way or the other, for a long time.

More than any of the drama I'm going through, or book sales, or building some buzz for our new group, what happened in that building was meeting her—meeting Everleigh. I haven't figured out my relationship with the universe just yet. Sometimes I feel like it's messing with me at every turn, testing my ability to stay positive and push forward in my life. Maybe that's just my own psychology that I need to let go. But occasionally, I feel like the universe just makes implausible things happen, and that those things can impact you for the rest of your life. I don't know if I really believe any of that, but what I do believe is that I met someone really special in that hotel bar, and that no matter if I become a successful author or end up greeting people at Walmart for a living, I need to see her again.

I need her again.

18

EVERLEIGH

I HOPE MICHAEL'S OKAY.

I mean, I know he's not, really, but how could he be? The poor guy finally writes something he's excited about and loses it in the same weekend. What pieces of shit people can be! On some level I feel a little guilty because he lost his computer on his way to see me. I know that he was just forgetful because he was excited—so was I—and that one careless move on his part cost him a story. Hopefully he'll remember what he wrote and can recover it.

He said he was going to use one of the other guys' computers to try and recover whatever he could on the way home from memory, I just hope he isn't so bummed about it that it takes away from his ability to write. I guess we'll see.

What I'm really sad about is how our night ended. That was the best sex I've ever had in my life, and it wasn't just some tawdry fling between a romance groupie and a scumbag male author. That stuff goes on all the time, but last night wasn't that. I'm not that woman, and Michael sure as hell doesn't seem like that guy. It was a genuine connection between two people, and an amazing weekend that sprung from it. I'm just upset that he was so upset, and that we couldn't even spend the night together because he left in a terrible mood.

"Are you ready?" Harley asks.

"Almost."

"Rowan, what about you?" All of a sudden Harley's become the organized one, herding us and keeping us in line.

"Yeah," Ro says, peeking her head out from behind the door of our bathroom. "I'm just making sure I didn't leave any of my stuff behind."

"And stealing the little soaps?" Harley jokes.

"Well, that too, but mostly the first thing."

"How about you Mrs. Knight," Harley says, turning towards me this time. "Did you pack your engagement ring and your extra special copy of his book?"

I look at her and make my angry face. "Stop it, okay. And don't joke about my annotated paperback, it helped me leave Jeremey, sort of. And yes, I'm done packing."

"That's a powerful book. Speaking of the devil, anything since that night he texted you?"

"Unfortunately," I tell her. "He doesn't like that I stood up to him at all. He keeps writing these weird and cryptic texts that he's gonna see me again, no matter what, and that I'm still his, and that he still loves me. A whole bunch of craziness."

"Does he know your new address?"

"Shit, I hope not," I say. Now I'm worrying that he does. "I mean, if he does he hasn't used it. No letters or random cases of him 'being in the neighborhood' or any other stalker excuse. All of our communication. . .scratch that, all of his communication has been via text."

"Wait," Harley interjects. "You don't write him back ever?"

"No," I tell her. "I'm afraid he'll take it as some kind of fucked up victory and think I'm encouraging him to text more."

"Yeah, you're right," Ro says. "I don't have any experience with stalkers, personally, but . . ."

"I'm not saying he's a stalker, Ro."

"I know, but he's definitely doing stalker-ish things. What I was going to say is that I saw a special on YouTube about stalkers once. . ."

"You watch that shit on YouTube?" This time it's Harley interrupting.

"Can I finish a sentence? Jesus."

"Sorry, sorry," I say. "Go ahead."

"Anyway, I saw this documentary that said what you just said. Basically that the psychology of creeps who do this kind of shit is such that they take any contact—even if it's you telling them to fuck off—as encouragement. Just how their brains work, so maybe don't text back unless you absolutely have to."

"And you don't have to," Harley says. "You've cut ties, right? There's nothing financial keeping you in contact?"

"No," I say. "We weren't married. Just a few things that we worked out already. There's really no reason to talk to him."

"Good, then don't!"

I love how protective they are of me, but I think they're over doing it a little. Maybe I shouldn't make Jeremey sound so crazy. He was really in love with me. I get how, sometimes in a breakup, people have trouble letting go. We were together for a while and some of it was really good, but once he started getting verbally abusive and controlling it changed how I felt. I hope he just stops contacting me once and for all.

"I won't, don't worry."

"Are we all ready to go?" Harley asks.

"You don't have to wait for us, Har," I tell her. "If you need to get back we understand, you took your own car, after all."

"I know. I just feel like walking out with you guys."

"Alright, then," Ro says, closing the last unpacked suitcase. "Let's get back to real life."

We get all of our belongings—our clothes, toiletries, and of course our book stuff—loaded up and down to the lobby. A few minutes later we're hugging goodbye, and the hotel fades into the distance as Rowan takes me back towards our real lives.

INTERLUDE

Sometimes, when you're lost, there's only one way to find True North.

In my case, all I have to do is pick up the phone. That's his name in my contacts—*True North.* It's a nickname, obviously. His real name isn't important. What you need to know is that he's an author like me. Actually, let me rephrase that. Saying he's an author like me is kind of comparing myself to LeBron because I play some pick up games on the weekends. We do the same thing, but he's way more successful than me.

He's quietly one of the best selling authors you've probably never heard of. The indie book world is full of guys like True North—people who've so carefully cultivated a rabid fan base and write such great books that they've made a career for themselves doing what they love. North is the coolest guy in the world—bald headed, double sleeves, and generally looks like a badass ex biker, but he's the sweetest dude in the world.

I met him when I was just getting started. Not everyone is nice to you when you're coming up, but he made himself accessible to me. He gave me advice. He told me his story. He helped me identify mistakes I was making in my career. He's just a cool motherfucker. Plain and simple.

He still helps me when I need it, although thankfully I don't dial his number as much as I used to. Even though he's only a few years older than me, he's like a mentor—a literary father figure of sorts. And his word is like gospel. There aren't many people whose advice I put such weight on, but he's one of them. Right now I need to hear his voice.

I text him first to make sure it's okay to call at this time of night. He's got a family and a full time writing schedule, so after he texts back that it's fine I hit dial. It doesn't take but a single ring before I hear his raspy voice on the other side.

"What's up, brother? How are you?"

"I've been better, man. But how are you?"

"I'm stuck on this fucking scene. I must've rewritten this shit twenty different times."

"What's the scene?"

"It's for my latest MC book. First sex scene between my two main characters. The woman's reluctantly attracted to the guy. He's a rough one—tatted up and a total badass. Anyway, I can't get it to read how I want it to. It needs some massaging."

True North is a perfectionist. I bet this scene he's talking about reads better than most of my books, but part of what makes him who he is is the high standard he has for himself, and his ability to tell a story like no other.

"You'll get it," I tell him. "You always do."

"Forget me. What's going on with you?"

I choose my words carefully because I don't wanna spill my guts or treat him like he's my therapist. He doesn't need to know every detail of the drama. "I lost a new thing I was working on."

"What do you mean lost?" he asks.

"Literally. I left my laptop somewhere and no one's been able to recover it. It was the first thing I'd written in forever. It was the end of my writer's block, and now it's gone."

"It's never gone, brother. The computer is a piece of machinery. It's a tool. The story is in you. Find it again. It's there."

This is why I called North in times of need. He had a quiet and wise simplicity that always made me feel better about whatever was bothering me. Although he was a prolific writer who's written millions of words, in person he was prone to short and truthful statements that didn't require a lot of follow up. He was the perfect person to talk to during times like this.

"This is why I call you. You always know what to say."

"I wish that were true. I just offer my two cents. You can take it or leave it."

"Well I haven't left it yet, and I'd be a fool to. You're the man."

"Thanks, Knight. What's the new one about? The one you lost."

It's a good question, and I'm not even sure exactly how to answer it. "I'm not sure yet. You know that old adage about the sculptor?"

"I know it well," he says. "That all the sculptor does is to shave away the stone to reveal the art underneath."

"Right. I'm in the shaving process now. But I'll tell you when I find out what's underneath all the crap."

"I look forward to it."

"How about yours?" I ask.

"The next MC book in the Rotten Scoundrel series. This is the best one yet."

"I've no doubt it is. I'll let you get back to it. Goodnight, North."

We hang up and I feel better. The last thing I need is to slip back into a bad head space. Even grown men need mentors from time to time, and True North has been there for all three of the Wordsmiths. He's a guy who pays his success forward, and who genuinely embodies the best that the book world has to offer. I know that we'll speak more soon. But for now I'm going to bed feeling better about everything. Before I do, I think of his words, and on my phone I open up a new note. I only write one thing before going to bed.

"Chapter One"

Then I close my eyes, excited as to what tomorrow will bring.

PART II

HOME

I let her call me Michael. "Let" isn't the right word—she just called me Michael, and at first it took me by surprise. Everyone calls me Knight. The readers only know me as Knight. But she didn't bother with my pen name. She broke right through the barriers that we sometimes keep up between us and the readers. She called me "Michael", and I never want her to call me anything else.

19

KNIGHT

ONE MONTH LATER

"What the hell does she want?"

It's a valid question Colton's asking me. Or, yelling at me. Getting a text—or any form of communication—from an ex, out of the blue, can be a complicated thing, and it makes you ask yourself some serious questions. *Should I answer this? What do they want?* A million little questions that are better to wonder about than to actually ask outright, but the first question is a good place to start.

"No idea," I tell him as we go over some ideas for a future Wordsmith signing. "This is the first I've heard from her since she moved out and into what's-her-face's place. Maybe she saw all of our activity on Facebook after the signing. She's still in the indie book world, after all."

"There's something I've always wanted to ask you about that whole thing." Colton looks at me hesitantly, which is not like him, so I'm curious what he's going to say. "I just never thought it was appropriate to ask, but since time has passed. . ."

"Go ahead, I'm over it all. I'll tell you anything you want to know."

"I'll remember you said that," he says. "Did the image of them hooking up turn you on, like, even a little bit? Not at the time, I know, but when you thought of it afterwards."

"No," I say squarely. I already anticipated where this was going when he hesitated. "Not even a little."

"Yeah?"

"Dude, I maxed out the deductibles on my mental heath insurance to make sure I didn't picture it too much. On top of that, even when I slipped up and that visual popped into my head after one too many, it was never sexual. If I want to see two women go at it I can click on the 'lesbian' tab on YouPorn, I don't need to see my wife getting eaten out by some chick I barely knew in my own fuckin' bed!"

"I get it," he finally concedes. "I didn't really think about it like that, I was just thinking like a dumb guy."

"Well that's what you are," I joke. "I appreciate you staying in your lane, but the answer is no, it never once turned me on."

I am intrigued by whatever it is Jenny might want. We don't have any more business together since the divorce was finalized and all of the financial assets were worked out, so it can't be about that. We split up the bank accounts and all those entanglements when she moved out, and the house was always mine, so I'm thinking that this has to be about something non-marriage related. But what could it possibly be?

"What did she text?"

I read it out loud. *"How's the writing going? Saw the event on Facebook. Glad you're doing well."*

"That's some bullshit," Colton say. "She doesn't give a

fuck how you're doing or she'd be here with you. She needs something."

"Maybe," I admit. "I can't imagine what else it could be other than that."

"I'm sympathetic," Colt says. "Jenny totally fucked you."

"Actually, she fucked that girl, but I get your point. But what I was going to say is that I've thought about how I should feel about everything that happened. Long term I mean."

"I don't know how you feel anything except anger and resentment, personally. But maybe I'm just a prick who holds a grudge."

"You're that too," I say, smiling. "In addition to being dumb like you said before."

"Haha."

"But, seriously though, I'm not talking about who was right and who was wrong. Obviously she was 100 percent wrong. I'm talking about my own state of mind. Should I just look back and get angry and have it ruin my day randomly? I know I have the right to, but is that the best thing for me?"

"Absolutely not," Colton reassures me.

"And, bear with me here, what if this isn't some phase? What if she's genuinely gay and just felt like she couldn't come out her entire life and it just clicked with this woman?"

"Even so, man, she didn't need to cheat on you. If she was going to cheat on you she didn't need to fuck that girl in your own bed, in your own home, and even if she was going to do that, she didn't need to do it at a time where you'd walk in. That shit has nothing to do with being gay, that has to do with having ethics and being a good person."

Colton's a lot of things, but he's usually correct in how he sees situations. He laid it out pretty clearly there and I can't really argue with him. He's absolutely right. As difficult of a thing as it would have been, she should have told me who she really was, and we could have at least remained friends, and maybe split up amicably. Instead, I got two shocks for the price of one—my wife was gay, and she was also cheating on me.

"Are you going to text her back?"

There's the six million dollar question, the only one really worth asking myself. The answers to those other questions —*what does she want, does she have an ulterior motive*— they can all be answered by how she responds to me. But it all starts with whatever I decide to do right now.

"I think so. I'm curious."

"Hey, listen, I know you're curious—to tell you the truth I'm a little curious myself—but the question is, like you said, is this the best thing for you? Maybe that curiosity leads to more anxiety or depression, or me and Grayson having to drag you off of your couch again."

"No, I'm done with all that." I'm feeling confident, and even though I really appreciate Colt's concern as a friend, I don't need it. I'm sick of questions, it's time to get some answers. "You won't have to drag me anywhere, don't worry. But I think I need to see what's so important as to drag her out from underneath her rock."

That last part was harsh, but I honestly feel no love towards her anymore, not after what she did. That wasn't the case at first, for a while I would have said or done just about anything to have her back in my life, lesbian or not, but that seems like a very long time ago. I was starting to lose that part of myself that harbored feelings for her slowly, but after I met Everleigh that all just disappeared. Gone. Never to return again. And I'm fine with that now, I really am. But I do want to know what's changed on her end that she'd reach out to me randomly after all this time. I guess I'll find out.

"Hey," I text back. "All's good. What's up?"

I leave it a little cold on purpose. I'll let her explain if there's more to be explained, but I'm sure as hell not spending any time on this unless there's a reason. I put my phone down and go back to Colton. "Where were we?"

"We were thinking of some cool events for the future and getting some swag made."

"I had this idea, but I want to save it for Grayson," I say.

"I'm not good enough?" he jokes. "Why won't you tell me and we can both run it past Grayson together."

I realize how it came out, like I'm trying to exclude him, but that isn't what I mean. "No, I didn't mean it like that, I meant it's one of those decisions we should all be in on."

"Kind of like the stuff we're discussing now," he answers. "Gray's at a signing. He's been a little strapped for cash, off the record, and he wanted to see if he could get some buzz going for his last book."

Books are like real estate. The longer they stayed on the market without selling the worse their prospects for the future. It's not a perfect analogy—there are some very high profile cases of already released books being discovered way after their publication date and becoming a hit—like *A Game of Thrones: A Song of Ice and Fire* by George R.R. Martin. That book sat on the shelves for hardcore fantasy and historical fantasy geeks to enjoy since 1996! Then it got picked up by HBO and became one of the most popular series and TV shows of all time. But that's obviously the exception, and for genres like ours, that shit never happens.

I worry when I hear that he's struggling financially, but the unspoken truth is that a lot of us are. Sure, we put our best foot forward on social media because that's what it's for. We take pics at just the right angle, we make sure most of our reviews come out 4 to 5 stars on release day through our

ARC groups, and we do our best to make it sound like we're fuckin' EL James on steroids. The truth? Most of us are struggling. There are literally thousands of authors and hundreds of thousands of books released each year. Standing out in the online world is a challenge, even when you do everything correctly, and it makes me sad to hear that people close to me are struggling to pay the bills.

"Yeah, totally off the record. How bad is it?"

"It's not great, man, not gonna lie. He's not filing for food stamps and government cheese or anything, but getting the next few books out is getting to be a struggle. You know how it is."

"Yeah." He's right. We all know how it is. Think of indie writing like one of those businesses that you see featured on Shark Tank, only we can't get venture capitalists to loan us money up front against future royalty rates or anything. When you're trying to make a name for yourself in this game it's like anything else—your expenses exceed your profit. It's that simple. Unless you write a hit—something that's getting harder to do in the Amazon era, and specifically with romance—you're going to struggle at first. The first goal is a net zero gain where you're just breaking even. But the ultimate goal? The ultimate goal is to be profitable, cash positive, being in a position where your royalties exceed all the expenses that go along with publication—editing, cover photos, cover design, social media banner design, swag, copies of your own books for giveaways, banners for signings, and a million other little expenses.

"I hope it's going well for him, but that's kind of what I wanted to talk to you about."

"I'm worthy," he jokes. "Even in a non-Grayson setting. Cool. Let's do it."

"I want to write an anthology."

"What?"

"A Wordsmith anthology."

"I like the idea," he tells me, but he says it in a way that makes me anticipate the . . . "But, there are only three of us. Is that enough for an anthology?"

"Not really," I tell him. "I haven't fully thought this through."

"I see that."

It's true. It's an idea I had yesterday and I haven't fleshed it all out yet. I know I like the idea of combining our ideas into a single book, but I don't really want to co-author anything. I don't even know how that works to tell you the truth. I like the idea of an anthology, but I'd need both the other guys on board—and probably a few more.

"But I like it. It could work. I just think we need more guys. I can think of a few."

"Me, too. But you see why I wanted to curb the conversation until the three of us were together. I don't even know if Grayson is into it, and it should be an all or nothing proposition, otherwise it won't be worth anything."

"Alright, I see now. I like the idea but it needs some airing out. A lot of it, actually. He's back tomorrow. I'll text him. How about we all get a nice dinner? Just the guys. We'll find an expensive steak house, even though we're all broke as fuck, and blow what little money we have on an overpriced good time in celebration of our success at the signing."

"I love it. That sounds awesome. Text him."

As I tell him that I hear my own phone vibrate. I know it's Jenny, so I roll my eyes and pick up my phone. I hope this isn't anything too dramatic. All it says is,

Jenny: I need to see you. I need to tell you something and it can't wait. Dinner at our old place?

What the hell? She went from passively friendly to

cryptic and weird really fast, but I guess that's a shift I should be used to with her. She's mastered the art of the pitch because she already has me interested. I decide to bite. "Alright," I text back. "I'll meet you there at seven."

I guess I'm having dinner with my ex wife tonight.

20

KNIGHT

Jade Fountain is a Chinese restaurant in town about ten minutes from my house. It's not a take out place—no egg rolls or any of that American bullshit. It's the place where Chinese people from all of the surrounding areas come to eat. Their menu is mostly seafood, served Cantonese style, and it takes a certain getting used to. I love almost everything they serve, but it took Jenny a while to make friends with the menu, so I'm surprised when it's here that she asked to meet me.

She called it 'our spot' because this is where I took her on our first date. If I'm being honest I wanted it to be a test of sorts. I knew that most people raised on American cuisine would find the majority of their dishes unpalatable, but I've always loved it, and I wanted to see how she'd react.

I get there first and sit down. I like to be first to uncomfortable meetings like this, I feel like it gives me some kind of home court advantage. When she walks in I have to admit how good she looks. She's a beautiful woman, I'll give her that, but as soon as I see her I know that her beauty doesn't effect me anymore. It used to be that a batting of her eyes or a sideways tilt of her head could get me to do whatever she wanted, but, to quote a favorite song of mine, now she's just somebody that I used to know.

"Hi."

I stand up to greet her. Even though I don't really want to be here I still act like a gentleman and kiss her on the cheek. Her hair still smells of Eucalyptus. "Same shampoo," I say, sitting down.

"My favorite. How are you?"

"I'm doing good, thanks." I don't ask her the same question because I don't really care how she's doing. I know that's petty as fuck, but I'd rather be petty than disingenuous, so I don't bother asking her back. I hope she's well, but what I really want to know is what's going on. "What's up?"

"Wow, you cut right to the chase, don't you?"

"Normally, no," I tell her, felling annoyed all of a sudden that I even agreed to this. "See, if we were old friends from college or something, and this was the first time we were seeing each other in a few years, it might be different. I'd be cordial. I'd be interested in what was going on with you. They'd have to ask us to leave because I'd lose all sense of time sitting here talking to you. But that's not the situation, is it?" I can't believe that I'm talking to her this way, but I'm feeling a bunch of things that I didn't anticipate after the text. I'm not depressed, or anxious, or sad, I'm angry.

"Wow," she says, looking down. "I guess we're skipping the pleasantries altogether. I really didn't think you'd still be this angry after all this time."

Neither did I. "What's up, Jenny?"

"You don't want to order something first? We might as well eat while we're here."

She's right. Just because it's unpleasant for me to sit with her doesn't mean that I can't enjoy the food that I love. I wave the waiter over to our table and order a few of my favorite appetizers. "Are we sharing?" I ask.

"If you're willing."

"That's fine, I'm not starving." I end up ordering three appetizers. I intentionally avoid ordering a full meal so we won't have to sit there too long. I don't want to be here very long at all, I have things that are way more important than whatever drama's going on in her life right now. When the waiter takes our order back to the kitchen I ask her again. "So what's going on? Why now? Why did you ask me here?"

"It has nothing to do with me, if that's what you were thinking when I texted you. It's about you."

I'm confused. "Me? What about me?"

"I'm such an idiot," she says. "I really worded that text badly. You probably thought I was in trouble or something, didn't you?" I nod. "It's not that. I know we don't speak anymore, but you know I'm still deep in the community, right?"

"I know. Just 'cause I don't read your blog or follow your page doesn't mean that I don't know you're out there."

"Well I've also been doing PA work for a few authors—some of them are on their way to a best seller list for sure."

A PA is a personal assistant. The indie book world is full of them. Most are loyal readers and book lovers who just want to help authors out with some of the grunt work of their jobs, things like promotion, organizing ARC groups, managing their pages, posting things for them if they can't, or if they're too busy, helping with release parties online, and so forth. Jenny was flirting with the idea of being a PA back when we were still together, but she always said that she was looking for the right authors to help out. Despite all of her many flaws, Jenny loves the indie book world, and she's hyper organized. I'm sure whoever she's helping out is thankful to have her.

"Okay," I say, not sure where she's going with this. Maybe she has an opportunity she wants to tell me about, but that seems a little unlikely.

"Do you know KL Steiner?" As soon as I hear that assholes name my blood starts to boil. He's this hack author who writes really dark erotica. He has a small army of readers who treat him like he's a cult leader, but he's not well known outside of his insulated circle. I guess none of us are, though.

"Yeah."

"I PA for an author who's very close to him. I don't know all the details. I didn't even know what they were referring to when I heard this because we haven't spoken. I wanted to call you. . ."

"Jenny, with all due respect, get to the fucking punchline please, I'm begging you."

"Sorry," she says. "I have it on good authority that KL stole one of your stories and that he's repackaging it as his next book. That's the word on the street, anyhow."

It's hard to describe my thoughts and emotions right now. I hear her words, but it's like I'm in a dream, or a nightmare. "I'm gonna need you to elaborate. What are you talking about?"

"Did you lose some computer? Your laptop that you used to write on?"

"I lost it the last day of the signing, but he wasn't. . ." Fuck! He was there! That little piece of shit. That's what Everleigh meant when she told me some author was trying to hit on her, but she wouldn't give me his name. I assumed it was just some guy trying to sleep with her and calling himself an author, but it was that piece of shit. He infiltrated our event just to fuck with me. "For real, Jenny, tell me everything you know." I'm looking at her intensely, only this time it's not directed at her. She's only the messenger, but I want to hear more right away.

"Look, Michael, this is all conjecture. Like, I couldn't prove it in court."

"You're not under oath, just tell me everything you've heard, whether it's true or not."

The waiter brings the appetizers over but I'm not hungry anymore. I'm the opposite of hungry, to the point that the smells of my favorite foods are actually bothering me. I push the plates aside and motion for Jenny to eat, but she also pushes them away. "Alright," she continues. "But my reputation is on the line, also. I know everything I'm going to say is gonna piss you off, but I'm breaking a few different confidences to tell you because, despite everything that happened between us, I still care about your career and want you to be successful. So I need your assurance that my name stays out of whatever happens after this."

I pause for a second, thinking about what she's saying. She really does seem upset for me. It softens my anger a little bit. It's nice to see that somewhere inside she still cares about what happens to me, but that's a back of my mind thought. Right now I need the story. I prompt her one more time and she lets everything out like a faucet—like someone who's been harboring a secret that she needs to confess. This isn't the first type of conversation we've had like this, but I do my best to not let it remind me of the past and just listen to what she has to say. I know that she's deeply embedded in the indie writing community, so I trust her word.

"From what I hear he found your laptop, took it with him when he left the event, and found a part of a story you were working on. Something like that. Did you have an unfinished story on there?" I nod. "Yeah, it seems like this is all true, then. Um. . .so, the rest of it is a little fuzzy because if this was a known thing it would look bad for him, but I heard that he took your story and is repackaging it to fit the genre he writes."

"My story was nothing like what he writes, how's he gonna pull that one off?"

"I have no idea, Mike, I can't ask him that. Maybe he's taking the setting, or the characters. I really don't know, but regardless he has your laptop and he stole your story."

"Who told you this?" I bark. I can hear the anger in my voice rising. It isn't directed towards Jenny for once, but I can see it's taking her aback.

"I can't, Mike, I'm sorry. I can give you what I'm giving you, but please don't ask me for more. Like I said, it's someone close to KL."

"So that motherfucker isn't just a hack writer, he's also a criminal. Jesus, I didn't think even he would go that far with any of this online drama we had." *The drama.* There's something everyone in our community who follows our work knows about—the day KL went off on his Facebook page about what assholes and bad writers me and the guys were, and how our whole Wordsmith group was bound to fail. That much is well documented.

What isn't known by the readers are the private conversations I had with the guy. No matter what he said in 'public', behind the scenes he was practically begging me to join. He saw that Colton's star was on the rise and he tried as hard as he could to hitch a ride. He knew that Colt would never co-write anything with him, so he figured the only way was to jump in the group with all of us. It was so obvious that he didn't think very much of any of us, and that he just wanted to boost his own career by using us.

That's not what kept him out, though. What kept him out

was his secrecy. Colt, Gray, and I go back. We're actual friends outside of our writing careers, and we spend time together that has nothing to do with romance novels. That's not a requirement, obviously. We can't just have our friends in the group, but the guy refused to tell us anything about himself because it was part of his whole shtick. It's one thing to play a mysterious character with your readers—that's just marketing—but it's just bizarre to do it with another grown man in a private conversation, especially when you're trying to get something. He wouldn't tell us his real name, or any personal information whatsoever. That was the game changer for us, not his writing. Ironically I was willing to give the guy a chance, but the Wordsmiths was Colt and Gray's idea originally, so I deferred to them, and both gave a resounding 'Hell No' when it came to the vote. I didn't care that much, but I offered to deliver the news. Needless to say, he didn't take it well, and the rest is history. Actually, the rest is my present.

"That piece of fucking shit."

"I agree," Jenny says. I can tell she genuinely feels bad for me. She had to know I was probably going to be less than pleasant towards her—we didn't end on good terms last we saw each other—but she was still willing to reach out just to give me the heads up. I guess that counts for something. I take a deep breath and exhale loudly so as not to freak out right here at the table and get myself barred for life.

I stand up, food still on the table, and drop some cash next to it. "I need to go handle this."

"What are you gonna do?" she asks.

"I honestly don't know. But I promise I won't explicitly mention your name." I start to walk off then stop myself. "And Jenny," I pause as she turns around. "Thank you."

"You're welcome. It's the least I could do."

"You're right about that. But still, thank you."

I walk out into the night ready to fucking hit someone. I'm fuming inside, with images of that fuck going through my head. It's not a healthy mindset to be in, but I can't help it. I walk to my car, take a deep breath, and promise myself that I can scream once I get home. When I pull into my driveway I don't even know what to do, but before I have time to think about it my phone vibrates.

"Hey," Everleigh's text says. "Am I ever going to get to see you, or are you too big for your britches writing that bestseller I know you're working on?"

Shit. There are no excuses good enough for why I haven't seen her since our hot weekend together at the signing. I've thought about her almost non-stop since we left, and we've texted back and forth a million times. I have been busy, really busy, both with writing and promoting, but that's not a reason to have not seen her yet, especially when we live in the same area.

Me: I'm so sorry. I'm going to dinner with the guys tomorrow night, but how about the night after that?

Everleigh: Sounds good. Where are you taking me?

Me: Fuck going out," I write her back. "I'll be your personal chef on Saturday. We're staying in.

KNIGHT

"I'M GONNA BEAT THE LIVING SHIT OUT OF HIM."

Colton reacts exactly like I thought he might when I tell him the news about my computer and KL. Like we'd discussed the other day, we're having a boys night out at a steakhouse a few miles out of town. It's an expensive place, fancy as hell, and we don't really fit in. We look very different from the crowd in here. A bunch of big dudes, tatted up, untucked dress shirts over our jeans, chest tattoos peeking out just underneath our necks. We get a few looks when we walk in together, but our money is as good as anyone's.

"For real, if I see him ever again he's getting taken down, choked out, and beaten the fuck down."

"You're too deep into your next book," Grayson says, being the voice of reason that he usually is in these situations. "You're not actually Aidan. In real life that kind of thing will get you arrested for assault. Not the publicity we need."

The person Gray is referring to, Aidan, is the male badass lead character in Colt's MMA romance series. The first book in that series, *Fist*, is the one that flew to the top of the Amazon sales charts, helping to boost his sales and his overall career. He's deep into the second book, *The Gentle Art*, right now, and he's started to train seriously again to help get into the character's head.

"I can kick your ass pretty handily, Gray, and there isn't shit you could do about it. But we're practically brothers, so I'll save my training for that scumbag."

Fist was based on a lot of shit in Colton's real life. In some ways we all infuse parts of ourselves into our characters and our books. In Colt's case, he really is a martial artist. He's from a family of martial artists, and it was his dad who introduced him to combat sports. Where most fathers and sons would sit on a couch watching football or basketball, Colt and his dad would watch mixed martial arts tournaments, or UFC pay-per-views and then train afterwards. They barely speak anymore—his dad is about the most fucked up person I know, but it's him who instilled a love of martial arts. Colton used to train like crazy five days a week, but since he's been focusing on his writing he's backed off some. It only made sense that the book he'd write the best would be about a world he knows well. If anyone could actually beat the fuck out of KL it's him, but I hope he controls himself.

"Seriously, Mike, I can't believe it, if it's true. That's some bullshit. It's not just shitty behavior, it's a crime. The fucker stole an expensive piece of electronics from you." Grayson's getting worked up talking about it.

"Not that expensive, don't worry."

"You know what I mean, Mike. And at our own event, just to add insult to injury. What the hell was he even doing there?"

"This," Gray interrupts. "Trolling us. Getting his bitch-ass revenge for us not making him a Wordsmith."

"Let's be clear," I say, looking both of them in the eyes

intensely, my anger and my voice rising. "If anyone beats this fuck down it's me. Got it?" They nod without saying anything. They can tell I'm serious and this revenge is mine. "But," I continue. "I'm moving on. We're moving on."

"That's. . ." Grayson stops himself, looking for the right words. "That's a really healthy attitude, man. I'm proud of you."

"Mike, all due respect, but if you don't fuck him up, I'm going to."

"Colt!" Gray yells, turning towards our angry friend. "Cool it. The man's trying to be an adult in this fucked up situation, think maybe we should help him and not get him worked up? We're not on the schoolyard. And the last thing you need is to get into another fight."

I clench up a little when Gray calls Colton out like that. Colt has a history of getting into fights, mostly in school before we both met him. His dad used to make him fight anyone he had a problem with. It got Colt kicked out of a few high schools. The only way he got into NYU was to hide those parts of his past on his application.

"Sorry," he says. "You're right. Sometimes I get back into my old state of mind when I'm heated. Your way is better, Mike."

"Look, I appreciate both perspectives. I'm worked up already, and I meant what I said—jail, getting arrested, bad PR—I don't give a fuck. This man has a reckoning coming next time we're in a room together. But in the meantime, we have success waiting for us around the corner, so let's order some fucking steaks and get after it!"

"I like this version of Mike," Colt says. "I like him a lot."

The waitress comes over to take our orders. We order steaks like men—Colton gets the porterhouse with creamed corn and steamed vegetables; Grayson, being a little more refined than both of us gets the filet, medium, with asparagus and mashed potatoes. Me? I go all out and fuck with the bone-in Ribeye, 30 oz., rare. I don't fuck around when it comes to steak, and I'm feeling like celebrating the success that I know is coming!

We sit around and talk business. Our WIP's first—Grayson's working on a new series, Colton has book two of his MMA series, and I have a stand-alone that I'm working on. I hear True North's words in my head as we speak. I took his advice and started a new story. It isn't much, but it's something. I don't have a title yet and I'm keeping the plot hushed for now. I'm a little weird with that stuff. I'm like those superstitious expecting parents that won't tell anyone their baby's name until it's born.

All I know so far is that my title-less book is going to be a standalone—meaning it's not part of a series of books—and it's a little risky to do a standalone in this genre. Readers love a good series. They love to fall in love with their 'book boyfriends', and to follow characters throughout a group of stories. Writing a series is your best chance for success, and it's the most lucrative way to write. I'll start a new series next, but right now I have to stick with what's inspired me, and that's Everleigh. "Mine's a standalone about a guy who's having trouble writing until he meets the girl of his dreams."

"I see," Colt says, taking a bite out of his porterhouse like a caveman. "You're writing your autobiography with a little fantasy thrown in. Good luck selling that."

"You're one to talk over there, how many times you hit the gym this week so you could get inside Aidan's head as a character? Breaking news, asshole, Aidan isn't real. He's you."

"Touché," Gray says, laughing at Colt who's now angrily

chewing on his piece of steak because I got the better of that exchange.

"It's not my autobiography, but it is obviously based on my life. I'm leaving the Jenny drama out, and you guys aren't in it—sorry. But I think readers will like to attach to something in our real lives. I think it'll help them connect to the story."

"For sure," Gray agrees. "I think we all put ourselves into our books, at least a little. Readers are interested in us. . .not just in the same romance story being told again and again. They want to know about us as much as they want to know about what we write. Combining those things can only yield good results."

"Thanks, man."

"So," Colt says after taking a huge drink from his beer, a blonde ale in the tallest Pilsner I think I've ever seen in my life. "When do we get to read this masterpiece?"

I usually tease readers with an excerpt from my WIP, but it's only a page or two, sometimes less than that. I'm always worried that it's too raw—too unedited, and that it'll turn off as many people as it entices. This one I'm keeping close to the vest. I haven't told anyone much about it, but I've been working on it, word by word, sentence by sentence, every single night since getting back from the signing. I can't wait until it's done and I can make it into a real book.

Colton gives me the eye. We'd discussed pitching Gray on the idea of an anthology with us and some of the other male authors that we're all cool with. I catch his look from across the table, and as soon as we're all done talking about our own books I transition. "Gray, I had this idea."

"Tell me."

I go through the pitch: five authors—us and two popular male authors that Colt and I are friends with—romance and erotica stories, all tied into some kind of central theme but otherwise different from each other. We'd sell it as the Wordsmith anthology, even though there would technically be guys who weren't in our group, and we'd try our hardest to get on a list with it, like the *New York Times*. Evidently the elevator pitch isn't even necessary. I see him smiling halfway through and I know we've got him.

"Sold. I think it's great fucking idea!" he says enthusiastically.

"Oh, shit, really? I thought I'd have to convince you a little more."

"Why?" he asks. "There's no downside. We'd just have to work out timing and ask the other guys. Just logistical stuff, but I'm in. I love the idea."

In my head I'm hoping to get True North on board, but that may be just a fantasy in my mind. I'll have to work on that.

Dinner winds down, and as it does we keep talking. Wordsmith things, our own work, and just friends shooting the shit. After a while my mind starts to wander, and I'm there in body only. My mind goes twenty-four hours into the future, when I'll be cooking for the woman who inspired this all. Even though I haven't seen her in person since we got back, she's been in my thoughts every day. Before I write, as I write, and after I'm done writing. We've been texting back and forth and we spoke a few times on the phone, but it's criminal that I haven't made more of an effort to have her in my life. I want her just as much now as I did then, so it's time to get my shit together and make her understand how much she means to me. What the hell am I gonna cook?

We skip dessert.

I know I'm too full for all of that business, even though a nice piece of chocolate or tiramisu sounds fucking delicious.

But I know everyone here already thinks we're a bunch of thugs, it'd be a bad look to throw up all over the place on our way out, and that's exactly what I'd do if I had another bite of food. There's always a next time.

The check comes and our eyeballs open up wide even though we kind of knew how expensive it would be. "Holy shit!" Colt jumps. He's right. That's more than any of us have ever probably paid for a meal individually, let alone collectively. To my shock Gray grabs the whole thing from us and hands it and his card back to the waiter, who's just a few feet away at the next table.

"Woah, woah, what are you doing?"

"Balling," Gray says, smiling. "I had a good weekend, and I want to treat my friends to a great—albeit expensive —dinner."

"Man, you don't have to do that, it's nuts, we can split it three ways." Colton reaches for his back pocket but Gray puts up his hands.

"When you hit number 1 in the romance category on Amazon with this series you're working on, or you, Mike, with this this standalone—you guys can take turns treating us all. Or maybe when we all hit it big with this anthology we can just rotate the expensive dinners. Who knows. But right now I'm taking out a loan on our future success. Just let me."

I'm legitimately touched by the gesture. I feel bad because I don't care how successful of a weekend Gray had, there's no way he sold that many books as to be able to afford the whole bill tonight, but after what he said I let him pay. Colton does the same, but he lets go of his wallet grudgingly. "Thank you."

"Yeah," I repeat. "Thank you, Grayson."

"You got it. Now let's pay this and get out of here before

anyone else stares at us like we're a biker gang about to rob the place."

After the bill's paid we hug it out on the curb and go our separate ways, with a promise to touch base that weekend so we can discuss future plans. Almost the second I get in my car my attention shifts to Everleigh and our date tomorrow night. I start the car and close my eyes. There she is, standing in my doorway, looking as gorgeous as the first time I saw her at the bar. Soon enough this fantasy will be a reality, I just have to make sure I don't blow it.

I open my eyes because I have an idea. I put on my signal, hit the gas, and I'm off to the grocery store to pick up a few things. Tomorrow's going to be amazing.

22

EVERLEIGH

I can't wait to see Michael tomorrow. I can't believe it's the first time since the signing that we're going to see each other in person. Things between us started out so hot and heavy, so intense, but then it seems to have fizzled out a little since we got back to reality. After the first few days of no contact I started to get seriously insecure. I thought sleeping with him was a mistake because maybe he didn't really want me. That's what I thought, anyhow. Maybe we'd just gotten caught up in the fake world of the signing, where everything isn't like it is back here in our real lives.

Then I told myself to just shut up. I know he's into me, and I'm sure as hell into him. I was starting to feel something for him that weekend, and I think he was feeling the same. I don't sleep with guys I don't have feelings for, so I hope he knows how I feel even if I didn't explicitly tell him. Plus he was going through some shit with his missing book and laptop that I knew he had to clear up. I have no idea what happened with that, but I'm sure he'll tell me tomorrow.

He texted me last night that he has something to tell me about his WIP. I'm excited that he even has a WIP. When we were leaving the signing I encouraged him to rewrite whatever it was that he'd lost on his laptop, but that was only because he seemed so worked up about it. I'm glad that he's working on something new because that means it wasn't a fluke, or some random idea that came to him. If he has a work in progress that means his brain is working like a writer's again, and he's producing things. That makes me happy.

But tonight it's just me and Harley. Michael told me that he and the other Wordsmiths are having a boy's night out, so I thought, why not have a girl's night in? I invited them both over but Rowan has to work late, so it's just Harley, me, and a bottle of wine. I've had enough going out and partying for a while, anyhow. To be honest a big part of all that going out was trying to meet guys and since I have Michael in my life I feel less guilty about not hitting up every bar in the area. My house, a nice glass (or two) of wine, and good friends are my idea of a great evening.

I dive into the wine a little early because Harley's late as usual. I'm so used to it that I told her to be here thirty minutes before I even want her to come. Even with that extra cushion she'll be twenty minutes later than she says. I give it about five minutes before my phone blows up with a bunch of update texts where she apologizes and tells me how she lost track of time and is on her way. My phone vibrates on the table. Sooner than I thought.

She comes in looking a little worse for wear, but then again she always looks frazzled. We order some pizza to go with all the wine I have. I'm already starting my second glass, and she brought a bottle also. "You got the blush?" I ask.

"You know it. I see you started a little early."

"I expected you to be your usual late self. I figured the buzzed version of me would get less annoyed at your tardiness."

"Very funny. I'm on time occasionally. And don't get blitzed, I'm not Ro. I'm not holding anyone's hair back. Vomit freaks me out."

"Deal."

We drink and eat once the pizza comes, and it takes Harley about ten seconds before she dives into the sex talk. "So tell me more about his dick, I'm curious."

"Jesus, Har, why the obsession with his dick?"

"I'm not obsessed. I think about dicks in general, don't you?"

"What?"

"Not like, random dicks. But when you meet a guy, or even when you're just talking to a guy, you never wonder what he's packing?"

"Sometimes, I guess, but not as a general rule, no." My two best friends are such contrasts, yet they're similar in some regards. Rowan's the closet freak. But Harley? She puts it right out there for everyone to see. It's funny, though, because now that she's talking about it I did have those thoughts about Michael when we met. But I usually don't. "And I already told you."

"No, you didn't. You told me you'd keep me posted once you'd finally laid eyes on it. I assume he's fucked you properly by now, so tell me."

"It's big, okay. Really big."

"I knew it!" She says. "And you're not just saying that?"

"Trust me, I'm not. It's. . .something."

"And?" She asks, looking at me like I should know where she's going with this line of questioning.

"And, what?"

"How was it? Having an impressive cock is one thing. Knowing how to use it is another. There's not always crossover in my experience."

"The man can do things with his penis that you only ever see in a porno, or some late night HBO special from the 1990's. I'm telling you, Harley."

"Shit, like what?"

I grab her attention with that line. Normally Harley's the one who's spouting off at the mouth in way too much detail about whatever sexcapades she's been on. But today it's my turn, and it feels nice to be the one throwing out the shocking statements instead of receiving them.

"Like this weird thing he did with his hips. It's hard to explain."

"Did he make you come?" she asks. I don't know why I get bashful all of a sudden, but I look down and snicker a little. Harley gets the point. "He did. He did make you come. Holy shit, he's not just good at writing, huh?"

"He's a man of many, many talents. Trust me."

"So, like, what else did he do?"

I tell her more detail than I'm used to spilling. Not that there's ever a lot to spill. I was with Jeremey for a few years, and our sex life had run pretty dry. In fact, if I'm being honest, it was never that amazing to begin with. It was fun in the beginning, like it always is at that point in a relationship. But Jeremey wasn't a giving lover. He liked to get off as fast as possible and roll over. He didn't give a shit about my pleasure.

Michael is nothing like that.

All he did was give. All he cared about was my pleasure. How many men care more about the woman's sexual pleasure than their own? I honestly got the impression that he didn't care whether he came or not, as long as he made sure that I did. When I orgasmed with him it was like he was. . .happy. It wasn't a conquest or an accomplishment to him, making me come was something that made him happy to do.

"He sounds amazing," Harley says, wide-eyed at my story. "I wish I could find a guy like that."

"Wasn't there that guy last month?"

"Gone. And not very good while he lasted. I mean that literally."

"And before that? Wasn't it James, or John, or. . ."

"Jason. Jason came and went. Again, I'm speaking literally. I haven't really been with anyone who's anything like what you're describing Knight to be. I'm jealous.

"Don't be," I tell her. "Outside of this I think you've got me beat in the sex department."

"It's not a competition, Ev. You found a guy who cares about you, and you obviously care about him. I'd trade all the good, anonymous sex in the world to have that. Savor it."

"I am. I really am. It's almost too good to be true except for one thing."

"What's that?" she asks.

"The secrecy. I'm not into the secrecy, but I feel like it's something we have to do to protect him. I'm not even sure what we are, or what exactly to make of what happened."

"It'll all work out. Right now, if you want my advice, don't make rules. Don't try to classify it. You're getting fucked properly by a hot male romance writer who really cares about you. Don't ruin that by analyzing it to death. Just enjoy it."

Harley's right. How lucky am I. Knight is fucking gorgeous. Before we officially met when he walked into the bar, all the women could talk about was how hot he was, how much they'd love it if he could reenact their favorite scene in one of his books with them, and how all he'd have to do was ask and they'd drop their panties right on his bedroom floor. But he doesn't want them. He wants me, and I can hardly go a second without remembering what the girth of his cock felt like inside me. I've never been that wet in my life. I get lost in the thoughts of what he was like. How hard he threw his hips against my ass. How he'd pull out of me fully just so he could experience thrusting himself back in all the way.

It didn't feel like sex.

And it sure as hell wasn't love making.

He was fucking me. And he was doing it like I've never experienced before.

And all I'm imagining is all of the techniques he hasn't shown me yet. The ways he could bring me to the brink of shaking in orgasm and then pull me back, only to take me there again. He has control, confidence, and more technique than Muhammad Ali. He was a master, and my pussy ached to have him in me again.

23

KNIGHT

THE NEXT DAY

I meant it when I said fuck going out.

There's honestly no need to pay a few hundred dollars for a nice dinner when I can cook it much better. I know that sounds cocky, but I can cook my ass off.

If I weren't a writer I'd say something trite like, "I'm a Renaissance man." The truth is I'm a Polymath, a man of many talents, few of them related, and long before I stepped into the world of writing and publishing books I was a chef...well, sort of. That might be a slight exaggeration. I went to culinary and pastry school, and I was honestly one of the best students in my class, but I was young at the time and like most young guys I was dumb, listless, partied too much, and didn't know exactly what I wanted to do with my life.

Culinary school sounded about as good as any other option available to me at the time. There was learning how to become a chef, sitting on my couch and doing jack shit, going to community college, or getting some other job. I'd done the other three things already, so before I ended up getting my bachelors in literature when I was twenty six, I entertained delusions of being the next Bobby Flay.

That wasn't in the cards. The long and early hours, the discipline, the shitty pay, none of it was for me. But I was damn good at the actual cooking part. Our chef instructors used to make competitions out of everything at school. Best prep, best meat cooked to the perfect internal temperature, best plating, best dessert. I won most of the competitions among my classmates. And even when I didn't win, I came damn close.

Listen to me, bragging like I'm about to open up my own restaurant chain. I'm not, trust me. I've barely been productive enough to write a book, but I do really love to cook. I don't know why I don't do it more. I do, actually. It's because I'm not willing to put in that type of work just for myself, and God knows I haven't had anyone else to cook for in a long time. But now that's changed. Now a lot of things have changed. Everleigh is on her way, and I think that even though we're staying in I still have a nice evening planned for us. A non-date date. And I'm not just cooking for her, either. But I'll wait to surprise her with that.

I do a bunch of prep work so that once she's here the meal is ready to cook. It takes me about twenty minutes to get everything set, and just as I'm finishing up my doorbell rings. She's here. I didn't think I'd feel this way after everything that happened, but I'm actually a little nervous to see her again. It's different now. Last time it was all about me and the signing. The setting was mine, the context of our meeting had to do with my career, and even the reason we couldn't be together out in the open had to do with me. Now, back in the real world, it needs to be about us, her and I together.

I open the door to see a vision that's far better than anything I could have possibly thought up in my limited imagining sitting alone in my car. Instantly those nerves that I was feeling seconds ago dissipate into nothing, and I feel something that's neither nervousness nor total comfort. I feel something in between, like a hybrid emotion that keeps me on my toes, but also makes me feel like we've had this date our entire lives, and now we get to live it out. "Wow."

She smiles. It's all I can think to say. It's three inept letters that make up a word any child would use to describe something, but it's the most honest reaction I can give. Just like that child, I'm in awe, and when you're in awe of something you say wow. "Thank you, you look great, too."

"You're too nice." I joke. I have crap all over my shirt, and my hair is a mess, and I really should have shaved yesterday, but this isn't the first time we're seeing each other, so I forego the perfect look for the perfect date instead, and I hope she'll forgive me on that. She steps through the doorway looking gorgeous. I stare at her while she takes a deep breath and comments on how good everything smells.

"Caramelized vegetables," I tell her. "Carrots, onions, and some garlic."

"Oooh, fancy."

"Not at all," I say modestly. "The oven does most of the work with those. Just a little olive oil, salt and pepper, and let 'er rip. I'm talking to you like I'm on some cooking show and you're a judge, aren't I?"

"No, you're good," she says, laughing. "I like hearing about it. It's making me hungrier than I already was."

She's facing my kitchen, but when she turns around to face me I wrap my arms around her and kiss her. She seems surprised at first, but it only lasts a second, and then her body submits, her lips press into mine softly, and her arms wrap my waist. "It's been too long," she says when our mouths separate. "Way too long."

"I know, I'm an asshole. I can't believe we're just doing this now. It's all my fault, I take full responsibility."

"I agree," she jokes. "No, it's never just one persons' fault. How about we call it both of our faults. I could have been a little more pushy, but I didn't want to bother you."

"It's never a bother," I answer, feeling terrible that she thinks of herself as some kind of burden. "Never. You hear me?"

"Yeah." She nods. "I know, but still. You left a little distant and preoccupied. I mean, I know why, all that shit with the book."

"It's no excuse," I jump in. "I love that you're giving me an out, but I own my shit. There's no good reason—not the book thing, not getting back into my normal routine, nothing —that should have kept me from you. All I've wanted to do is be by your side since I got back."

"So then, why not call sooner? I felt like you weren't interested anymore and didn't know how to let me down, or something. I wasn't sure."

Fuck. I feel really terrible when she says that. I've been so caught up in my own bullshit that I haven't done a good job making her understand how much she already means to me, and how much I want to keep getting to know her. "No. Hell no." I grab her by the chin and angle her face up so that our eyes are locked together. "Never, do you understand. I apologize. I couldn't want you around more than I already do. Okay?"

She smiles and we kiss again. "Okay. I believe you. After all, how many guys will invite you over and cook for you? I guess you must be serious."

"Oh, I'm not cooking for you."

"Huh?" She asks.

I said it that way on purpose, I know that it'll take her off guard. As she's looking at me puzzled I smile. "I'd be happy to cook for you anytime. But tonight, we're cooking together. You and me."

"Really? I'm a terrible cook, I have to warn you."

"I'll teach you a few things."

"I'm sure you will." She's looking at me seductively, like that look she gave me the last time we were in a room together. I've missed that look. The one that can bring me to my knees. It's a rare thing to have a woman who can make you think about getting married and having a life together, and also make you want to bend her over a table every time you see her. It sounds like the two things would always go together but in my experience they often don't. Everleigh has both qualities. She's the the most beautiful woman I've ever laid eyes on—someone whose eyes make me see into my own future, and I can hear the footsteps of babies running around our house. She's also the sexiest creature ever, and a few shifts of her weight as she walks makes my dick so hard that I can barely contain myself.

"So," she says. "When do we start?"

"Right now. We're making filet mignon."

I take her into the kitchen where I have all of my stations set up. It's less romantic if we have to do any prep work, so I took care of all that before she rang my bell, leaving nothing but fun for us. "So what do I do first?"

"Come over here."

I motion for her to stand next to me. Once she's at my side by the counter I take a step back and position myself so I'm behind her. The roundness of her ass is just touching my cock, enough to tease and make me a little hard, but not enough to distract me too much from getting through some of the cooking. "First," I say, taking her hand in mine. "You have to heat the pan. Cast iron, always."

"Why?"

"It conducts heat more evenly, and gets hotter than any other type. It's just a matter of letting the fire do it's work and getting a slow burn going."

"I see." She lets me guide her, and I turn on the gas stove to high. The sounds of ignition sparks are followed by a large orange and blue flame that dances in circles underneath the bottom of the coal black pan, getting it nice and hot. "Now what?"

"Patience," I whisper in her ear. "Now we wait for it to get hot enough." I press into her ever so slightly, not enough to be too sexual, but enough to let her know that I'm talking about more than just steak. She responds, pressing her ass into me with just enough push to get me going a second time. I'm behind her, and she turns her head in my direction.

"How do we know?" she asks.

"Like this." I reach over and turn the faucet on low. The cold water drips over my hands for a few seconds, and when it's time I position my dripping skin over the cast iron pan. A single droplet of water falls, hitting the metal and splitting into a million little hissing pieces, until it dissipates entirely. "Now it's ready. But first. . ." The steaks are sitting next to me on a plate, coming to room temperate. If you put the meat on too cold it'll seize up and toughen, but if you let it warm slowly before heating it'll caramelize and cook perfectly when the warmth of the pan radiates through it. "First we have to get them ready."

"I see," she says softly. "And how do we do that?"

"Filet is delicate. It's slender, and it needs to just be appreciated for what it is. You can't dress it up with too much seasoning. You'll get the most out of it if you just appreciate it's subtle beauty. A little olive oil, salt and pepper, and you're done. Let it speak for itself."

She reaches over and grabs the bottle of olive oil I have sitting next to the stove. "Like this?" She starts to drizzle some over the top of both steaks. The stream hits the center and pours off the side, bathing the steak in its wetness.

"Perfect. But you have to make sure it's even. Like this." This time I put my hand over hers, and guide it to the meat that's waiting, warm and dripping on the counter. She keeps her fingers wide and lets me direct her hand. I put it squarely on top of the steak, which is almost at room temperature. I squeeze her just a little bit and she starts to massage the steak with her fingers, digging them in and rubbing the oil over the entire surface. "You're good at this."

"I bet you tell all the girls that."

"No," I say, laughing at her joke on the inside but staying serious on the outside. "Just you. You're a natural." After she's rubbed it enough I let go of her hand and she asks me what to do next. "I've got this part," I tell her.

I step in front of her and take care of the seasoning. Salt, pepper, and nothing else. I take out a pat of butter and let it melt before placing the steak in the pan to the sound of sizzling as the caramelization forms on the bottom. As that's sizzling I step behind her again. I wrap my arm around her waist and lean my head into her neck to give her a kiss. She turns her head up to me and our mouths meet. Her lips are soft, gentle, and she smells incredible. I have an expensive piece of steak on the stove and vegetable roasting in the oven, but all my nose lets in is how great her hair smells. "I think your steak might be burning."

"Nah," I whisper in her ear. "It can sit there for at least two minutes. It's forming a nice crust. Don't worry, I won't let it burn."

A few minutes later the food is done and I'm turned on as all hell. I haven't seen her in a long time and having her close to me again is making me hard. All I want to do is rip her clothes off, but I have to wait and it's driving me nuts. I am excited to be having dinner with her, though. I miss sitting and talking to her as much as I miss being with her physically. I take the steak off and let it rest a minute while I get everything else ready. I made garlic mashed potatoes, roasted vegetables, and now the steak that's cooked perfectly. I plate everything and we go sit in my dining room.

I bought a really expensive bottle of wine for tonight at the store next to the grocery in town and I break it open. "Here." I put the plate and the glass of wine in front of her and then serve myself. She swishes the glass around and breathes in deeply.

"Everything smells wonderful," she says. "This was a much better idea than going out to a restaurant. I really enjoyed cooking with you."

"Me, too. We should do it more often."

"That's up to you." That stings a little. The tone of her voice is a little less sultry and sweet than it just was, and I realize that I may have fucked up a lot by waiting so long to contact her again.

"I'm sorry, again. Listen, unless you don't want to see me anymore there will never be a time when I'll go this many weeks without seeing you, okay? You have my word on that."

"Promise?"

"I promise, and I don't break promises."

"Oh, come on, everyone's broken a few promises here and there. There must be some."

"Never. Not once. Not ever. And I never will." She thinks I'm joking or that I'm exaggerating. Everyone does when I tell them my promise thing. They basically have the same reaction that she's having, which is to project their own behavior onto me, but keeping promises is like a religion to me. If I say that I'll do something and give my word, then it's gospel.

"That's a rare thing, Michael. You might be one of a kind."

We finish our dinner. Everything tastes amazing, if I do say so myself, but more than the food it's the company that I'm enjoying. When we're together our conversation flows seamlessly, like we were meant to talk to one another. She understands all of the difficulties I have as an author—all of my fears, my worries for the future, my concern that I'm never going to amount to anything but another hack romance author. Even though she's never written a word down herself, she listens closely to everything I'm saying, and gives me such focused attention that it's intoxicating. Her eyes rarely look away when I'm speaking, and I return the favor for everything she's telling me.

"It's the last thing I want to bring up, but how's all that drama that was causing you some distress back at the signing?"

"Better," she says. It's the first time she looks away from me, staring at her plate and pushing the last few carrots and onions around with her fork. "Better, thanks for asking." I don't push any further than that. The topic of her ex seems to push all of her buttons, but then again, it does the same thing to me. I let that line of questioning go.

"How's it coming?"

"The book?"

"No, the cure for MS. Yeah, the book, silly."

"I can't believe that I'm going to say these words, but it's going really well. I keep writing more and more each night and I've been going on these crazy three hour runs, where my fingers never stop banging the keyboard."

"Holy shit, that's amazing!" She jumps up from her seat and gives me the biggest hug ever. "I'm so proud of you."

"This is going to sound corny as all hell, but it's because of you. If I didn't meet you I'd still be crawling my way through some bullshit novel that probably would have been terrible by the time it went to print."

"I appreciate that," she says. "But this is all you, do you understand? I'm glad I inspire you, but it takes a lot more than some inspiration to write a book, or a lot of books at that. Do I get to know the title?"

"No way."

"Oh, come on! I inspired it, how can you not tell me the title?"

"If there is anything you need to know about me as a man and a writer its these two things: I never break my promises, and I never reveal the title of a new book until I'm finished with it. And neither of those things are going to change."

"You suck," she jokes. "But I understand. It's fine, keep me waiting, it'll just build up my anticipation."

"That's my plan. But I think it'll be worth it."

"I know it will," she answers. "And even more than the title, I look forward to reading whatever it is that I inspired."

"You will, trust me. You'll be the first to read it when it's finished. I have an ending in mind, but I need to edit and finish a few parts first. I was thinking of doing that later on tonight, actually."

"If I have anything to say about it," she begins, "you'll be pretty occupied most of the night." She leans over and kisses me again, only this time there's more passion in her kiss—a promise of something more to come. While we're kissing my heart races and my dick gets rock hard. I can sense the urgency in her as she wastes no time running her hand up my thigh and smothering my cock. She starts moving it, massaging in small circles, her grip tightening as she does. It feels amazing.

Her sense of urgency gets mine going. We haven't seen each other in a while, and I've wanted her ever since that day I left her hotel room in a panic. It kills me that it's been so long, but we're going to make up for it right now.

Her pussy is magical. Crack. A thing I need my cock to live inside of. Before Jenny I was with my fair share of women. Don't get it twisted, I wasn't anywhere near approaching fuckboy levels of action, but I also wasn't exactly unpopular with the ladies. But I've never felt anything like Everleigh's pussy before. It's small, tight, and feels like something that I was meant to fuck, as though my cock were a key, fitting perfectly inside her wetness.

Every time I slammed into her the first time I went deeper —deeper than I've ever gone with a woman before. Her wetness just let me in without any effort, and when I felt my tip break through, I thought I was going to come right then and there. Thank God I didn't, because then I wouldn't have felt what fucking her could really be like.

I lift her up and carry her up the stairs. She's as light as air in my strong arms, and I'm turned on before I even hit the top step. I stumble, distracted by how beautiful she looks, and fall forward slightly. I don't drop her, but she looks at me and tells me to put her down. She sits on the third to last step and turns around, lifting up her dress. She's not wearing any underwear, and as she points her perfectly round ass towards me I stare and rip my pants off. Her little pink pussy is staring back at me, waiting like a prize between her legs, if only I can get my clothes off fast enough.

She's on all fours, looking back at me with a look in her eyes that's begging me to slip inside. I reach down and tickle the outside of her pussy with my middle finger, warming it up for what's about to come. She starts to moan as I hit her clit, rubbing in smooth, strong circles again and again. After a few seconds I reach with my hands and spread her legs open, and she lifts her ass up. I don't waste any more time with foreplay. I slide right into her, my knees on the step below her and my arm balancing on the bannister to my right. I start fucking her furiously, her pussy clamped around my cock as I thrust in and out of her. I'm moving her whole body, and the slap of my hips and balls against her ass is ringing through the hallway.

"Fuck me harder, Michael!" she cries out. I start to go faster, and each time I hit against her I push a little deeper inside, lingering there for a minute so she can feel the whole length of my manhood filling her up. The last time I hold the position, not moving at all, and I grip her hair with my left hand. When I pull back I pull her hair with me, and her body arches as her head leans back. I start hitting her pussy again, faster and harder while I hold her body in place by her hair. I let go of the bannister and her hair, grabbing both of her shoulders with my hands while I fuck her. I'm pulling her body back as I thrust my hips forward, and the sound is turning me on.

I take my hand and put it on her face, letting my fingers dance close to her mouth. That's all it takes. She knows what to do. She opens up and starts sucking my finger. The feeling of suction is turning me on even more, and she takes my whole finger in her mouth as I lay waste to her soaking wet cunt. That feeling is driving me nuts. I stop what I'm doing and pull out as she turns herself around. She knows what I want, and I know what she wants.

I take one step up so that I'm over her body. Grabbing my cock I inch it towards her already open mouth. I slide right inside and let go, and she starts applying that hot, wet suction to my shaft, the saliva from her mouth dripping out the sides and hitting the step. I move my hips forward and back slightly, fucking her face. She moves with me, taking every inch of me all the way down to her throat until she's gagging. I pull out and pick her up so that we can finish in the bedroom.

I throw her on the bed—literally. She bounces for a second and then I climb over her, inserting myself right where I belong. I sit back and grab both of her heels and rest them on my shoulders. I'm on my knees, holding onto her legs, and I start thrusting every inch of my rock hard cock into her, over and over again. She reaches down and starts rubbing her clit in hard, fast circles. A few minutes later we're both close. She's rubbing herself furiously as I fuck her, and the sight of her beautiful tits bouncing around is enough to make me come. "I'm almost there," she pants. "Don't stop, Michael. Fuck me harder."

"I'm not stopping."

I keep going until her whole body lifts up toward me, and the feeling of her pussy clamping down on me gets me there fast. I hold off as long as I can, and when I see that her body relaxes I reach down and pull myself out, shooting my hot cum all over her. "Oh fuck." I scream as I watch my cum hit her sweaty, white skin. When I'm done I lean over and kiss her. We're both breathing like we've been deprived of air for minutes, and as our lungs fill up again, I feel more satisfied than I ever have after sex. It's not just physical. It's mental and emotional. I'm falling for this woman, harder than I ever thought I would.

24

EVERLEIGH

I WAKE UP TO THE SMELL OF MICHAEL, ONLY IT'S NOT Michael himself, but his pillow I'm smelling. I open my eyes and see that I've stretched diagonally across the bed, my head still on his pillow, and my naked body carving the shape of the bed into two triangles. It's morning, I know that much, but I'm not sure exactly where Michael is.

I sit up and rub the sleep out of my eyes. I slept like the dead. Last night was amazing and I was pretty tired out by the time I finally lost consciousness. I don't remember if I dreamed, but I usually don't remember my dreams. What I do know is that I feel more rested than I have in a long time. I have that euphoric, post-amazing-sex feeling going on. Our date was everything that I'd hoped it would be. Is there anything sexier than a man who can cook?

But the best part was after the meal. He's such a great lover—attentive, compassionate, and rough when I want him to be. I think he almost pulled my hair right out of my head! I could sit here forever just waiting for him to come back, but I need to get my lazy butt up, literally. From inside the bedroom I can hear the clicking of a keyboard. I put on my shirt from last night and leave the bedroom.

Down the stairs and to the right is Michael's living room, and as I turned the corner I see his profile, hunched a little bit over and hitting the keyboard of his laptop as quickly as he can. He must be finishing the book. I don't interrupt him. I stand at a distance, admiring a master artist at work, as if I were watching Picasso paint a picture. He doesn't notice me at all because he's so focused, and his fingers are dancing along the keyboard seamlessly, without any pause whatsoever.

I turn around and go back upstairs to take a shower. I grab some towels from his linen closet and make my way to his bathroom while he finishes. Maybe when I come out he'll be done. Twenty minutes later I'm toweling off and letting a cloud of steam out into Michael's upstairs hallway. I listen closely and don't hear the sounds of a keyboard any more, so I get dressed as fast as I can and head down the steps. Michael's still in the living room, only he's not writing any more. I peek around the same corner and see him sitting back and staring at the open laptop in front of him. He has a smile on his face, and the happiness in him is reaching me even from across the room. This time he sees me standing there.

"Good morning," he says, catching me creeping just around the corner. "Did I wake you up?"

"I was already up. I hope you don't mind I took a shower when I heard you down here writing."

"Of course I don't mind. And yeah, I'm sorry I was finally getting to this last part I've been wanting to write."

"Don't apologize, I'm so happy for you. It was a great sound to hear first thing in the morning. So when is it coming out?" I ask.

"Well, if I factor in the time for my edits, sending it to my actual editor, getting it formatted, and then having advanced readers get a look at it, I'd say probably two months or so."

"I can't wait. Do I get to be one of the advanced readers?"

"Nope," he says, looking at me with a devious grin. "It'll be a surprise."

"I hate surprises," I tell him. "I'm too impatient for them. I need instant gratification, okay?"

"Well I guess you're going to have to practice some self control then, huh?"

"If you weren't so good looking I think I'd slap you."

"Lucky me, then."

"So when is the book ready? Signed, sealed, delivered?"

"I'll have early copies printed after editing in a week or so, but the wide release is going to be timed for the week of the signing."

"RAAC?"

"You know it."

RAAC stands for the Romance Authors of America Conference, and it's easily one of the biggest signings of the year. It's held annually at a different location around the country. I've only been once but it was a real experience. It's usually held at a giant convention center, and there are literally a few hundred authors and several thousand readers and fans that attend. When I went I came home with 75 signed books and Harley had over 100. It was insane. "You got a table?"

"I think we're going to get one," he tells me.

"You and the guys?"

"Yeah, I think it would really help give us a push. It's still a few months away so I think we can swing a table. I wasn't going to ask you this until later on, but how would you feel about assisting me at the table?"

"Like, be your PA?" I ask.

"No, not as my PA."

"As what then?"

"How about as my girlfriend, Everleigh? How does that sound?"

He says that so confidently and so smoothly, as though it's always been my title. We haven't seen each other that much, I know, and usually titles like that have certain timeframes and behaviors associated with them. We haven't really 'gone out' on any dates, or curled up on a couch watching Netflix. He hasn't met my family and I haven't met his. Hell, I haven't even properly been introduced to his friends and fellow writers as anything yet, but I guess in some ways all of that is just extra. I feel strongly towards Michael, and I think we could really be something.

"As your girlfriend. I love that."

We kiss, and my whole body starts to tingle. "Is it weird that I asked you to be my girlfriend? Was that too high school of me?"

"I thought it was really sweet, and I'd be honored. But there is one thing."

"What's that?" he asks.

"Your career. No one really knows about us except Harley and Rowan, and they're obviously not going to say anything, but I have a lot of friends and people I've come to know pretty well in the book world. People are going to gossip about this, I'm telling you. I don't want to hurt your career. Maybe we should stay a secret?"

It kills me to even ask that when he made himself so vulnerable just now by asking me to be with him, but what I'm saying is true. The book world is a collection of some of the most caring, giving, and wonderful people I've ever encountered. But, like with any large group of people, it can also be a place of gossip, pettiness, rumors, and hate. Things like this won't get posted publicly, but people will talk about it. Michael Knight is banging a reader? Is she with him just to get free books? Those are the kinds of things that will be whispered in private messages and at conferences.

He thinks about what I say after I say it. His mood doesn't change, he's still really happy and even relieved that he finished, but I can tell that he's weighing the pros and cons of what I just brought up in his mind. "I see what you're saying," he begins. "And I know how petty some people can be." He stops his speech and turns his body towards mine so that we're facing each other rather than sitting next to one another, and he continues. "But those people exist everywhere and we can't live our lives around them. If my experiences from the past few years have taught me anything, it's that you can't make decisions and base your emotional health on others' perceptions or actions. It's not a good way to live."

His words touch me, but I still have some reservations. "I know what you're saying, and I agree, but regardless those people do exist, and they're not just like some co-worker or distant family member who you can ignore and never have to see and just go on living your life as you want to. These are readers, bloggers, publishing company owners and employees. Basically they're the people who can impact your career, for the positive or the negative."

"That's true," he answers. "But you know who else are readers, bloggers, and publishing company owners? Good people. Good people who are in this business for all the right reasons, and aren't concerned with the personal lives of writers. They may have an opinion, sure, or, to be honest, they may have no idea who either of us are. This could all be over exaggerated."

"Yeah, but. . ."

"No," he says, cutting me off. It surprises me a little but it's the way he does it that makes me stop and pause rather than try to speak over him. He's never quite spoken to me that way, and in this case I can tell that he needs to tell me something important. "Listen, we don't have to debate this. I see your points. I see all your points, and they're good ones. I'm not disagreeing with you. What I'm telling you is that we're talking about my life and my career, and I'm not willing to compromise either because of some social media trolls. Even if that means a few less book sales, or a few days of whispers behind the scenes. I'm not going to lose out on someone great just so some yentas can feel better about me. Do you understand?"

He takes my hand in his and holds it gently. I do understand, I understand completely, but what I understand even more than his words are the meaning and emotion behind them. He really cares for me. Most ambitious writers —hell, most ambitious people in any field will put their career first, especially when they're trying to grow it into something big. But Michael's different. He has all the ambition and drive in the world, which are two things I find painfully attractive in him. But he's also caring, sweet, and he wants whatever our relationship is going to be to be given a chance to grow, just like his career. I realize in that moment that he's not going to cast me aside, or treat our last few meetings as some meaningless hookups that helped him write some book. He really wants a relationship with me.

"I understand," I tell him. "More than you know. In that case, Michael Knight, I'd love to assist you at the signing—as your girlfriend, or whatever else you need me to be."

"That's great, because it wouldn't be right for you not to be a part of it. It just wouldn't."

I lean in and kiss him, and as soon as I hear him moan a

little I swing my left leg over and straddle him. He's wearing nothing but his boxers and a tee shirt, so as soon as I sit down I feel his hardness hitting me in just the right spot. I'm not usually so aggressive, but I grab onto his shirt with my fist and bunch it up like I'm controlling him. My hair is falling around his face as I kiss him, and he lets me do whatever I feel like doing.

We kiss for a few more seconds before I decide to stop teasing him. His dick is even harder now and I can feel it poking me. I'm wearing a loose skirt and no underwear, so I let go of his shirt and reach my hand into the front slit of his underwear and wrap my hand around that monster. I squeeze, hard, and move my hand up and down a few times. I don't feel like foreplay and neither does he. This man, this hot, beautiful man who I've admired for years just asked me to be his girlfriend, and I'm not just happy, I'm fucking turned on! I want him bad, and I'm going to have him right here and right now.

I take his cock and place the head right on the outside of my pussy. I'm already as wet as I've ever been, I can feel it. As soon as I position him he grabs onto my hips and thrusts upwards. He slides right in, and I gasp as I feel it go into me. He's huge and thick, and when he thrusts deep into me, hands on my hips, I just lean forward and start to ride him. My hands rest on the top of the couch in front of me, and Michael starts pumping me from the bottom with all of his might. He's fucking me so fast that I barely process how good it feels. I stop moving and let him thrust, again and again, until I feel like I'm going to scream. When he tires I take over and do all the work.

I grab his wrists and push them against the back of the couch so that he can't move. He's so big and strong that he could break free of my grip at any moment that he wants to, but I know that he won't. Instead he lets me ride. I move my hips back and forth, pressing down and feeling the girth of his cock fill me up, and fill me up it does. I know this isn't going to take long. I keep riding and pressing, and his cock is hitting my clit perfectly, and within a few seconds I know that I'm right there. "Oh fuck, I'm gonna come!" I scream. I can feel my orgasm building quickly, and before I know it my body's convulsing, and I swear my eyes roll back in my head. It's like every nerve ending is on fire, and I scream out, "Fuck!" as I hold still and let the pleasure take me away.

When it's over I don't collapse because I know he's not finished yet. So I take a deep breath and keep on moving. But before I can get any momentum he flips me over unexpectedly so that my back is now against the couch and he's standing above me. He's still inside of me, so I lie there while he slams his hips into me a few times. I must have done my job because before too long he's also about to come. He pulls out at the last minute and sprays the outside of my wet pussy with his hot, white cum, moaning uncontrollably as he does.

He falls over next to me, and both of us are out of breath. At the same time I feel energized. That's a hell of a way to start a morning—a finished new novel, being asked to be a great guy's girlfriend, and an amazing quickie.

Things are looking up.

KNIGHT

"WAIT, SO THAT GIRL AT THE BAR AT THE SIGNING IS, LIKE, your girlfriend? What the fuck, man?"

Sometimes I'm amazed that Colt is a writer—thank God he can be more elegant when he writes than when he speaks, but I get why he's more than a little surprised. I would be too. I didn't really tell them much about Everleigh, just that I was seeing someone who I met around the time of the signing, but I didn't give them any details. It's for her protection as much as mine, but since things are getting much more serious with us, it's time to spill the beans.

"Yeah, her name is Everleigh." It feels great to say that out loud to someone, but I'm sure there are going to be some serious follow up questions.

"You sound like you're in high school, do you know that?" Grayson is sounding a little more judgmental than he usually does, but I guess he's just being a good friend and putting what I'm saying to some scrutiny.

"Yeah I heard it, too," I say. "But I wouldn't have said it any other way. I'm so happy, dude."

"I see that," Colt says. "It's great to see you smiling, man, it really is. I think we're just a little taken aback. You haven't said shit about this—not at the signing, and not even in the weeks after. Why the secrecy?"

"We hooked up at the signing. She was a fan of my work, but more than a fan. She was touched by it. We hit it off and just got to talking. She's really special."

"Sounds like it," Gray says. "I've never seen you like this with a girl before. But, still, you need to be careful with fans."

"It's not like that," I tell him. "You just need you to trust me. I'm a grown man, and I'm telling you she's not some groupie. She's legit one of the greatest women I've met. She's the reason I just finished my first book in a long time. She's the reason I can't stop smiling right now."

Colton and Grayson look at each other and grin. "Our boy is all grown up!" Leave it to your best friends to quote Vince Vaughn in *Swingers* just at the right time. "I guess he doesn't need us anymore."

"Hey," I tell them. "I need all the good people around me I can get. We have business to discuss."

This beer garden in Astoria, Queens just opened. It's a few towns over from my place, and it's gotten some killer reviews. I was never a beer guy before, but the boys got me into it when I was deep in my funk. It was one of those fun activities they dragged me to, only this one stuck. It was my idea to come back today, because there's nothing like a beer with your best friends to celebrate something, and I have a lot to celebrate.

"So we're doing RAAC, correct?" Gray asks.

"Yeah, I think it's a great opportunity to build some buzz," I tell him.

"Agreed." Colt waves the waitress over to order another IPA.

"Okay, then I'll get us a table. Then we just have to decide what we're bringing. Where is everything with the WIP's? And what about the anthology?"

The waitress comes over and takes Colton's order. Gray is also working on his second drink—a Guinness—while I'm still sipping my first. She asks me if I want anything and I wave my hand. "No, thank you, I'm still nursing this one."

"Bitch," Colton jokes.

"Don't make me knock you out when I'm in such a good mood."

"I'd love to see you try," he says back, giving me the crazy face he thinks makes him look tough. I just laugh, and so does he, then we get back to the signing talk. "My next book won't be ready by the signing, but I'm almost done with my story for the anthology. We have three months, so if we're all almost done that's plenty of time to get the wheels in motion. Where's everyone else with that?"

"I'm in the same boat," I answer. "But my book is done as of yesterday."

"Holy fuck, congrats!" Gray and Colt raise their glasses and make way too much noise. I get embarrassed, but it's really cool how supportive they're being. They've been here through all the shit of the past year, so more than anyone besides me they know how much what I just said really means.

"Thanks, guys. And I'm on a run with my writing. I'm basically done with my part for the anthology also."

"I'm in the same boat," Gray says. "I'll have my library and the anthology. Ironic doesn't begin to describe it, Mike, but it looks like you'll be the only one with a new book at the signing."

"Who would've guessed?" Colton asks.

Not me. Sure as hell not me. I realize that sometimes you

need to get on the other side of trauma to see how fucked up you really were at the time. You lose perspective quickly when you're hurt. Everything gets distorted—time, your own emotions, how good or bad things really are. Your entire worldview is distorted like a funhouse mirror, and it takes good friends and a great woman to see you safely to the other side of that bullshit.

"I know, it's crazy, man. But enough about me. I can't wait for this anthology. If we can get it edited and formatted in time, it'll be big. I think the women will love it."

"For sure," Colton says. "Then we just have to decide on a cover. I have an idea on that if no one has any objections."

Colt is friends with a lot of models, and has connections in that pocket of our industry. If the indie romance world were a country, the cover models and photographers would be their own region. Despite the old adage, most people actually do judge a book by its cover, and the shots that appear on the front of our books are as important to sales as the words contained inside them—maybe more so. Ask ten different readers what they use to make a decision on what book to one-click, and most will tell you a cover that really grabs their attention. I'm fine with Colt taking the lead on it.

"Yeah, I trust you," I tell him. "Just show us when you find someone."

"I'm gonna text G. I think he just had a new shoot with Jameson."

The 'G' Colt's referring to is Greg—Greg Olden, but we all just call him G. He's an author himself, mostly of male/male books, and he dips his toes in many genres that aren't just pure romance. He's got a huge following, an amazing backlist of books, and he takes some of the best photographs in the industry. Greg owns a successful photography company, and Colton is close with him. I trust him to get us a great cover shot."

"Sounds good," I tell him. "And have fun trolling Greg's website full of half-naked dudes. I know you'll enjoy it."

"You know what I hope?" Colton asks. I expect him to come back at me with another insult, but instead he reminds me of something that I'm trying actively to forget. "I hope that mother fucker who stole your computer is there. I hope he's at the table next to us so I can fuck him up in front of his readers." I get concerned when Colt doesn't jump at my invitation for some witty banter. He's had a real problem with anger in the past, and I can see the rage in his eyes right now.

"Calm down, man," Gray says, jumping in. "That's Mike's issue to deal with. Correct me if I'm wrong, Mike, but I'm guessing a public spectacle where one or more of us gets arrested isn't the kind of publicity that you want for your new book. Am I right?"

I nod. Just like last time he brought it up, I appreciate Colton's protective nature, but if anyone is going to handle the situation it needs to be me, and in my own way. "Yeah. I love that you wanna beat his ass, Colt, but getting arrested isn't going to bump our sales, it's just going to mean we're going to have to spend any profit from the signing for bail money. We're professionals, let's try to act that way." Colton nods his head in agreement, but I can tell he doesn't totally agree. At the same time I know he'll do what I want him to do. "But," I continue, looking at him. "If push comes to shove, back me up, okay?"

A huge grin shows up on his face. "Do you even need to ask me that?"

"Hey, look," Gray says, jumping. "If it comes to that we've both got your back, you know that. We can share a cell. It'd be worth it to hit that asshole. But at the same time, let's call that Plan B, alright?"

"Agreed," I say.

We finish up our drinks and food then go our separate ways. Grayson has another signing this weekend, and he's prepping for that. I swear he's a straight road dog, always doing the damn thing. Colton wants to write, but first he has to train, of course. He's got a standing lesson now with his Muay Thai, boxing, and Jiu Jitsu coaches. He really is getting into that new book.

As for me?

I have a date with Everleigh. It's time that she and I went on a proper date, and I have an awesome idea that I know she's going to love. I mentioned it the other day, even though she had no idea what it was. It doesn't matter what we do together, as long as I'm with her. I'm a better version of myself when we're together, that's all I know.

I have a few hours. I'm going to go home, finish my anthology story, and then pick up Everleigh at her place. I can't wait to see her again.

EVERLEIGH

"WHAT THE HELL IS ACRO YOGA?"

Harley asks a great question, and I'd love nothing more than to answer her, but I'm still not totally sure myself. "I Googled it before, it looks like you have to be more than a little coordinated and flexible. All I know for sure is that I'm doing it later with Michael."

"You need to be coordinated? Oh, then you're screwed, Ev!"

"Shut up, I've done Yoga before. I was on a Yoga streak for a while, like a year ago. Remember?"

"It's not a sport," Harley says. "I don't think you can call it a streak. It's not like you're winning the Yoga class. And even if you wanna call it a streak, you only went for like two months."

"For me that's a legit streak."

"I don't know how this Acro stuff works, though, maybe it's competitive."

"No, it's like couples yoga, but the poses are using both of your bodies. Look."

I take out my phone and open up YouTube and type in

Acro Yoga. "Holy shit, you're gonna fall!" Harley laughs at me and she might be right. I'm watching the video I saw before with her and even though it says that these are normal people, they look like trained Cirque de Solei performers.

"You might be right."

"Or," she continues. "This might be the coolest date that you've ever been on. He's original, I'll give him that."

I'm really excited to be going on a date with Michael. We've never been out in the open, just the two of us, but I'm a little worried I'm going to spaz out with this yoga date he planned.

"That's a distinct possibility. Honestly, I'm just happy to be going out with him without having to hide anything. It felt weird doing that."

"I still can't believe that you're dating Knight!"

"I know. It's weird to even think of him as my boyfriend. I never would have seen this coming. Honestly I just wanted a chance to look him in the eye and tell him, face to face, how much his work has meant to me. Then maybe a selfie, and a couple of signed books. Hooking up with him was never my intention or idea."

"You say it like it's a horrible thing, Ev. Do you feel bad about it?"

"No," I tell her. "Not bad."

"What then?"

"Worried. I'm worried about how our relationship is going to look to people. You know how catty some people can be." At first I felt bad, mostly because I was thinking of myself. I didn't want to be that girl, the groupie, the one who was on the prowl for hot male authors. I didn't want to be seen in this community as that kind of woman. But now I'm still worried, just not about myself. "I don't want his career to suffer for this."

"I get that, but I think that you're going to be fine. You and I both know there's a lot more dramatic shit in this world than that. Plus, it's some hookup. It's not like he's got a reputation for sleeping around. And we all know you don't. So what's the worry? You can't live your life around other people's issues."

"That's exactly what he said to me."

"He's right," Harley says. "You guys do you, fuck the rest of the world. There'll be a few petty bitches who'll gossip, but who cares. Aren't there always? You have the right to be happy and you finally left that asshole. Do you."

"You're right. Thanks, Harley, I needed to hear that."

"What are best friends for?"

"This," I say. "Exactly for stuff like this."

We finish our coffee and I leave feeling better about the whole scenario. Once that stress is gone it allows me to just let myself be happy and excited about our date. I have to stop home first and get ready.

KNIGHT

I'M SUPPOSED TO PICK UP EVERLEIGH AT FIVE, BUT I THINK I'm going to stop by early and surprise her. I'll grab some flowers at the florist in town and swing by a few minutes early. I don't know what's come over me, even when I was with Jenny I wasn't really the romantic type. She used to complain all the time that I was great at writing romance but terrible at actual romance. Maybe she was right. But Everleigh makes me feel like I'm in high school, like everything is new, like I'm a better version of the man that I want to be. All of a sudden I want to cook for her, and buy her things, and get her flowers and candy. What's going on with me? Whatever it is I'm going with it, 'cause I feel great.

I finish up the last few chapters of my anthology story pretty quickly. The words are really flowing from me lately. Hopefully they're good words. That's two original works finished in a matter of weeks. To think that I wasted a year of my life basically writing nothing makes me sad, but it reminds me of how far I've come, and how far I still have to go. It's a short story, only about ten thousand words, so I take a half hour and give it a quick read through before emailing the file to my editor. She hasn't heard from me in a while, and now I have two different stories for her to fix.

After I send the email I get ready and head out to Everleigh's place. We really don't live that far from each other, I can't believe we'd never met before the signing. I grab the flowers and follow the GPS directions on my phone until I'm in view of her apartment. Parking in Queens really sucks if you don't have a house like I do. I remember how stressful it was to find parking when I used to live in a building like this.

It must be my lucky day because there's a spot only a block away. In New York, finding a spot that close to where you're going is like finding $100 bill on the street—rare and awesome. I don't want to just pop in, in case she's in the shower or something, so I text her that I came early to surprise her. She writes back that she's on her way home from running some errands, and that I can wait for her in the building if I want. Sounds good to me, so I grab the bouquet of flowers I got and head over. Her apartment is on the ground floor—1C— so I won't be climbing any steps. When I open the front door to the building I stop for a second.

Wait. Who the hell is that guy?

Outside of Everleigh's door is some dude, just standing there and looking a little creepy. He's little, and he's wearing an overcoat. He's facing her door, but when I open the door to the complex he turns and looks at me, and then goes right back to standing underneath her door. I can see his hands moving frantically, his back still facing me. I can tell he doesn't realize that I'm here for Everleigh, but I walk right towards him because something about this is giving me a weird vibe.

"Hey, man," I say, stopping about a foot behind him near Everleigh's door. He turns around and looks at me nervously.

He has a squirrelly look to him, and I can see that what's in his hands is a small notepad and a pen. First I think he might be a solicitor or a delivery guy, but he's not wearing a uniform. Besides that, he's just acting super weird. I don't like this at all. And I really don't like that he just looked at me and then turned around without answering. "You a friend of Everleigh's?"

"Yeah, something like that." This time he has no choice but to answer me because I tap him on the arm. He pulls back like I'm grabbing him or something, even though I just touched him lightly, but I finally get his attention. I want to know just what the hell this guy's up to.

"What does that mean, exactly?" I ask. I know I'm being a little aggressive with this guy, but I'm getting a bad feel from him.

"It means it's none of your fucking business who I am, guy."

"Guy?" I take a step towards him so that I'm really close. I don't like this person, whoever he is, and I don't like his fucking attitude. I can tell he doesn't expect it because he takes a small enough step back for me to notice, even though he's trying to be tough. I can see right through his facade. Tough people are confident in themselves. They don't talk to people like he's speaking to me, and they don't take a step back. "Who are you talking to? Forget that question. What the fuck are you doing outside of my girlfriend's door when she's not home. Who are you?"

He looks at me intensely when I say the word girlfriend, and then it clicks. This is the ex. He looks enraged at me using that word, and I can see in his eyes that his anger is making him want to lash out at me, but he's too much of a pussy to actually do it. "Your what?" he asks.

"No, I'm not the one who needs to answer questions right

now, bud, you are. Like, who the fuck are you, and what the hell are you doing creeping outside of Everleigh's door?"

"Jeremey," he says. "I'm Jeremey. And I'm just dropping something off."

"Oh yeah, what?"

"None of your fucking business, new boyfriend."

That's it. This fucker is about to get some.

EVERLEIGH

I'M DRIVING A LITTLE FAST BECAUSE I KNOW MICHAEL'S waiting for me. I came home and got into my workout clothes a little while ago, but I forgot that there was nothing in my fridge but some expired milk, so I decided to bum it and go to the grocery store in my leggings and tee shirt. I don't want him to have to wait too long for me, so I treat a few yellow traffic lights like they're green so I can get home as quickly as possible.

There are no spots, of course, so I park around the block and walk. I text Michael that I'm on my way but I don't hear back. I hope he isn't pissed that he's had to wait. As soon as I get to my doorstep I see something happening in the hallway. It looks like two male bodies in a violent dance. It takes me a second to realize what's happening, and I'm horrified.

Holy shit. Michael's fighting Jeremey. The sight is so weird that I don't even have time to process. I just start screaming. "Stop it, stop it!"

Men fighting is scary. They're all over each other, their bodies intertwined and violent. Michael gets on top of Jeremey and starts punching him while he's on the ground. I don't even think he heard me, so I run over and grab his arm. "MICHAEL, STOP!" This last scream and the touch of my hand breaks him out of his frenzy. He looks like a wild animal. His hair is all messed up, his face is red, and the tattoo on his forearm is sprinkled with Jeremey's blood. I don't know what to think or feel, but I know that I can't stand violence. "What the fuck is going on here?"

"This maniac attacked me!" Jeremey yells. "I was just here to leave you a note."

"You shouldn't be here doing anything," I yell back, focusing my anger on him first. "We've been broken up for a while now, and I told you that I don't want to see you anymore. Do I have to get a restraining order?"

"No," he says, speaking really quietly as he gets back to his feet. "Of course not. I. . . I just wanted to talk is all."

"Oh bullshit," Michael yells. "I know a creepy ex when I see one, and trust me, this guy doesn't want to just talk. Who the hell comes to their ex girlfriend's empty apartment and just stands in the hallway writing notes while she's not home. You're fucked up, man."

"And who are you to be calling anyone that?" I yell, angry that Michael is acting like this. "Who threw the first punch, huh? Did he attack you first?" He doesn't answer, just stares at me, and I have my answer. "Right, so you think it's okay to just start wailing on someone outside my place. What was he even doing?"

"I was writing you a note, like I said."

"Shut the fuck up." Michael lunges at him again, and I stand in between them to stop his advance. I've never seen this side of him. Jeremey looks bad. I don't know how long they were going at it, but he definitely got the worst of it. His eye is bruised and there's blood coming out of his nose, dripping onto his shirt.

"Stop it. Get out, Michael!"

"What? Me? What are you talking about? That's bullshit!"

"I don't want to talk to you right now. I'll text you later. Just, please go."

My heart breaks when he looks at me. He's got a tear in his eye, but he's holding it back. He's still breathing heavy from the fight, and now that he's totally facing me there's even more blood on him. I can't even look at him right now.

"Fine, I'll go," he says. "But watch out for that one."

He points at Jeremey for a second, then turns and leaves. Now I have to deal with this one. What happened to the great day I was supposed to be having?

"So you're dating a criminal, huh?"

"He's not a criminal," I tell him. "He probably thought you were here to hurt me or something."

"What's his name? He looks familiar. Is he one of those porn writers you were always reading, even though I told you not to?"

"It's not porn, Jeremey, and I'm not getting into this again. You don't get to tell me what to read, and you never should have tried to begin with. That's why we're not together anymore. That's one of the reasons, anyhow. Why are you here?"

"I just wanted to leave you a note."

"That's not appropriate. We broke up. You don't get to see me anymore, and sure as hell not just popping up unannounced at my new. . ." I stop in mid sentence because I realize he shouldn't have this address. I'm unlisted, and I haven't posted it anywhere on social media, of course. I was so caught up in their fight that I didn't even think about that. I shouldn't be asking why Jeremey's here, I should be asking how he's here. All of a sudden I regret sending Michael away, and I feel afraid, like Jeremey might try something. I can't scream or yell, and that's not even something I'd normally do, but I really need him to leave right now.

My heart starts racing but I stay calm. Michael's not even visible anymore. "I'll look at your note, but I need you to respect me and go, alright? I can't have you just showing up here, but I promise I'll read it. Alright?"

"Fine," he says, huffing and seeming a little agitated. "I'm out of here. Until next time."

"There's not going to be a next. . ." He's out the door before I finish my statement. I take a deep breath, still a little rocked from that encounter, and go inside. What the hell was that? I almost kill myself as my foot slips out from underneath me and I have to grab the wall to stop from falling. I flick the light switch and look down, not believing my eyes at first. There's paper everywhere. There must be ten different sheets from a note pad, all slipped under the door.

I squat down and start picking them up, one at a time, until I have them all gathered. Each has a sentence or two on it. As I read them my heart starts to race again. One says, "We'll be together again." Another reads, "Mistake to leave me." And a third says, "Soon. Very soon."

I feel nauseous when I'm done. I put them in a drawer and sit down on my couch. There are so many emotions running through me right now that I'm not sure how to sort them. I need my girls. I text Harley and Ro and just ask them to come over. As I wait for a response I start to think a little more clearly. I can touch base with Michael tomorrow.

But I know what I need to do about Jeremey now.

29

KNIGHT

I FEEL LIKE SOMEONE IS PUSHING A POWER DRILL THROUGH one of my temples. Jesus. I don't remember my head hurting this bad in a long time. I did this to myself. I think I remember. *Right*. I got into a fight with that creep and Everleigh got mad at me just for trying to look out for her, and I decided to come home and make friends with all of the leftover liquor I had in my house. The last thing I actually remember is breaking open that bottle of Jager I have in the cabinet. After that it's kind of a blur. All I know is that the bottle is sitting next to me half empty, and I feel like I just went the distance with a world class boxer.

I can't believe it all went down like that. I was just trying to defend her, and this is the thanks that I get. If she can't tell that person is a dangerous creep who's obviously stalking her, then I'm not sure what we're doing together. I hate to say that, and it breaks my heart to even have that thought, but I can't help it. It's been an entire day since that happened, and no text. I thought I'd hear from her in the few minutes after I left, but it's been a full twenty-four hours and nothing. God, I feel like total crap right now.

Demons come back to visit at our weakest moments. It's like they're always there, just hovering on the periphery of our lives, even at the times when we've convinced ourselves how happy we are and how well everything is going. And then all it takes is one fight, one disaster, one tragedy, and our old friends come knocking at the door, waiting to throw our lives into total chaos. I haven't gotten wrecked like I am right now since I was recovering from my divorce. I guess self-destruction lies just on the other side of love.

Suddenly I hear a knock on the door—a pounding to my ears even though it's probably just a normal knock—followed by the calling of my name. "Mike! Mike you in there? It's us." It's Colton's voice, I can hear it clearly, and it sounds amplified because of the headache I have. I don't want to yell back because I feel like if I do my head will burst like a scene from some B-horror movie. I get to my feet, my body aching, and take a few steps towards the door. "Mike!"

"Hold on," I say, not raising my voice too much, but projecting it enough so that maybe he'll stop screaming through my walls. I open the door to see Colton and Grayson standing in my doorway looking borderline panicked, and before I can even say another word to them they rush through the doorway and hug me.

"Where the hell have you been, man? We've been texting and calling since yesterday."

"Why?" I ask, puzzled at this whole situation.

"Why?" Grayson repeats. "First of all, we had a Facebook live video we were all going to do together to promote the anthology, remember?" I actually didn't remember. But there isn't much that I recall after leaving Everleigh's house yesterday and hitting the liquor cabinet. "But besides that, we were worried. You never disappear. We called and texted about thirty times. We thought something had happened to you."

"I'm sorry. I really am. I'm okay." I can hear the tone in my voice—defeated, bitter, feeling a little sorry for myself, but I can't help it.

"Okay is the last word I'd use to describe your right now, Mike. You look like a warmed up bag of shit." Leave it to Colton to tell me the unfiltered truth. "You look like you looked last year. What's going on? Is it that girl you're seeing?"

"I don't even know if I'm seeing her anymore."

"So it is her," Grayson says. "Mike, you can't keep acting like this every time you have a girl mess with you. What happened?"

I explain the situation to them both as Colton makes a pot of coffee to help sober me up. I tell them everything in as few words as my pounding head will allow. Me going to her place, encountering that douche, getting into a fight, and her telling me to take a hike. They just sit and listen, but I'm starting to judge myself a little, especially the part that came after all that. "Okay, now that I said that all out loud I can hear how bad it sounds. I might have thrown me out also."

"The good news is that parts of it sound much worse than others." Grayson is trying to be comforting, but that's not what's happening at all.

"Oh, great," I say sarcastically. "So none of it sounds good."

"Fuck no," Colt jumps in. "It sounds like you fucked up some little guy in an apartment hallway because he wouldn't answer your stupid questions, and then you went full blown alcoholic on yourself, and here we are!"

"God, your honesty stings sometimes," I tell him. "But I

think it's what I need. I don't like how I feel or how I acted at all. That's not me. Not the real me."

"You're a hothead, dude. You've always been a hothead. Remember that time in college you wanted to brawl with that guy?"

"He called me a dick in class!" I yell.

"You were being a dick in class. He was right. And you were ready to get thrown out of school and jeopardize your future 'cause you couldn't control yourself. Leave the brawling to me." Gray looks at Colt and rolls his eyes.

"Stop it," he says. "You're not brawling anyone either. Jesus you're too into your book. I think you need to change the theme a little."

"Shut up, man, I'm being serious. We're here for Mike. This shit can't keep going on. I'm sorry, I know you're a grown-ass man and I can't tell you what to do, but we can't have this as business partners, and you can't have this if you want to have the kind of success you say you want. Real shit right now. I love you, brother, but you're fucking things up."

I just look into his eyes as he lectures me, but it's a lecture I need. If he were anyone else I'd shut my ears to everything he was saying, get super defensive, and maybe even physical. But from a guy I consider my brother they're sobering words —literally—and I try to soak them in. "You're right. That's exactly what I'm doing. I'm fucking things up, and I can't have that. The Wordsmiths can't have that."

"So what are you going to do about it? Don't tell me you're not going to do shit like this anymore. I already know that. Tell me how you're going to fix things."

"I like the tough love, Colton. It's a nice kick in the ass." He doesn't smile when I smile. He doesn't respond at all. He just keeps looking at me like a parent waiting for their kid to answer them. "Alright, no joking around, I get it. First thing

I'm doing is throwing out all of my booze. I only drink at home, I'm not really a bar guy anymore."

"On it already!" It's Grayson. He's in my kitchen searching all of the cabinets for bottles and gathering them in a large black plastic bag. "I got you, don't worry. Keep going."

"Yes, sir. And take it all. I don't need any of that shit lying around. But besides that I need to make amends with Everleigh. I haven't heard from her and I'm really worried that I've ruined things. It's been like a day."

"Text her, then," Colt says. "Tell her you fucked up and beg her forgiveness. It was an extreme thing to do but not necessarily a deal breaker."

"True," I say. "I don't know why I was waiting for her. I need to take action. It's not like me to be passive. I really like this girl. I'm falling in love with her. That's the truth. I can't lose her."

"Then don't." Grayson steps out from behind my kitchen counter. "Don't. Make it right. That's what men do."

"Alright," I say, jumping up. "Enough of this bullshit. Enough talking. You're both right, and it's time to get my shit together. Thank you. Both of you. This shit won't happen again. I'm sorry it's happened at all."

"That's what I wanted to hear," Colt says. He takes a step towards me and we hug. "Go get that girl."

I am.

I'm not just going to clean my shit up.

I'm going to go get Everleigh.

30

KNIGHT

SHOWING UP AT HER PLACE ISN'T THE KIND OF THING I WOULD normally do, but I didn't think that this was a text or call kind of situation. I'm returning to the scene of my fuck up, twenty-four hours later, only this time I'm here for redemption. I don't see Everleigh's car in front, but that doesn't mean anything. Spots in this part of Queens are few and far between. It's not that I want to surprise her, but I don't want to give her time to think of reasons not to see me. It's too important, and I have some apologizing to do.

I walk into the same lobby where I beat the fuck out of that guy, only now it's empty except for me. I walk up to her door and stand there for a second. I'm not even sure what to do or say. I'd rehearsed what I was going to say in my head on the drive over here, but now that I'm here I feel frozen, and I just stand there.

"Are you just gonna stand there, or are you going to knock?" I hear Everleigh's voice behind me, and I turn around right away.

"Hey."

"Hey. I didn't expect you," she says.

"I know. I was doing a surprise attack. I'm sorry."

"It wasn't a bad thing. I'm happy to see you, actually."

"Really? I was worried that you were going to tell me to take a hike."

"I'd never tell you to take a hike, Michael. I mean, I'd never do it outside of you beating my ex bloody right in front of my door. Other than that."

"We're golden."

"You wanna come in and talk?"

"I'd really love that."

I can't tell exactly what she's feeling, but she doesn't seem too angry. Thank God for small miracles. She motions for me to sit down on the couch and I feel like I'm about to get another lecture, but that's not how she begins the conversation. "I want to apologize," she says, and my heart sinks.

"What? You want to apologize to me?" I'm shocked.

"I overreacted. Actually, we both overreacted. You to him and me to you. Jeremey is the ex I told you about, and I know that I didn't paint him in a very good light. I know that you were just trying to look out for me—to protect me, even. But that was not okay."

"I know it wasn't. And you're really kind, but it's my turn to apologize now." I take a deep breath and consider what I'm about to say. "I need you to know that no matter how you described him, or how much of an asshole the guy may be, I had no right to beat him up like that, and that isn't on you, it's 100 percent on me."

"Thank you for saying that," she says. "I think I needed to hear it."

"Well, I heard a few things that I needed to hear from Colton and Grayson yesterday afternoon, and it made me consider some of the decisions I've been making recently."

"Like what?"

"Like my anger. Like my drinking. I didn't really tell you this before because I'd convinced myself that I was past it, but I have a tendency to drink too much when I'm under stress."

"Oh," she answers, and I'm not really sure how to interpret it.

"Yeah, I'm not a full fledged alcoholic, but my father was, and I used to drink to excess all the time. I'd kicked it for a while, but for a year after my divorce I was basically on one long bender. I was depressed and angry, and I turned to the bottle to try to forget everything that had happened. That's really why I didn't get much done, but eventually Colt and Gray helped pull me out of it and I basically stopped drinking. Until. . ."

"Until?"

"Yesterday. I was so worried that I'd lost you that I freaked out and went a little crazy."

"Like, how crazy?"

"Like Colt and Gray had to wake me up out of a drunken stupor 'cause I'd blacked out. That kind of crazy."

"Michael!"

"I know, I know. It was shitty of me, but I was really screwed up, and I thought I'd hear from you. Why didn't you text me yesterday?"

"That's why you drank? Michael, I'd never cut you off just like that, no matter how mad I was. I just hate violence and I needed time to figure out what was happening with Jeremey. I wasn't breaking up with you."

"Then why didn't you text?"

"Because I was at court," she says.

"Court? For what? Are you in trouble?"

"No, but Jeremey will be if he ever tries to come within

50 yards of me again. I was at court getting a restraining order against him."

"Is he that bad?" I'm here to apologize for being overprotective and violent, but as she's telling me about this I start to get really concerned.

"Not in the way you think. I mean, I don't think he'd do anything crazy, anyhow. He was always a little verbally abusive and very controlling, but he never touched me."

"That's when you were together," I say, still concerned. "What about now? What does he do with his control issues now that he can't have you? Maybe he's capable of more than you think."

"He left some creepy notes under my door. That's what he was doing when you found him here. I took them straight to a judge with Harley and Rowan and asked for a restraining order. I texted him from court and he promised to back off. I honestly don't think he's a dangerous guy, just a bad guy."

"Is there a difference?" I can see the concern in her face. I don't want to make her doubt her intuition about this guy, but I can smell danger a mile away. "That's rhetorical. I guess if you say he's safe then he's safe. But at least I feel better about you not texting me."

"Jeremey was only part of the reason," she tells me. "I could have texted you also. I thought about it. But I honestly didn't know what to say. You scared me. I hate violence, and especially when it's brought literally to my doorstep."

"I'm sorry. I can't say it enough."

"I know you are. I can see it in your eyes. But it's not just that I was scared."

"What else, then?"

"Michael, you have to understand—I spent years in a relationship where I was controlled. I can't stand that feeling.

I'll never allow myself to be in a situation like that ever again."

"I'm not trying to control you, Everleigh, I hope you know that."

"I do," she continues. "I know you're not Jeremey. But it felt very controlling. I'm a big girl, and I don't need protection that I don't ask for. When you took away my ability to deal with Jeremey myself—however noble or protective your intentions were—it still felt like you were taking away my ability to run my own life. I know that's not what you meant."

"No," I say emphatically, realizing that I messed up even more than I thought. "Never. And I'm sorry. For everything. Can we just. . .can we just move on from this? Did I mess things up beyond repair?"

I almost don't want to look at her after I ask, so I look at the floor instead. I don't know what I'm expecting when I ask that, but I'm terrified of the answer. I can't imagine what I'd feel like if I lost this woman—she's become everything to me. I hold my breath in anticipation of her answer.

"No," she says. "Of course not, Michael. It's never beyond repair. You think I'd just throw what we have out because of a little fight? I was just angry and scared. But we've talked and things are good. I can't imagine my life without you right now."

"I was just thinking the same thing." The smile on my face is unmistakable and large. I can feel my cheeks pressing upwards and my mouth parting just slightly. I probably look like a fool in love, but that's exactly what I am.

"Come here."

I rise from my end of the couch and sit next to her. As soon as I get close to her body I feel excited, not only because that's how I always feel when I'm close to her, but because

I'm so happy. It's been a rough couple of days. But they fade away quickly as I'm sitting here, and the bliss of the previous days comes flooding back to me. My finished book, my story for the Wordsmith anthology, and my relationship with Everleigh—all of it becomes this entity that I can feel inside of my chest, warming me and making me smile uncontrollably.

We start to kiss. Really kiss. Something comes over me that I've never felt before, and something I don't even try to fight. It's like there's a caged animal inside of me, screaming to be let out—as if every drop of desire that I've ever had for Everleigh rushes to all of my nerve endings at once, and I know that I have to have her right then and there.

I pull on my shirt so hard that the top buttons shoot off, and I claw at it until it's off. My pants follow. She's undressing almost as fast as I am, and before I know it I'm on top of her, naked and hard. I waste no time. It isn't a foreplay situation. I use my hand to guide myself right inside of her. She's soaking wet, and my cock slips right into her, and I thrust my hips forward as hard as I can. She screams and arches her back as I wrap my hand around the back of her head. I start kissing her as hard as I can as she plunges her tongue deep into my mouth. My hips never stop working, and as we make out I keep fucking her as fast as I can.

There's no space between our bodies, and she reaches around my back and claws into me as I thrust, faster and faster, until I know that we're both almost there. I can hear it in the sounds she's making. I can see it in her eyes. I can feel it with every clench of her tight, wet pussy. She's close, and so am I. I feel her body explode towards me, like every ounce of strength she has is concentrated at once, and then as soon as it begins it also ends. She collapses onto the couch, and I keep fucking her for another minute until I'm ready also. Just as I get there I reach down and pull out, spraying my cum all over her stomach, my eyes rolling in my head.

I fall next to her as we both take in as much of the surrounding air as our lungs will allow. I've never felt so satisfied, as if the troubles of the last few days never happened. She shifts her body towards me and snuggles up against my naked body, and I wrap my arm around her.

"So I guess this means we're good?"

"Yeah," she says, laughing. "We're golden, Michael. We're golden."

"WELL, WOULD YOU LOOK AT THIS SHIT?"

I don't mean to wake Everleigh up, but that's exactly what I do. I stayed over last night. I woke up early to get some work done, but instead I blurt out some shit that wakes her right up. It's another one of those impulsive moments that I should probably be controlling, but unlike beating up her ex, I think she'll give me a pass on this one. I usually don't bring my computer into bed—I like to keep writing separate from other activities in my life, but my phone was dead when I woke up and I felt like clicking around social media a little.

Turns out I should have stayed off. "What's wrong?"

"Oh, I'm sorry," I say, feeling bad that I woke her. "Nothing, go back to sleep."

"Yeah, that's not happening now."

"I'm really sorry."

"No, it's fine, I was starting to wake up anyway."

"Liar."

"Okay," she says. "You're right I was dead asleep, but I should probably get my butt up out of bed anyhow. What time is it?"

"7:00 am."

"For a Saturday that might as well be three in the morning."

"How did you sleep?"

"Well, I think, but I'm still half dreaming." She lifts her arms over her head and yawns. She's still naked from the night before, and my eyes are drawn to her breasts, and the way her hair is all messed up and falling over them. It's so beautiful that I almost forget the bullshit I just saw on Facebook. Almost.

"I think I'm having a nightmare, myself."

"What is it, Captain Dramatic?"

"Come here, look."

She scoots over towards my side of the bed as I shift my computer to her lap. She looks at it and I look at her, waiting to see the recognition on her face. It takes about three seconds. "Oh, hell no."

"Now you see why I woke you up?"

"Now that I'm seeing this I'm amazed you didn't yell louder."

"I'm practicing my self control."

"I'd fucking lose it if I were you."

The post is from last night, but I'm only seeing it now. It's on KL Steiner's author page, and it reads:

"Readers & Followers—I have a double announcement. First, I'm pleased to announce the formation of a new reading group I've created called The Brotherhood. I'm pleased to be joined in this group by author Roland Rays and author Johnathan Logan, whom you all know and love from their takeovers in my reader's group. I can't wait to get some great writing done with my new brothers. Please see the link in the comments of this post to join our new

Brotherhood Facebook group. Secondly, I'm excited to announce that my new book is available for pre-order and will be released a few weeks before RAAC."

I read the whole thing one more time because I'm not sure which part I'm more offended by, the fact that he stole our idea for an all-male fraternity of authors, or that he literally stole my WIP and is now going to publish a book he basically pirated. The second. Definitely the second. But the first one is a bitch move, too. "What an unbelievable piece of shit," Everleigh says.

"I guess I shouldn't be surprised. What did I think he was going to do with my story?"

"Was it a full book?"

"Not even close, no. Maybe that's why I'm not so bent out of shape about it."

"I'd be loosing my shit."

"Aren't you supposed to be helping me control my anger?"

"I am," she says, smiling. "But we can get back to being calm after this. This is some. . ."

"Fucked up shit, I know." I understand that I should be raging right now, that I should be able to justifiably throw this computer across the room in a fit of rage. I'd be justified in doing that. But I don't. I don't do anything of the sort. I don't scream, or yell, or punch anything. In fact, the longer I stare at the screen I start to notice the weird reaction I'm having internally—which is no reaction at all.

"Should I be worried?" I ask her.

"Worried about what?"

"About the fact that I'm not bothered by this, I'm not upset. I don't feel like tracking him down and beating the shit out of him."

"I guess you got that out of your system already this week, huh?"

"How long is it gonna take to live that one down?"

"Don't know," she jokes. "Check back with me in a month or so."

"Seriously, though, I don't feel like I thought I would have. I feel. . ."

"What?"

"At peace. I feel peaceful."

"Is that a bad thing?"

"No," I say, contemplating her question. "Not a bad thing. The opposite. I think what was really bothering me was the idea of losing you. I honestly haven't really thought much about the stolen laptop or anything else in the book world for a while. I've just been focused on finishing my book and my story for the anthology. And now that I'm basically done with both I don't really care about this other shit. Let him have his group. Let him have whatever few pages he stole from me. He can have it." I look over at Everleigh. "I have the only thing that matters to me."

"That's. . .that's amazing of you to say. I feel the same way."

"So when do I get to tell everyone?"

"We talked about this already," she says. "You know how I feel."

"I do. But I also know that I'm not going to treat you like some dirty little secret. It's time that the world knew about us, Everleigh. I'm sick of hiding it."

"That's up to you, Knight. I'm not going to tell you what to do. It's your career. I'm okay with whatever you choose."

"Listen," I say, changing the subject quickly. "How about we all go to dinner. I should have my book back from my editor and formatter within a week and a half. Why don't we go to dinner with the guys? You and me."

"I have a better idea," she says. "How about we go to dinner with the boys, and I invite some special guests."

"Okay," I agree. "Who did you have in mind?"

EVERLEIGH

"No way, Ev. I'm not getting set up with some author."

Harley protests too much. At least Rowan gave in right away, even though this isn't technically a set up for either of them. "It's not a blind date, it's just dinner. Michael wants to celebrate his new book with me and the guys. I'd feel more comfortable with you guys there. Then we'd be all balanced out. Three guys and three girls."

"Ha! See, I knew it. It's a set up. You're pairing us off."

"I am not, what's wrong with you? There are three of us and three of them. It's really just about the math."

"Uh-huh," Harley says. "I just don't like being set up. It's never really worked out for me."

"Okay, Harley, you have to listen to my words. I'm-not-setting-you-up, okay? I just want my girls around me like he'll have his boys. Plus he's paying for everyone, and that's kind of a big deal."

"Why?" Rowan asks.

"Because he believes in this book so much that he knows it's going to make money. That might not be the smartest thing to do with money you haven't even earned yet, but I'm going with it because he finally believes in himself again. That's worth more than a dinner. Come on, Harley, you'd be helping his career, for God's sake."

"Ooooh," she says sarcastically, as her humor fills the room. "So by going to this not-a-set-up-at-all dinner, I'll actually be making Knight a better writer, is that it?"

"Yeah, you get it."

"Jesus, Ev, did you ever consider going into politics?"

"That's a hard pass for me, but thank you?"

"Not sure it was a compliment," Harley says. "But I'll go because you're my girl and I'm here for you, always."

"You're the best!"

"Hey, what about me, I said yes right away. Why aren't I the best?"

"You're also the best," I reassure Rowan. "You're both the best."

"We can't both be the best. Then there's no best."

"Well I make up the rules and I say you can be. Seriously, I love you both."

"We love you too," Harley replies. "But one question."

"Yes?"

"Which one is for me? I have a preference but want to make sure we're on the same page."

"Wait, what do you mean?" I'm confused, but Harley is unpredictable like that. She goes from hating an idea to loving it within seconds sometimes, like now. I'm not sure what she means, though.

"I want Chase. He's the hottest one. No offense, Ev."

"None taken. I'm surprised, though."

"Why so shocked?" she asks. "You don't think he's hot?"

"He's gorgeous, don't get me wrong, and Michael has said nothing but good things about the guy, I just didn't think. . ."

"That I was interested? I know, I wanted to fool you a little. I'm in."

Enter Harley. She can be weird, aloof, and sometimes says things just to throw whoever's talking to her off a little. I should be used to it, but sometimes she can even throw me for a loop, like today. "That's great. I mean, I don't know if he's looking. I think Michael just invited him out to celebrate the release of his book. I don't think he's going to think of it like a set up."

"Don't worry, I'll let him know."

"How are you going to do that?"

"Don't worry," she tells me. "I'll figure it out. I have my ways. He'll get it."

Her words scare me a little, but I don't follow up. I learned a long time ago that Harley is her own person—a free spirit in every sense of the word. She's a big girl, and I've been there for more than a few questionable decisions when it comes to guys, but she's done the same for me. I realized a while back that trying to dissuade her from anything is a waste of time. Best to let her make her own mistakes when it comes to these situations, if there are mistakes to be made. I'll just let that one play out however it's going to play out.

"Are you excited?" Rowan asks me.

"I'm so excited. I really am." I hate to say it, but I'm not used to being so genuinely happy for another person's accomplishments. No matter what happens with the book, what matters is that it exists, and that he wrote it. I know he wants more than that, obviously, but I'm just happy that he'll have it out there.

33

KNIGHT

TWO WEEKS LATER

"THIS PLACE IS FANCY AS FUCK. I APOLOGIZE FOR BEING MAD at you for asking me to wear a suit."

"It's weird to see you in one to be honest."

Colton and I get there first. He looks good in a suit, but he gave me shit when I told him we were going to that type of restaurant. Had it been up to him we would've just gone to the local pub for a burger and a beer. On most days I'd have agreed with him. I like casual places, too. But finishing this book is more important to me than almost anything else I've written. I need to go fancy.

I found the place on Yelp. It's a new fine dining place that just opened in my part of Queens three months ago. So far the reviews have been great, so I decided to give it a try. Gray gets there dressed to the nines a few minutes later. I offered to come with Everleigh, but she wanted to bring the girls. Apparently she thinks that Harley and Colton will hit it off, but I didn't mention any of that to him. I'll let that play itself out, I have bigger things on my mind.

The boys and I get seated and wait for the girls to arrive, and all I can think about is how satisfied I feel right now.

Colton leans in and asks "Is it, like, weird to order a beer in this kind of place?"

"I'd go with wine tonight, even though you're not a wine guy."

"What about something stronger?"

"That's fine," I tell him. "Just don't over do it."

"Look who's talking." He ribs me in the side and I laugh. He's right. I'm the last person who should be dispensing drinking advice. I swear I still have a headache from my bender a few weeks ago. We all get our drinks and wait, making small talk for a few minutes, when I see Grayson raise his glass.

"Before the ladies get here, I just wanted to say something." He looks right at me and smiles. "It was a year ago—a fucking year ago—that you were a messed up pile of shit, wasting away in your house and practically drinking yourself to death."

"I really hope this is going somewhere," I joke.

"It is, I promise you. Just listen."

"Okay."

"You were a mess. You know that. But to see where you are right now is something I find truly inspiring, and I can't wait to see what you've come up with."

"I couldn't have said it better," Colt says. "It's amazing. You're one of the strongest people I know, man. You've overcome some obstacles that would've crippled other people, and here you are now, thriving."

"I don't know if I'm thriving yet," I say, feeling touched by the intensity of their words. "But I do know one thing. There's no way I'd be sitting here right now without you guys. You got me off my ass and writing again, and I can't ever thank you two enough."

"What are best friends for?" Colton asks. "Here's to the

Wordsmiths, and to many more celebratory dinners—only someplace where I can wear regular clothes."

"You have such a way with words, Colt," I joke. "You should maybe consider being a writer."

"I will look into that. Cheers."

"Cheers!"

We sip our drinks and talk for a few minutes. I see a few figures walking in. I start to stand up because I think it's Everleigh and the girls, but I sit right back down as soon as my brain accepts what my eyes are seeing. "I don't fucking believe this."

"What's the matter, Mike?"

"Turn around."

"Why?" Grayson asks as he shifts in his seat. "Oh, fuck, you've gotta be kidding me."

He sees it. I see it. And in about two seconds Colton is going to see it also. It's them—the Brotherhood. I see KL leading the charge, a cocky smile on his face like he just landed the *New York Times* bestseller list. Behind him are the other two, who I have nothing against except for their alliance with such an unethical asshole. And trailing behind the whole group is. . .is that Jenny? What the holy fuck? I see her right behind Roland Rays and our conversation the other week all of a sudden makes sense. She must be PA'ing for him. Wait, but was it him who told her about the stolen story?

Colton finally sees what we see and I catch the expression on his face changing rapidly. He doesn't say anything, he just stares, and so do I. It's about as unexpected a turn of events as I can think of, and I'm not sure how to handle it. It's the three of them, KL, Roland, and Johnathan, followed by Jenny and other women I assume are the other guy's PA's. All my eyes can focus on is *him*.

This is the piece of shit who stole my laptop and almost

ruined the momentum I had with my new book. On top of that he's publishing the parts he stole and passing it off as his own. I'm feeling so many different things that I'm not sure what to do with myself. As they take a few more steps into the dining room KL and I lock eyes. It's like everything freezes except the two of us—our eyes locked in something like I imagine animals experience when the prey catches the predator looking at them from across the prairie. My body feels a rush of anger, and I have to force myself to take a deep breath to control it. "Fuck that guy!" Colton says, and I can hear that he's just as mad as I am, maybe more so. My anger tends to lead to self-destruction, but Colton is prone to actual destruction. The truth about the two of us is that we've saved each other many times—me when I take to the bottle too hard, and him when his anger gets him into some very dangerous situations.

"Take a deep breath, Colt." Grayson's trying to keep us calm, but there'll be none of that right now. KL gives a nod of recognition our way, the arrogant smile still adorning his face. "They're not worth it. This is just the worst coincidence ever. But let's just leave it at that and try to have a good time. The girls will be here soon. Agreed?"

"Agreed," I say. "But if it's all the same to you, can we switch spots so that my back is to the room? I don't need to look at that bastard all night."

"You got it."

I switch positions with Gray so that I'm sitting next to Colton and my backs to the Brotherhood's dinner party. As I'm transitioning I see the girls walking in on cue, looking as beautiful as ever. They all look great, but there's only one whose beauty matters to me. Everleigh. This night is really about her. Not just her. This night is about *us*. They make their way over and I step forward to give her a kiss.

"You look incredible." She really does. She's wearing a red dress that fits the contours of her body perfectly, accentuating her curves and daring my eyes not to look. I say hi to Harley and Rowan and introduce them formally to the boys.

We all sort of 'met' at the signing, but not really. To be honest Harley and Rowan were just Everleigh's friends to me, just two other readers in a room that was filled with people all day. But I'm happy that we all get to hang out and get to know each other.

"You're not looking so shabby yourself. But what's wrong? You look tense."

"Nothing," I say, lying just to avoid getting angry. "I'll tell you later." She doesn't notice who else is in the room and I have no desire to call attention to it just yet. Right now I have introductions to make. "Harley, it's great seeing you again."

We hug and Colton steps towards her. "Hey Harley," he says. "We didn't get to talk too long at the signing."

"I know," she says. "You saw a lot of people. I wouldn't expect you to remember too much. I love your books. Especially the last one."

"Oh I remember. You think I'd forget you? No way." She smiles when Colt turns the charm on. There's definitely a vibe between them. She's abrupt and speaks in a very blunt way, but there's an unmistakable warmness to her— something that's hard to quantify but easy to detect.

I turn to Rowan to give one last hug. "And you must be. . ."

"You can call me Ro, Knight. And it's great to meet you for real." She also gives a huge squeeze and by the time I let go some of my stress has been taken away. I should have known that Everleigh's friends would be this nice. Good people surround themselves with other good people, and now it's my turn.

Now that the formalities are done I find myself staring at Everleigh. I can't wait to celebrate, but in the back of my head I'm thinking about the asshole sitting across the dining room next to my ex. But even in the midst of all that mental noise I still notice Colton checking out Harley. He's not looking her up and down, or doing his I'm-a-sexy-male-author thing to her. That's usually how he is with beautiful women, but like I said I notice micro expressions in people, and his are of something I've never seen in him before-- something antithetical to his personality: he seems submissive to her.

What does that mean? Even though Colt's one of the kindest human beings I've ever met, he usually leans toward the braggadocious, at least outwardly, and especially when it comes to meeting women. He's had some BAD experiences with his exes over the years. I haven't seen him look at anyone like he's looking at Harley since. . .

When I look to my other side I see Grayson chatting it up with Rowan like no one else is in the room. Everyone seems to be hitting it off. We shift seats a little bit so that I can sit with Everleigh, and I guess that I'm not hiding my dissatisfaction with our company well because she asks me again, "What's the matter? And don't tell me 'nothing', I can see that it's something."

"Did you look around the dining room at all?"

"No, why?" She turns her head and starts scanning, and I wait until I see that she sees them. "Oh. Oh, wow. Really?"

"My luck, I guess."

"What are the odds? Look, don't let this ruin anything. You want to go somewhere else?"

"No, it's fine, we're all here already. I can get past it."

"If you get too distracted I want you to just look here." She places her fingers on my face and turns me gently from looking at KL to her. "Right here."

"That sounds like a plan."

Even though I'm still secretly seething, dinner is going off without a hitch. We order drinks and food, and everyone seems to be getting along. Next to me is a package I brought. It looks like I'm giving a gift, which I guess I kind of am. It's my new book. No one's seen it and no one's read it but my editor. Thank God for her I still can't format dialogue correctly!

As dinner goes on I find myself getting nervous. Insecurity isn't really something that I ever really feel, but as the time for me to show the cover and the title gets closer I start to worry that no one will like it. Then I look at Everleigh and tell myself to shut the fuck up. It seems to work.

We order dessert. It's not nearly as good of a spread as what I could make if I were the pastry chef, but it's decent enough as these places go. Everleigh gets the Tiramisu and leans into me as the waiter puts it down in front of her. "You would have killed this dessert."

"Thanks." I smile. Great minds.

As the meal winds down I stand up. I don't have a prepared speech or anything, but there are a few things that I want to say. All eyes are on me, and I swallow audibly. I don't know exactly how to express what I'm feeling, so I just start talking. "Everyone, listen up for a minute, I have nothing planned here except to show you what's sitting next to me. Without getting all warm and squishy."

"What's wrong with warm and squishy, Mike?"

"Shut up, Colt!" I yell. "But seriously, I don't wanna get overly emotional, but I do wanna give credit where it's due. Tonight is about you guys as much as it is about me. To

Colton and Grayson, there's no way I'd be here right now if you hadn't picked my tired ass up, several times, and made me join the Wordsmiths."

"It was our pleasure, Mike," Grayson says. "That's what brothers do. They help each other out."

"Still," I say. "It wasn't something you needed to do, but it was something that I needed to happen. And really, more than anyone else here tonight, I want to dedicate our own little cover reveal to you, Everleigh. I can honestly say that without you this book in my hands wouldn't exist. I think you're going to love it." She smiles and looks up at me, and I decide that it's time to take off the paper wrapping. "Here it is." The paper pulls off easily, and underneath is my book. I think it one more time just so that I know it's real. I'm holding my new book. I hand it to her so that she can read the cover.

"Oh, Michael," she says.

"I thought you might like the title."

I watch her read it again and again, even though it's only a single word.

ForEver.

It was the perfect title, and it came to me as soon as I finished the last page.

"I can't believe you named it. . ."

"For you?" I ask. "Why not? It is for you, and I hope that you love it as much as I do."

"Congrats, man, it looks amazing!"

"Thanks, Gray. That means a lot." I forget for a minute that anyone else is even in the room until I hear Gray's voice. I'm lost in Everleigh's eyes, swollen with tears that I named a book in dedication to her.

I pass the book around and everyone tells me how much they love it. I couldn't be happier. Colton looks at his phone and I can see his face change. I look over to see what's wrong but he won't look back. He's looking at his phone like it just robbed him—like he wants to smash it on the floor. I'm still celebrating and happy, so I look away, but then I see him get up and excuse himself. . .

34

COLTON

I LOOK AT MY PHONE AND SEE THAT THE PIECE OF SHIT excuse for an author took a pic of us from across the room, right when Mike was holding up his new book, and he uploaded it to his Brotherhood Facebook page with the caption "Hey Brotherhood members—here's a pre-cover reveal from a washed up author. Who's cover do you like better, his or mine???" Underneath that hateful post are 11 comments and counting, mostly the scumbags who joined that group tagging KL and telling him how great his cover is, and how much Mike's sucks.

I'm so fucking angry that I don't know what to do. Mike finally got his life together, wrote what I'm sure is an amazing book, and dedicated it to the woman he's falling for, and this guy tries to go negative on social media! Let me revise what I said. I do know what to do. I know exactly what to do.

I watch him escape to the bathroom and I follow him. I avoid making eye contact with Mike because I don't want him to talk me out of what I'm about to do. I wait until KL passes out of sight before I get up. I just keep looking at my phone so nothing looks suspicious. When I open the men's room door I see that there's no one inside but us. KL's at the urinal draining his little dick, and I stand by the sink pretending to wash my hands. A few seconds later he's done. I keep my head down at first, still pretending to wash my hands and planning what I'm going to do next.

"Well, Colton Chase. Fancy meeting you in here." The sound of KL's voice is grating, and not only because I'm fuming. He has a high pitched, annoying voice that sounds really bad when he does live videos on Facebook. In person it might be even worse. "What brings you boys here tonight? I saw you all from across the room. Small world." I feel my fist balling up even though I try to stop it.

"We're celebrating, KL." I tell him, making eye contact in the mirror only. "Michael is releasing a new book soon, but you already know that, don't you?"

I'm looking at him intensely in the mirror, not moving my eyes from his to see how he reacts to what I just said. "I have a new book also," he says with an arrogant smile creeping up on his face. "Coincidences all around tonight. We're also here celebrating."

I've had enough of this charade. Banter is cool in a Tarantino film, but right now I'm just about done talking. "Did you tell them where you got your story from? Or were you planning on coming over and thanking Mike for his contribution?"

He doesn't like that one. "What are you talking about?" he asks. I turn towards him. "Don't fuck around with me. I'm not Michael. I will beat the fuck out of you right where you stand." I take a step closer to him so that we're only inches apart. "I know you were the one who stole his laptop at the signing. I know that you took what he'd been inspired to write and built your new book around it. And I know that you just posted to Facebook making fun of his new book. None of this shit is okay."

"The Facebook thing was a joke," he says, looking nervous. "I just did it to hype up my group. It's called marketing, genius. Maybe you could learn from me. But about the other two things, who the hell do you think you are accusing me of committing a crime and not writing my own book? You have some balls."

"Yeah," I say, inching even closer to his face to make him uncomfortable. "I do. Much bigger than yours. And if you deny what you did one more time something bad's going to happen to you, do you hear me?"

"Oh, I like the tough look on you, Chase. It's sexy." He starts laughing hysterically. "It's like you're starting to believe your own hype a little too much. You write shitty books about fighters, Chase, you aren't one."

"That's fair enough," I say, calm as can be. "But I know enough to kick your ass. Now, what's going to happen is this. You're going to wash your filthy hands—the same ones that swiped my best friends computer. Then you're going to walk out to the dining room, past your little entourage of losers, walk up to Michael, and tell him what you did in front of all of us."

"Is that right? Is that what I'm going to do?"

"Only if you have half a brain. Which, knowing you, means that you won't. But you should, trust me."

"Fuck you, Chase. Fuck you, and your stupid Wordsmith bullshit group. And I wouldn't want to interrupt Michael while he's making googly eyes at that dirty bitch sitting next to him. . ."

He doesn't know what's happened until he's buckled over in pain, struggling to breathe. If he'd had the time to process he might have seen my fist shooting full force into his abdomen, knocking the wind right out of him. I don't know what's coming over me, but I send one more shot his way as he tries to grab at my pant leg, this time into his face. I can feel his nose break as soon as I hit him, and pretty soon the blood is flowing out of it. I lean down and put my face next to his. "Fine, have it your way. Stay the fuck away from us or this is just the beginning of the beating I'm going to put on you, you piece of shit."

I leave him there, bleeding and embarrassed, and walk back out. As soon as I clear the bathroom I realize what I've done, and I start to panic. I'm not worried about him or about getting in trouble, I'm worried about escalation. As soon as one of his boys sees what I did to him this is going to turn into a thing none of us need it to turn into. I don't want Michael's moment ruined, so I hurry over to the table.

Thank God, he's paying the bill.

I PAY FOR EVERYTHING AND WE ALL HEAD OUT. COLTON seems to be in a rush and I can't really figure out why, but he's trying to hide it from me for some reason. I can always catch up with him later. Right now Everleigh and I are going to split off from the group. We have some celebrating of our own to do.

"Well, Knight, it was great meeting you. I love your book. And I love that you're with my girl." Harley extends her hand like we're at a business meeting, but I scoop her up in a big hug. She reacts right away and hugs me back. "Sorry," she says right after I let her go. "I have no idea why I went to shake your hand. I can be a little awkward. You'll get used to it."

"I look forward to it. Goodnight Harley."

"What are you guys up to?" Grayson asks.

"Everleigh and I are going back to my place. How about you all?"

"Not sure," Colt says, still looking a little nervous for some reason. "You ladies wanna hit up the bar a few blocks over? Feel like a goodnight drink?"

Harley and Rowan look at each other and grin, hesitating for only a second. "We'd love to. Show us the way." Rowan is interesting also. She seems to have struck up some pretty easy conversation with Gray over dinner. He's a total nerd so I'm sure they were talking politics or literature or something. They look good together. Now, Colton and Harley? They look good together also, but each of their personalities is like a time bomb waiting to go off. I wonder how that's going to work out. One thing I'm sure of though—Colton's into her.

"Great," I tell them. "Thanks for coming tonight, guys. Have one for me."

"Will do," Grayson answers. "We'll catch up on some business tomorrow. Night."

"Night, guys."

◇ ◇ ◇

We get back to my place, and I have a little surprise waiting for Everleigh. But first, a trip to the fridge where I put in a bottle of champagne to chill before I left.

"That dinner was delicious," she says. "The whole thing was really wonderful, even with that douche bag sitting across the room."

"Not my ideal dinner company. When he walked in I wanted to kill him. But then you guys arrived and I just let it go. I thought of what we talked about and I just did some breathing and it didn't matter to me anymore. I think I might be growing as a person." I laugh and so does she.

"I think you might be. I like what I see."

"Here." I grab my champagne flutes from the cabinet and get ready to pour us each a celebratory glass. The bottle pops like a firecracker when I open it, the foam pouring out of the tip so fast that I hold it over the sink. When the foaming stops I pour her glass first, and then mine. She looks so beautiful standing here in my kitchen. Her dress accentuates her body, drawing my eyes to every curve. But there's one thing missing on her. I think I can help with that. "To new beginnings!"

"New beginnings."

"Let's go into the living room, I want to show you something."

I set everything up before I left so that my little plan would work perfectly. Dinner, drinks at my place, and now a few gifts that I hope she loves. I left the packages strategically positioned on the couch so that she'll see them right away. It works.

"What's this?" she asks when she sees the two of them sitting side by side.

"Open them up."

She sits down next to them and opens the one on the left first. "I love it." She unwraps a special hard back copy of *ForEver* that I had specially printed for her. Inside the front cover I made a special dedication.

To the woman whose name this title bears,
I was a broken man when we met. My face needed a razor
and my blank pages needed inspiration to fill them with
words. And then I met you. You filled my head with words
and my heart with feelings. The words in this story are a
tribute to you.
I love you.
-Michael

When she turns to me there are tears in her eyes. I sit down next to her on the couch and put my arms around her. "I love you, Everleigh. I don't know why it took me this long to say it, but it's true."

"I love you, too, Michael. So much!" She leans over and

we kiss. Saying those words means everything to me, so much so that I don't even consider whether the timing is right, or whether its too early, or whether or not she'll say it back. I feel nothing but trust and passion with her, and as soon as she says it back to me I know that it's real. "This book is so beautiful. I'm going to put this on my shelf and never ever touch it again!"

"Whatever you want to do with it is fine with me, it's yours, forever, and in more ways than one. But, hey," I mention, "that's just the first thing, open up the other."

"Michael, this night is about you, you really didn't have to get me anything at all."

"You're wrong on both counts, Ev. This night is actually about you, and I couldn't help but get you a little something. Now open it up."

She looks like a kid on Christmas, and I watch her tear at the small box I wrapped terribly. "I'm sorry. I'm shitty at wrapping gifts."

"I don't care about that," she says, opening it up. "Oh, Michael."

The little blue box reveals itself under the wrapping that now finds it's place on the floor. There's no mistaking that Tiffany light blue color. Inside is a necklace—a heart pendant —that I had inscribed on the back. "This is so beautiful."

"Turn it over." On the other side the words read, "*ForEver* yours, Michael.", which is also on the dedication page of the book. "Can I put it on you?"

"You'd better."

She turns around and lifts her hair up. I reach around and drape the necklace over her naked neck, so that my heart rests firmly on top of hers. "Let me see."

"How does it look?"

"Not nearly as gorgeous as you." We kiss some more, and

I want nothing more than to take her upstairs to the bedroom, but first there's something that we need to do. "Here," I say, taking out my phone. "I want to remember this night. Let's take a pic." She leans in and I hold the phone up at just the right angle. It comes out perfectly, no filter required. "Before we go upstairs, I want you to know that I need everyone to know about us. This isn't some secret thing we're doing. It's not some tawdry affair or some shady hook up. We're in love, and I'm not hiding that from anyone."

"I love you. And I trust you to do whatever you feel is best."

"This is what's best." I take my phone and type up a little something and hold the phone so that Everleigh can see the screen. I have the Wordsmith Facebook page open and she can see that I've made a post with the pic I just took of us. I let my thumb hover over the "POST" button until I see her reaction.

"Do it," she says, smiling for the first time when it comes to this topic. I'm glad we're on the same page, finally.

"Posted. But I won't be waiting to see any likes or comments."

"Oh yeah," she says seductively, giving me that same look that first drew me to her at the bar. "And why's that?"

"I have more important things to do."

"Well, then, do them already."

I don't need to be asked twice. I stand up and scoop Everleigh into my arms. She's light as a feather as I carry her upstairs to the bedroom. She's holding on tightly around my neck. At the end of the stairs is my bedroom—the location that became a horror show for me not too long ago. Tonight? Tonight it's the place where my life begins anew.

<><><>

Love. I haven't said that word to any woman in. . .well, forever. It flowed off my lips, and it was like being freed to say it to her. I lay her down on the bed and we start to kiss. I pull back for a second—just the briefest of moments—I want to just look at her. I want to take her in. I want to remember every second of this encounter. She doesn't even wait for me this time. She takes off her clothes and I do the same. I'm standing and she gets to her knees on the bed and pulls me down for a passionate kiss. As our tongues smash together I run my fingers through her hair. My cock is hard, and she reaches down and grips it tightly. I can feel it pulsating in her warm hand as she strokes it. She pulls her mouth away from mine and leans down to suck me off. My pulsating head slides into her mouth, and the suction she creates has my whole body tingling. I push my hips forward as she cups my balls with her hand. I love the feeling of my cock in her willing mouth. She looks up at me, making intense eye contact as she lets me slide further down her throat.

After a minute she stops and I pull her up again and whisper in her ear, for the second time tonight, "I love you." She latches onto me and pulls me down on top of her. I slide my cock in her easily and start to slowly fuck her, driving as deep inside of her as I can go with each thrust forward. I stay there, my hips pressed intensely against her pelvis and I feel her pussy clamp down and squeeze me. I pull back and repeat the whole thing, again and again, going in as deep as I can each time. It's a different kind of sex. I want to go slow. I want her to go slow. I want to savor every inch of her body as she lets me fuck her.

The feeling of her wet pussy clamping down on me is making it impossible to hold off for much longer. I know that with a few more thrusts it's going to be over. I slam my cock into her with all the force I can muster, and she takes every inch of me willingly, moaning my name as she does. "I don't think I can hold off any longer," I tell her.

"Why would you? I want you to fill me up with your hot cum. Right now."

I explode inside her! I can feel the intensity of my orgasm as I shoot deep into her, and I feel the incredible release when I'm done. I have no energy left, and I collapse on the bed. She rolls over and puts her head on my chest as I pant my way back to normal. What happens next is something I don't anticipate, and it's not what it sounds like. I feel myself starting to fall asleep, only it's not in the typical, male I-just-had-sex way. It's the type of feeling that happens when you're truly content and truly happy. Normally I'd fight to stay awake, but I'm going to be just a little bit selfish. I close my eyes, the happiest man I've been in ages, and I fall contently asleep next to the woman I love.

EVERLEIGH

I WAKE UP GROGGY AND A LITTLE HUNG OVER. I'M NOT JUST hung over from all the drinks during and after dinner, either. I'm hung over from the entire night. That was some of the best sex I've ever had. Michael was a beast—passionate, powerful, and it all came on the heels of each of us saying that we love each other for the first time. I can barely walk, but in the best possible way.

Michael wakes up at the same time as I do.

"Good morning," he says.

"Morning. I have to go into work. I've been leaving everything up to my employees and pastry chef team too much over the past few weeks. But I have an idea I wanted to run by you before I go."

"What's that? I'm in already, but tell me."

"I'm closing the place a little early today. I'm sending everyone home at 5. Why don't you come by and you can. . .show me some of your skills."

"Is that a challenge I hear? Did you just lay the smack down?"

"Ummm, I think I might have done exactly that, yes. I wanna see what you've got."

"Oh, it's on now. You don't know what you just got yourself into. I'll be there at 5:30."

"It's a date."

I walk out into the cool morning air with a whole different perspective. I feel all sorts of things that would've been unthinkable just a few months ago before I met Michael. I feel happy. I felt content. I feel in love with the best man I've ever met. And on top of all of that I feel excited about what the future is going to bring for us.

As I get into my car I remember that he posted right before the night took us away. I grab my phone and open Facebook to see. My notifications are blowing up! I find the post he tagged me in and I can't believe my eyes. There are over 500 likes and over 200 comments on our picture. I'm so amazed that I start to scroll a little. Every comment is positive and supportive—amazing, you 2 look great together, gorgeous pic, congrats, I love this. This makes me so happy because I was still genuinely afraid that this would hurt Michael's image. If anything it seems to be helping. I text him before I leave in case he hasn't looked yet.

Me: Might want to check your Facebook page.

I can't wait to see him later.

37

KNIGHT

Two Weeks Later

Have you ever had a moment in your life that you didn't believe was real while it was happening? I had one of mine this morning.

Here's how it happened.

I woke up for release day, pretty confident that my sales would be abysmal as shit, as they've been in the past, at least by my standards. I'd done all the behind the scenes legwork —I'd assembled my 'pimps', which is the book world term for the people who help you share your posts and get the word out, sometimes also called a 'street team.' I also contacted bloggers, did some minor paid advertisements, sent out a newsletter, and generally did everything I could to spread the word. I'd done all of those things before to mixed results, so when I logged on two days ago and saw the following just under my book's description, I literally didn't believe my eyes:

#1 Bestseller in Kindle ebooks—> Romance—> General

#1 Bestseller in Kindle ebooks—> Biographies & Memoirs

Those little tags were everything that I've ever wanted to see. It's the first step to the next big step. The beginning of the kind of success I've always dreamed of, validation of. . .well, of everything. I let myself have the realization: my book is a number one bestseller, and now I'm a number one bestselling author. It seems like a dream but I know it's real. I know it's real because it came from Everleigh, and my feelings towards her are the most real I've ever experienced in my life. She brought me back from the depths of some darkness, and now I'm doing better than I ever have.

That was a few hours ago, and now I find myself sitting in the reading section of a bookstore by me, sipping coffee and feeling my heart race with excitement. I don't think Everleigh has seen yet or she would have texted me for sure. So that means it's time to text her. She needs to know about this ASAP.

Me: You working hard?

Everleigh: Hardly working. How's the book doing? Haven't had time to look.

I send her the link to the amazon page and just wait. I know it'll only take a few seconds for her to. . .

Everleigh: OH MY GOD! Michael! Holy Shit! You're a bestseller!

Me: Not me. We. We did it.

Everleigh: I didn't do anything. This is all you.

Me: Why do you think people connected to this book so much? They knew it was about you. About us.

Everleigh: Where are you?

Me: Local bookstore. The same one who agreed to carry

Into Your Eyes last time gave me some shelf space for a few copies of *ForEver*. When I tell him it's a bestseller he might give me even more space.

Everleigh: I can't text how happy I am. I want to show you. Meet me later for dinner?

Me: Do you even need to ask? I'm there. When are you out?

Everleigh: I'm closing at 6 today, but I can probably get out a little sooner. I'm doing a happy dance right here in the bakery. People are looking at me like I'm nuts.

Me: Tell them your boyfriend just hit it big. They'll understand.

Everleigh: I love you Michael.

Me: Not as much as I love you. I'll see you later.

I take a sip of my coffee as I wait for the owner to meet me. I have to tell him about all this, but I already have some books sitting out. I stand by the counter sipping coffee and day dreaming about the future—about the next book that I already have ideas for, about my future with Everleigh, and about the Wordsmiths. Of all of those things it's the last that I'm worried about. Not because I don't believe in us, but because of Colton's behavior. Everleigh's made me realize that I have to ignore the haters and the assholes of this world and just do me. I think Colton hasn't internalized that yet. Nonetheless, I'm excited about publishing our Anthology soon, and about the RAAC signing shortly.

The future is bright right now. I just hope it stays that way.

I hear some women next to me talking loudly by the display of books in the middle of the room. I pretend not to be eavesdropping, but I'm really listening to them talk books. I used to do this kind of thing before I ever published. It sounds creepy but I'd go hang out in bookstores and listen to people talk about the displays—covers they liked, books that caught their attention. It gave me a good idea of how to market some of my own work. Today I didn't come here to do that, but I listen while I pass the time.

"Look at this one," the short woman says to her friend. "Michael Knight. I love these kind of books, have you ever read one?" I look over and see her friend nod in affirmation, but not want to acknowledge her verbally. "Well I just read the back of this one and I'm grabbing it. Sounds sweet and sexy at the same time. I think I'll like this author."

I smile, and internally I'm doing the same happy dance that Ev was doing on the floor of her bakery. For the first time in a long time I'm truly happy.

Bestselling author. Great Writer. My favorite.

Yeah, I could definitely get used to all this.

I have one more stop before going home. . .

38

KNIGHT

I DIDN'T GET TO VISIT EV AT WORK THE OTHER DAY LIKE I wanted to, so I decide to surprise her now. With the traffic moving the way it is I should get to the bakery just before closing. That's the plan. I don't want anyone around. After leaving the bookstore I made one more stop before heading over here, and I don't want anyone to see what I'm bringing inside.

I pull up just as the last customer is leaving, a white package of goodies in their hand to take home for dessert. I'm sure whatever they have in that box is delicious, but I have pure magic in my little white box. I peek inside the window to make sure that really was the last customer, and the place looks empty. I get out, nervous as can be, and head inside.

Everleigh's there counting register, and as I walk through the door she greets me. "Hey!" she says. "This is a nice surprise. Hold that door."

"Okay." I keep the door open behind me as she comes over to flip the sign from "OPEN" to "CLOSED."

"Sometimes that's the best feeling in the world," she says.

"When you know your day is done and all you have to do is clean up."

"I haven't had that feeling in a long time," I say.

"Writer problems," she jokes. "Some of us with real jobs still have normal hours, you know."

"I remember. How was your day?"

"Good," she answers. "We basically sold out of everything. We get busy this time of year."

"That's great." I can hear the nerves in my voice, and I'm holding this package behind my back like a creep. I can tell she caught on because she stops looking me in the eye and starts looking towards my back.

"What'cha got there?"

"Did your staff leave already?"

"Yeah. I let them get home to their families a little early. I can handle the last few customers and closing the place up."

"Aren't you the best boss in the world?"

"And aren't you good at avoiding a question. What's behind your back there, Houdini?"

Little does she know that I wasn't avoiding her question at all, I was just buying time and gathering info. I don't want anyone around for this, and my heart is racing a mile a minute. "Sorry, you mean this?" I pull my hands out from around my back and she just stares at what I'm holding.

"Are you kidding? You brought pastries from another place?"

"I'm sorry, but it's my favorite bakery in the world. Ever since I was a kid." That part is true. The bakery I got the cupcake from has been there since I was little. My dad used to bring home all sorts of desserts from there when we were kids. It's still a special place for me, which is why I asked the owner to make a very special cupcake for me about a week ago. It's what I have with me right now.

"It's still a little weird, isn't it? Bringing a pastry from one bakery to another. We have cupcakes here you know. Good ones, too."

"I know. I just love these. Ever since I was little. My dad brought them home from time to time. Share one with me. I have a lot to celebrate."

"Alright." She says, grabbing two plates from behind the counter. We sit down at one of the little tables in the front. There isn't much room, but there isn't meant to be. It has an intimate feel to be here alone right now, and that's exactly what I want. I open the box to a single, oversized cupcake. Everleigh puts two plates and a large knife on the table in front of me. "You wanna do the honors?"

"You bet. But first. . ."

"Yes?"

"First I want to tell you something."

"Okay. What is it? You're freaking me out a little bit."

"That's the last thing I want to do." I take her hand in mine across the table. "It's Nothing bad. I was just thinking, while I was standing around the bookstore, thinking about this journey that I'm on. I was thinking about how much I love you. About how improbable meeting you was. And about how lucky I am to have you in my life."

"Aww, Michael. I feel the same way. I love you too. What brought all of this on?"

"Thoughts," I tell her. "Thoughts of yesterday. Thoughts of today. And, more than that, thoughts of tomorrow. Which is what I really wanted to say."

"What's that?" she asks.

I let go of her hand and grab the knife. Opening the box I slice the oversized cupcake straight down the middle. "Which half do you want?" I ask.

"It doesn't matter."

"Take the larger one. I think it's the one on the left. You can pull it apart."

She does what I ask her, having no idea the surprise that's waiting inside. I look down as she pulls the two halves apart. I hear the sound of it hitting the table underneath, and when I do I look back up at her to see her recognition. It takes a few seconds of disbelief, but once she realizes what she's looking at I see the glow in her eyes as she looks across at me.

"Michael. . ."

I pull out my chair, taking the icing covered ring in hand, and drop to a single knee. "Everleigh, will you be my wife? I can't imagine the rest of my life without you."

She contemplates only for a second, a tear forming in her eyes. She's never looked more beautiful than she does right now. "Yes, Michael. Of course I'll marry you!"

I stand up after putting the ring on her finger, and we kiss the best kiss we've ever had. It's a moment that I never want to forget for the rest of my days.

"So, wait, I just realized something," she says.

"What's that?"

"Now I don't get to go to RAAC as your girlfriend."

"No," I say, finishing her thought. "You get to go as my fiancé. As the future Mrs. Knight."

"I like the sound of that."

"Me too."

We kiss again, alone in our little place. I can't wait to tell everyone tomorrow. I can't wait for all of our tomorrows.

EPILOGUE

COLTON

I DON'T KNOW WHY I CALLED HER AND NOT MIKE OR GRAY, but that's what I did.

It's weird, I barely know her, but Mike was right, even though I wasn't about to admit it. I was into her the other night, and I'm into her now. What Mike and Gray don't know is that we talked for a long time the other night—really talked. She's an amazing woman, and she really seemed to get me. Maybe that's why I called her to help me, or maybe I'm just too embarrassed to call Mike or Gray just yet. It's his release day. I hope he's killing it. I hope he's doing better than I am right now.

I always wondered what a jail cell would look like.

You watch those shows like *Lockup* and you think you know what it would feel like to sit in a holding cell, but it's way worse than it seems on TV. Some of the people in here are just scary, and half of them smell like total shit.

I got picked up for assault last night. I guess KL decided to file charges. He really is a pussy, but right now I have bigger issues to worry about. I need to get the fuck out of here. That's why I used my phone call on her, and she didn't even ask any questions or hesitate. I see the guard approach, a surly looking fat guy who looks like a guy they'd cast in the role of a cop on some bad TV show.

"Chase, Colton?"

"Yeah."

"You're free. Let's go."

They process me at the front desk. It only takes a few minutes. I'm exhausted from being up all night surrounded by some pretty shady individuals, all of whom were looking at me like they wanted to beat my ass. I need to go home and take a shower. As I walk towards the front I see Harley waiting for me. It's weird, I barely know this girl—literally met her twice—but she's the one I thought to call right away. Even in the state of mind I'm in right now I notice how beautiful she looks. More than that, I'm just really excited to see a familiar face.

"Hey there," she says, grinning at me like I'm in trouble or something.

"Hey."

"Who'd you kill?"

"No one, unfortunately. Just a minor beating."

"Is that an oxymoron?" she asks.

"Actually, not in this case. It could have been a much worse beating for him, trust me."

"You're kind of hot when you're tired, mad, and just released from prison, you know that? You wear the outlaw thing well."

I know she's joking, but I'm not in a joking kind of mood. "I'm not an outlaw. This whole thing is stupid. I need to contact Mike and Gray and tell them what happened."

"How about breakfast first. You'll need some calories to confess to your best friends. That, plus I'm really being selfish because I'm starving. There's a diner around the corner, what do you say?"

"I say yes. Do I smell bad, though?"

She leans in and sniffs me. "Not to me. But this place does, let's get out of here before I start to smell like a criminal."

We walk outside into the cool mid morning air. I take a deep breath like I've been doing hard time or something, but the smell of fresh air is weirdly comforting at the moment. "Where's this diner?"

"Just over here. It's on me, just like your bail."

"Oh, I'll pay you back for that, I promise."

"You can pay me in some signed books—the ones I didn't get from the signing."

"You got it. Speaking of signing, it's not too long to RAAC. Shit. I have a lot to work out."

"Before you call your boys, how about you confess to me? It can be part of the debt you owe me."

"Now I'm in debt to you?" I joke.

"Yeah," she answers, smiling. "That's how it works, but this will be easy to pay back. Just get me some signed Colton Chase originals and confess your crimes over pancakes. Easiest debt to get out of."

"Alright. I hope you have a few minutes."

"Colton, if I were busy I wouldn't be hanging out with you outside a jail I just bailed you out of. So silly. Let's start walking, it's this way."

"Life takes us in strange directions sometimes, doesn't it?"

"Sometimes?" she answers. "Try, all the time. But I've learned to go with it. I've been where you are."

"You mean jail."

"It's not my time to confess yet. Show me yours and maybe I'll show you mine later. Pancakes first, of course."

"I don't even know how I got into this shit. I mean, I do know. It's my fault, obviously, but still, this feels super confusing."

"I'm sure it does," she says. You'll tell me about it over some coffee."

"There's one thing that I do know."

"What's that?" she asks me innocently, stopping right outside the diner.

I feel a sudden rise in my throat, and I look up at her. "This isn't over between the Wordsmiths and the Brotherhood. No. This is fuckin' war."

COMING SOON

COLTON—BOOK 2 IN THE WORDSMITH
CHRONICLES

Colton

I feel like Matt Damon in *Good Will Hunting*.

Not the genius parts where he's doing complex math in the hallways of MIT. Hell no! Right now I feel like him in that scene right after he and his friends get arrested after getting into that brawl on the streets of South Boston. That was how it went down for me also, minus the friends and the schoolyard. Truthfully, it wasn't a fight at all. I assaulted a guy—punched him in the gut in a restaurant bathroom, but he fucking deserved it. Anyhow, that's old news. The update is that I got arrested. And now I'm sitting in this court room with a cheap suit on and my court appointed public defender, who looks like he got out of law school about five minutes ago, sitting next to me, looking as nervous as I am. I'm going to address the judge before he hands down sentence. My lawyer told me I have the right to do that. Hopefully he knows what the fuck he's talking about.

I'm a writer, so I'm good with using my words to manipulate emotions. I don't always speak as well as I write, but using language to my benefit is like a super power I can turn on and off at will. Right now I need to turn it the fuck on. Everyone in the room rises as the judge makes his entrance into the courtroom. "Stand up, Colt." my lawyer instructs me as the judge makes his way behind the bench. This whole thing is weird—why does one guy have the power over my freedom? I guess I can ponder that while I get ready to convince him to let me go.

A month ago I beat the shit out of another author—KL Steiner—in a restaurant bathroom while I was out celebrating the cover reveal of my best friend, Michael Knight. It was the wrong thing to do, there's no getting around that. I threw the first and second punches without any provocation except for him being a dick. I should have controlled myself, but I didn't. I gave KL what was coming to him, and I really didn't think anything was going to come of it. Wishful thinking, I guess. A few days passed with nothing, and then the cops showed up at my doorstep and took me to jail.

Harley bailed me out, and I was given a court appointment for today. "The honorable judge Scofield, presiding!"

"Please be seated." The judge instructs. We all sit down and I have that same feeling I did like I'm back being dragged to church when I was a little kid. All the standing and rising and ritual. Let's get on with this already! My case is up first on the docket. "Colton Chase?"

"Yes, your honor?"

"Council, how does your client plead?"

"Guilty your honor, but he would like to address the court if you'll allow it."

"That's fine," he says. "As long as he keeps it brief. I have to hear a lot of cases today."

"Certainly, your honor." My lawyer motions for me to speak, and all of a sudden I get really nervous. I'm feeling the importance of this situation in a way I didn't think that I would. Normally I'm a pretty cool customer—not really prone to anxiety or feeling self-conscious, but right now I feel like I'm on stage, naked, with everyone staring at me, making fun of the size of my dick or something.

"Mr. Chase," the judge says in a deep voice. "Go ahead."

"Your honor, I don't want to waste any of your time. I committed the assault that I'm here for today. I'm not going to deny that or waste the court's time defending an indefensible action. I shouldn't have hit that man, and I regret doing so. I wasn't defending myself or anyone else. I lost my temper, plain and simple, and I never should have done that. All that I request, Your Honor, is that you take into consideration that I have a completely clean record up to this point. This is my first offense—a stupid and regrettable mistake—and I'm willing to do anything I can to avoid jail time, sir."

I stop talking and I feel really dumb. I basically just asked him to not do what its his job to do—send people away for breaking the law. I'm just hoping that I got the right judge on the right day, and that he takes pity on me in any way possible. It's only a few seconds that he ponders my request, but in that courtroom it feels like an eternity. I'm expecting the well worded judicial equivalent of 'fuck off, asshole, we've got your jail cell all ready for ya', but instead he looks at me with kind eyes.

"Mr. Chase. I've heard your request. I thank you for taking responsibility for your actions. Trust me, it's a refreshing thing in this court. And, while I agree that assaulting another person is in no way ethnically or legally acceptable, it shows character that you're willing to simply admit to it and not waste the Court's time. Mr. Chase, I have a son your age, and he's struggled with similar issues

. Although it's within my power to take your freedom, I don't feel that it's in anyone's best interest to do so."

His words feel like a giant exhale. I'm not going to jail!

"But," he continues. "Just because you're not going to prison doesn't mean that you're getting off scott-free. There are consequences to your actions."

"Yes, Your Honor. I'm willing to do anything to stay out of prison."

"Be careful what you wish for, Mr. Chase." There's something about the tone in his voice that's freaking me out. "I'm sentencing you to 50 hours of a community service, as well as court-mandated anger management therapy for a span of no less than three months."

"Therapy?" I ask.

"Yes, Mr. Chase, therapy. If you think those kind of impulse and anger issues are going to just resolve themselves then maybe I'm wrong to be taking a chance on you. You're welcome to reject the deal I'm offering you, Mr. Chase," he tells me. "But the alternative is a jail cell upstate. Your choice."

This is a no brainer. "Therapy and community service are fine, your honor."

"I thought that you might see it that way. And I'm glad that you do. Good luck to you, Mr. Chase."

"Thank you, Your Honor."

I walk out into the hallways of the court house a free man, but I'm a little bewildered at what just happened. Now I really feel like Matt Damon in *Good Will Hunting*! Therapy. I've never even considered going, but now that I'm thinking about it I could probably benefit from it. What I said to the judge is true—I don't have a criminal record, but a lot of that is honestly just because I never got caught doing things I shouldn't have done. I used to get into fights in high school.

A lot of fights. The only reason I haven't been to jail on ten different occasions is because there's a code among guys when it comes to physical altercations—no one calls the cops. Calling the cops or suing someone over a fight that both people went into willingly makes you seem like a complete pussy. I guess KL never got that memo.

But just because I never faced any charges doesn't mean I was doing the right thing or living the way I should have been living. In fact, I was pretty unhappy most of those times. My attack on KL was the first time since my first year in college that I've gotten into it physically with another man outside of a martial arts training situation. I know it was wrong, but I'm not sorry that he took a few shots to remind him that there are costs to being an unethical asshole.

Maybe I do need therapy.

"So how does all this work?" I ask my attorney. I never met this guy before today, but he seems nice enough. I'm not exactly rolling in money so I don't keep an attorney on retainer, meaning that I had to go with a public defender who's clearly younger than I am. Thank God I'm good at talking. "The therapy and community service, I mean."

"You have to check in every week and provide evidence that you're going to both until you fulfill the court's directives. There are a few community service places I can recommend if you need."

"Thanks, that would be great."

"And for therapists. . ."

"Actually, I think I'm good with the therapist part, believe it or not."

"You have a therapist?"

"I think I just might."

After I got out on bail I started hitting the gym hard. I'd vowed to myself that all of this drama wasn't going to impact the writing my new book, *The Gentle Art*. It's about an MMA fighter who finds love on his way to getting a UFC contract. I've been training a lot of Jiu Jitsu to get into the mindset of Aidan, my alpha male character. My main training partner also teaches some of the advanced classes on Tuesdays. He's a retired cop, and I remember shooting the shit with him after class one day, and him mentioning that his wife was this famous psychologist in the city. At the time I barely paid attention—it was just some getting to know you chit chat. But now the memory comes flooding back to me.

I step out of the courthouse into a beautiful summer day. There's nothing like the early summer in New York. Give it a month and the air will be thick with humidity and mosquitoes the size of small birds, but right now it's perfect. The chill of spring has thawed, and everything is starting to grow. I reach into my wallet. I grab the card Calem gave me at Jiu Jitsu and I see her name—*Cordelia Summers, Ph.D.* I guess I'll be calling her soon.

But there's another woman that I need to call first.

I walk down the steps of the courthouse feeling every bit the extra in an episode of *Law & Order*. When I reach the bottom I grab my cell and get ready to call Harley. I don't know what it is or why, but she's gotten in my head. She was who I called to get me out of jail before I called Mike or Gray, but more than that she was who I confided in. I told her things at that diner that only a few people in my life really know. She just has something about her that makes me trust her. And it doesn't hurt that every time I see her my pants get a little bit tighter.

She's a fucking dime piece—a 10–a girl who can turn heads when she walks in the room. And she certainly turned mine when we met at Mike's cover reveal party. I couldn't stop staring or talking to her, and I definitely felt a chemistry between us.

I hit 'send' on my phone and wait for her to pick up. It rings four times before it goes to voicemail. Damn. I guess I missed her. I'll try again later.

Pancakes with Harley sounds like the title of a bad novel, an even worse podcast, or the shittiest band ever. But pancakes with Harley was the one ray of hope in an otherwise terrible series of events for me—it was the thing that started me on the road to where I am now. It wasn't just because she was there for me, either. It's because she told me things about herself that were some of the most personal things someone can share. She told me her secret. The thing no one else in this world knows. It's a secret I'll guard with my life, and it's something that made her feel like my girlfriend even though she isn't.

I have two stories that need to be written—my next book, and my real life story with Harley.

I'm not sure how either are going to turn out, but I can't wait to see.

Here I go.

This is a series about us—the indie book community. As you just read, a lot of the characters are based around real people who I've had the pleasure of meeting and interacting with, and real experiences that I've been lucky enough to have. For each of the books in this series I'm going to include some spotlights of the people who helped make each book possible, either directly or indirectly. It's my way of honoring those involved. I think you'll know most of them pretty well.

Golden Czermak
Amazing Author/ Great Photographer/ Cool Motherfucker

Golden is not only a colleague, he's also an amazing human being and one of the nicest people I've had the pleasure of meeting in this community. On top of that he takes some great photos (seriously—if you're an author get after @furiousfotog), including the cover images for this series. I had the honor of meeting him in person and hanging out with him over a weekend at the Gettysburg signing. His books include: The Journeyman Series, The Secret Life of

Cooper Bennett, Cade (The Agency Book 1), The Swole Series, and others.

From Golden,

"In the beginning, I worked the standard corporate rat race, completed college for a Chemical Engineering Degree, and if that wasn't enough to fill anyone's plate, began a small photography company on the side. Since then, and with the growth of the FuriousFotog brand, I became an internationally published modeling/fitness photographer with a following that reached 2 million fans worldwide. Eventually, I began working as a book cover model (after getting bitten by the gym bug - you are what you immerse yourself in I suppose. LOL)

Having been in the industry for at least six years, I've interfaced and networked with countless authors and other clients. As part of my work as a photographer, I've worked with them to capture and create book cover images - now numbering over 550 at the beginning of 2018. The cover of this book is one of those special images, and it's an absolute honor to have my work grace the cover of Chris' novel. However, the model is another matter entirely, causing me to break out in sweats and heavy panting every time he looks at me with "those eyes." Thank goodness they are closed on this book cover, otherwise, we would all be in trouble and Chris' words would be forever locked away behind Josh McCann's stare. I must take steps in future to prevent the threat of that happening...

Learning the ins and out of the book world, along with being an avid reader and storyteller myself, I also decided to write and publish my first book, Homeward Bound, in 2016. 16 have since followed in a surreal adventure that Chris also has the pleasure of experiencing. But enough about me, let's return this book to Chris where it belongs. Follow me on social media below for more."

www.onefuriousfotog.com(Photography)

www.facebook.com/furiousfotog

www.goldenczermak.com (Books)

www.facebook.com/authorgoldenczermak

Josh McCann

    Cover Model—*Knight: Book 1 in the Wordsmith Chronicles* and many, many others.

Josh is one of the most popular cover models out there. A great guy who's been a pleasure to talk to, I couldn't be happier to have his image be on the flagship book of the series.

Jessica Hildreth

Cover Designer/Formatter/Swag Designer/Mother of Dragons/Breaker of Chains

Chronologically I haven't known Jessica that long, but it feels like I've known her forever, and she's already become an integral part of my books. My cover and swag designer since Calem, Jessica (like Golden) is one of the best people in the industry. Professional, easy to work with, and great at her job. I can't imagine my books without her. You can see all of her wonderful work at www.jessicahildrethdesigns.com

Lauren Lascola-Lesczynski

PA Extraordinaire/Beta Reader/Dispenser of Wisdom

Lauren is everything noted above and more. An inimitable part of the success of the R&E Fraternity and my career, she's been supportive in all the ways I've needed her to be. Hyper organized, critically minded, and always available, she's one of the best in the business! Thanks to Lauren for all of her help!

Stephanie Albon

Beta Reader

An avid reader, I first met Stephanie at the Gettysburg signing. I can't thank her enough for taking the time to read Knight, offer me some critical feedback, and help catch my mistakes. Thanks again!

The Readers

Like an Oscar speech, there are too many people to name and upload pictures of individually, but the sentiment we feel towards all of you is the same: you make this possible. With every page turn, book purchase, like, comment, share, ARC read, blog review, and other types of support, you make events like Gettysburg manifest—a thing that can exist. Without you, the simple truth is that there would be no such events.

Personally, the greatest inspiration that I took outside of the amazing conversations I had with other authors was getting to see readers in person. That may sound silly, but we're visual creatures, and being in an environment like that - my first- where there was nothing but love and support, put human faces to what is far too often just a series of icons on a social media page. Interacting with readers on any level— whether it was just signing a mug, or taking a picture, or going in depth over the plots of my books—made this all real, it made me feel successful, it made me want to write more stories for everyone.

Though I speak for no one but myself, always, I'm certain that the BT, Jackson Kane, Golden Czermak, Mickey Miller, Rob Somers, Seth, SD Hildreth, Derek Cromwell, and all the guys share in these sentiments - without you we're just a bunch of guys with a laptop and a dream. With your support, however, we're authors, capable of publishing book after book, story after story, knowing that there' an audience who appreciates the labor put into our work as much as we appreciate the labor you put into reading it and helping us. Thank you, from the bottom of my heart. Not only those who attended the signing, but everyone. But to those at the signing, in particular, thank you for making manifest what was simply just a dream not too long ago. Stay tuned.

ACKNOWLEDGMENTS

So many people inspired this work—readers and writers alike. All of them deserve to be thanked. So, here it goes, in no particular order.

The members of the Romance and Erotica (R&E) Fraternity who I got to meet and talk with during the Gettysburg signing— BT Urruela, Scott Hildreth, Golden Czermak, Seth King, Derek Adam, Mickey Miller, Rob Somers, Chris Genovese, and Jackson Kane. Our talks inspired these words, and for that I'm eternally grateful.

To Harlan's Readers and the loyal supporters of the R&E Frat—your support of this book will help keep my fingers poised over the keyboard for the next few books. Keep reading and I'll keep writing.

Ellen Farrelly, Jennifer Beeley, Elizabeth Gray, Nora Fresse, Debbie Victorino, Crystal Shunk, Mary Dikeman Probst, Ches Daniele, Mandy Tregaskis, Heather Schrader, Monica L Murphy, Katie Sullivan, Angel Davis, Mindy Knadler, Kristina Olsen, Kimberly Field, Lyn Liddell, Michelle Lambert, Julie Jacobus, Erin L. Grant, Amy Darragh, Jennivie Wirries, Maria Nevarez, Cindy Hughes,

Liz Black, Christina Burrus, Jill Bourne, Julie JA Lafrance, Maria Rivera, Misty Yancey, Kellie Conway, Lisa Pleines Cochran, Tiffany Greene Elliott, Linda Rimer-Como, Raven Johnson, Marla Corniels, Melinda Evans-Mcleroy, Amber Marie Brazell, Selena Lanovara Scott, Heather Swan, Connie Walsh Beeson, Clare Fuentes, Athena Engel, Lea Winkelman, Crystal Matz PA,Denise Long, Courtney Fogle , Elise Heness, Danielle Brass, Tammy Dalton, Karla Monahan, Dawn L. Roether, Mina Parmar Kalidas, Sonya Hardin, Angi Burns, Jennifer Rusher-Minton, Cindy Bearor, Deanna Wilson Thompson, Elizabeth Bell, Gina Marcantonio, Samantha Beson, Melissa Eastep Myers, Heather Fueger, Angie Davis, Jessica Seibel, Jenn Haines, Amanda Wilson, Michelle Titherington VanDaley, Carrie Spear Trupp, Kristen Lee Kucera, Joanne Coughlin, Amanda Cunningham, Heather Rollins Himmelspach, Claire Jenni Alexander, Katie Hindmarch, Nadine Keedy, Deb Meade Cechak, Sarah DeLong, Charlotte Isaac, Sharon Aldrich, Debbie Herron, Mike Urbat, Elaina Lucia, Kathy Lemecha Brown, Melanie Stevenson, Keri Roth, Jamie Spencer Harbison, Cathy Lane-Zaffuto, Suzette Prescott Dynko, Angela Crowell, Lauren Mitchell, Lisa Hemming, Diana Green, Laura Albert, Debbie Eichler, Cassy Kubehl, Shirley Werner, Joann Sterns, Stephanie Starkel, Kari Ann, Stephanie J Bird, Jessica Laws, Tiffany Reed, Teri Ditchman, Luetta Lyons, Monica Randau, Chris Cox, Lg Reads

Meghan R. Deppenschmidt, Any Jenkins, Lisa Carotenuto-Mark, Cat Wright, Shelly Reynolds, Jennifer Willison, Kelly Vidito, Marcia Gray, Jamie Marguilis Speck, Julie Leopold, Carol Lynn Scheufler, Jodie Coman, Mina Parmar Kalidas, Tammy Lynn Cuppett, Kristina Bonham, Kristi Van Howling, Sara Miles Mason, Megan Asmus,

Brenda Pratt, Sharelle Lovato, Catherine Ingalls Hussein, & Beverly Gordon.

My ARC TEAM

And, finally, to the members of my ARC & Beta teams, who took the time to read, review, spell check, and offer feedback before it was released! Without you the book wouldn't be what it is.

Lauren Lascola-Lesczynski, Stephanie Albon, AR Bailey, Amanda Lee, Amanda O'Brien, Amanda Rambusch, Amy Horton, Andi Smith, Andrea Flatness Kollmer, Angel Davis, Angi Burns, Ann Leeson, Ann Zimmer, Anna Lee, AnnaMarie Hay, Arien Johnston, Bente Elin Bendiksen, BiancaMarie Brown, Bonnie Bracken,Carly Pedersen , Carol Lynn Scheufler, Carolyn Nunley, Cat Wright, Catherine Ingalls Hussein, Cathy Lane-Zaffuto, Ches Daniele, Chris Cox, Chriss Prokic, Christine Valentukonis Geier, Cindy Hughes, Clare Fuentes, Crystal Matz PA, Danielle Brass, Darlene Carroll, Dawn Brian Roether, Deanna Hunt, Debbie Eichler, Denise Fackler Van Plew, Dora Harvey, Elizabeth Bell, Hanna Abskharon, Heather Swan, Ingrid Duebbert, Janet Clark, Jenni Copeland Belanger, Jennifer Rusher-Minton, Jessica Estes Ingram, Jessica Laws, Joann Stearns, Julie Leopold, Karen Tartaglia, Kathy Webber, Katrina Haynes, Keri Roth, Kristen Erickson Eckard, Kristi Van Howling, Lacy Laurel, Lacy Mercado, Laura Albert, Lauren Mitchell, Leanna Cummings, Lesley Robson, Leticia Hernandez, Lg Reads, Linda Rimer-Como, Lisa Hemming, Lisa Pleines Cochran, Mandy Demaree, Marcia Gray, Maria Nevarez, Maria Rivera, Megan Asmus, Melanie Stevenson, Michaela Zankl, Michelle Lambert, Mina Parmar Kalidas, Missy Noecker, Misti Jo Runyon, Monica Cottrell Randau, Monica L. Murphy, Nichole Watson, Nikki Wilson, Nora Fresse, Phyllis Smith, Samantha Beson, Sandra Cohen,

Sandra Foy, Sara Gross, Shaleen Gray, ShannonChris Colin, Shelly Reynolds, Shirley Werner, Stephanie McKnight-Bailey, Stephanie Starkel, Stephany Snell, Sue Ouellet, Susan Duran, Suzette Prescott Dynko, Syndi Hutchinson, Tammy Lynn, Teresa Guthrie Lara, Teri Ditchman, Tiffany Greene Elliott, Tina Laurelli, Tori Jo Carlson, and Vickie Beams.

Thank you all, from the bottom of my heart. #potato

CONNECT WITH CHRISTOPHER HARLAN

Where You Can Follow Me To Hear About New Releases

My Website/Newsletter Sign up
www.authorchristopherharlan.com
BookBub
https://www.bookbub.com/authors/christopher-harlan
Amazon
https://www.amazon.com/-/e/B01M1KU74Y
Instagram
www.instagram.com/authorchristopherharlan